SIMPLE SIMON

Also by Ryne Douglas Pearson

Cloudburst
October's Ghost
Capitol Punishment

SIMPLE SIMON

A THRILLER

Ryne Douglas Pearson

WILLIAM MORROW AND COMPANY, INC.

NEW YORK

It is the policy of William Morrow and Company, Inc., and its imprints and affiliates, recognizing the importance of preserving what has been written, to print the books we publish on acid-free paper, and we exert our best efforts to that end.

Library of Congress Cataloging-in-Publication Data

Pearson, Ryne Douglas.
    Simple Simon : a thriller / Ryne Douglas Pearson.
      p.   cm.
    ISBN 0-688-14296-6
    1. Government investigators—United States—fiction.
  I. Title.
PS3566.E2343S57 1996   95-50106
813'.54—dc20   CIP

Printed in the United States of America

FIRST EDITION

1 2 3 4 5 6 7 8 9 10

BOOK DESIGN BY CATHY AISON

For Dominic and Melissa

acknowledgments

Thanks are due now more than ever to R. H., S. H., and M. G. Also to my family and friends, for believing and turning books face out at every bookstore they visit. To Clyde Taylor, for the start. To Chuck Verrill, for guidance. To Howard Sanders and Richard Green, for making dreams come true, and to Joe Singer, Maureen Peyrot, and Karen Kehela, for seeing the pictures a story sometimes paints. And as always, to my wife, Irene, for simply being, and for being with me.

SIMPLE SIMON

Prologue

Rising Son

North of Tokyo . . .

Keiko Kimura stood near the foot of the bed, a sheer white peignoir hanging from wispy straps to veil her still-enticing form, thinking both that the American's fledgling erection was unimpressive and that his blood was going to be the devil to get out of fine silk.

But she could not deny the rapture of that warm red wetness rolling over her, or the heights to which a scream could take her, and looking upon the pale body that was willingly four-pointed to the bedposts, she knew that ruined lingerie was an acceptable trade.

"Do me, mama-san." The American beckoned with eyes hungry and limbs tugging joyously at the bindings he had insisted upon in pursuit of some masochistic fantasy. "Hurt me."

"You want Keiko to spank you?" She skated one foot across the wood floor, then the other, until she stood bedside, black hair draped over either shoulder and dark eyes sweeping his body. As she sat upon the mattress, her tongue slid into view and slowly wet her lips.

He smiled, teeth bared, chest heaving. His erection began to improve. "I want you to *punish* me."

Primal forces boiled within her as he spoke *that* word. *Punish*, she thought. So perfectly did he speak it, so clear and pure was his desire for it, that Keiko replayed the intonation over and over in her mind. After a very few repetitions she felt herself getting wet.

"Come on, mama-san, I'm needin' this bad, and I'm needin' it soon. . . ."

Keiko rolled her head once and then looked squarely at the American. His face was dotted with glistening beads of sweat. She imagined each tiny drop as a pearl of redness— blood tears that he was crying . . . crying for her.

Ooh, sweet one, she thought, the warmth rising within, lifting her almost to the precipice before she called retreat. *Too much. Too much so soon.* There would be time enough for pleasure, but as was necessary, business had to come at some point before her plaything was dead.

"Come on," the American demanded now, with gritted teeth.

"You gotta do something for Keiko first," she said, and slid a hand through the black curls on his chest. She found his nipple and squeezed it between thumb and forefinger.

"Unnhhh," he groaned, his face contorted in the beginnings of an ecstatic agony. Or so he believed.

On the end of each finger was a perfectly filed natural nail, and with these Keiko now pinched. Hard, very hard, so much so that the American was drawn from his burgeoning erotic state to recoil from this *real* pain.

"Hey! Easy!"

With a force less impressive than might seem necessary, Keiko dug deep into the nipple and jerked her hand away, tearing it from his body, flinging the bit of soft pink flesh aside. It hit the off-white wall, leaving a bright red starburst on the slick surface before falling to the floor.

"You crazy fucking bitch!—"

He pulled and bucked and twisted and fought. Blood sprayed from his wound, flecks dotting Keiko's face and the peignoir she had briefly fretted over. Her tongue appeared again and licked spots of blood from above her lip. Its taste, its simply being *on* her, made staying focused on the business end of things very difficult. Almost impossible. "You gotta talk to me, Joe."

"Joe?" the American asked through the pain. He didn't know that all American men were Joes in his tormentor's mind.

"You not the only one paying Keiko tonight, Joe." Her mouth tingled with the salty, coppery taste of his essence. *To bathe in it*, she thought. Soon, though never soon enough. "Someone wants to know what you know."

His brow wrinkled at her words. A warm crimson trickle ran down his ribs. "You're a fucking psycho! Know what?"

Keiko's face expressed something—not a smile or a scowl. Nothing easily identified. *A beastly look upon the human form*, the American thought. Then he saw a knife come up from the side of the bed in her bloody hand.

"You know," she said, holding the knife delicately by its shank, drawing slow figure eights in the air above his face.

"Know what?" he shouted, nearly pleading now.

Now she smiled, lowering the knife to begin a hard night's work. "It don't matter, Joe. You gonna tell me everything about everything, and I'll sort it out." She pricked the tip of his nose and drew the blade slowly across her tongue, savoring the taste. His being was so fleeting, as would be her own ecstasy. In the morning, with this job behind her and with this plaything cast aside, the cravings would begin

3

anew. With the cravings there would come a need. And for that need there would be someone, somewhere, who would provide satisfaction. Until then . . . "Just enjoy it, Joe. We got all night."

Art Jefferson had been back in Chicago less than two months when he made an enemy of United States Attorney Angelo Breem.

"What in God's name was that, Jefferson?" Breem demanded after catching up to the FBI's number two man in Chicago on the courthouse steps and grabbing him by the elbow.

Art looked seriously at Breem's spindly hand, and the U.S. attorney wisely withdrew it. "What was what?"

Breem, still exasperated by his sprint to find Art after court had adjourned, pointed a shaky finger at the man he considered a turncoat. "You know exactly what I'm talking about. What you testified to on that stand is going to let Kermit Fiorello walk!"

Art turned and took a step up so that he stood on equal footing with Breem. He towered over the zealous prosecutor by six inches. "I told the truth."

"Christ, Jefferson! You know Fiorello's guilty! Guilty as sin! He's responsible for at least six contract murders, two of which we could have nailed on him, plus the racketeering charges, if *you* hadn't gone soft!"

"Soft?" Art asked, his head cocking. A vein rose beneath his left temple. "Listen to me, Mr. U.S. Attorney, if you had had your *P*'s and *Q*'s straight, there would have been no need for me to testify at all. Your case was weak from the get-go. And so you decide to call me in to dredge up some ancient history on Fiorello? That was fifteen years ago, Breem. It had nothing to do with the paper-thin case you had until ten minutes ago. I didn't kill your case; it committed suicide."

Breem seethed, his fists balling at his side. He would have loved to swing at the cocky black agent. Mr. Big Shot coming back from his time on the Coast. "He is guilty, Jefferson."

"You think I don't know that?" Art asked, leaning to get in Breem's face. Breem's features were pale and abrupt. "I was chasing Fiorello when you were at the prom."

"Then why did you say he had nothing to do with the Carerra murder?"

"Because he didn't!" Art backed off and shook his head. "If you'd bothered to check with me before calling me to the stand, I could have set you straight on that. But no, you base your whole case on that one crime. If Fiorello had Carerra whacked, then he had to do the same ten years later to Tangini, and then to Picone, et cetera. He did Tangini and Picone, but not Louie Carerra. Any agent who was around back then could tell you that." He stabbed a solid finger at Breem's red tie. "You didn't do your homework, and because of that, Kermit Fiorello is a free man once again. Thank yourself, Breem, before you blame someone else."

With that Art showed the U.S. attorney his back and trotted easily down the steps, ignoring the visual daggers being thrown his way. He cared little for people like Breem. All high-profile talk, all grand drama in the courtroom, and no real smarts to carry the basics of a case from start to finish. Breem wanted to go places as fast as possible, and in this case he'd gone a damn sight too fast. It seemed that every damned U.S. attorney wanted to get to D.C. and a nice office in the Department of Justice as quickly as he could. Well, Angelo Breem's path to the top had just been detoured, and Art had no illusions that the pipsqueak would blame him for it until the day he died.

So what? Art asked himself as he reached the bottom of the steps and headed down Dearborn to grab a bite at Nico's. He'd made worse enemies in a long career with the bureau. What could one measly U.S. attorney do to him?

Number 6601 needed surgery.

Circling the earth at 150 nautical miles in a ninety-eight-degree sun-synchronous orbit, the two-billion-dollar piece of electronic and imaging wizardry known as the KH-14 was just a year into its planned ten-year life span when the same shuttle that had placed it into orbit, *Atlantis,* blasted off from Florida's Cape Canaveral an hour before dawn. On the fourth revolution *Atlantis* rendezvoused with the reconnaissance satellite and precisely matched its course and speed. They were man-made moons in tandem orbit of Mother Earth.

As the sun set on the East Coast, two men from the planet Earth exited *Atlantis* and moved via MMUs (manned maneuvering units) the ten yards to number 6601. One astronaut carried tools. The other carried a small case the size of a shoe box. It shone silver in the clear sunlight of space.

The astronaut with the tools opened an access panel on the huge satellite's side, below and aft of its number two solar panel. He worked carefully and removed four bolts that held a red box in place. One cable went in the red box, and another came out. He disconnected these and pulled the red box free.

It took him twenty more minutes to put the silver box in and reconnect the cables.

After finishing the surgery, the astronauts took the red box with them and reentered *Atlantis.* They were to continue with the "scientific" activities of Mission 98-A for another eight days, then land back at Cape Canaveral, weather permitting.

Number 6601 required only five minutes to recover from surgery, just long enough to recalibrate itself with controllers on the ground at several secret installations across the United States. The first thing it did was spit a stream of electronic gibberish toward the earthbound receiving stations. All of them answered back with the same gibberish. They understood each other. But no one else did.

Number 6601 had just been taught a new language.

It was very late when the father sat in the rocker in the corner of his child's room and helped his son onto his lap. The son wore white flannel pajamas highlighted with tiny blue snowflakes, and when he curled up in the strong arms, his nose pressed into the crook of his father's neck. The son detected the faint scent of motor oil, and this comforted him. He slid his thumb into his mouth and closed his lips around it.

"Wander boy, wander far, wander to the farthest star," the father began to sing softly. His pitch was off, his rhythm tortured. The son found assurance in the song sung his father's way; it was the only way he knew. "Wander boy, wander far, dreams are what you're made of."

Eyes closed, and the son began to suck his thumb. The father stared blankly at a bare wall and continued the melody. He had long ago stopped asking God to heal his son. He accepted him now. "Under a tree by a house, by a field washed with rain, lies a boy all alone with his thoughts and his dreams."

The father loved his son. He had sung to him every night of his life but one. It was their special time. "Wander boy, wander far . . ." At this point he continued only in a hum. "Hmm-hm-hm-hmm-hmm-hmm-hm-hm-hmm."

The son fell asleep in the safety of his father's arms.

Half a world away there was no safety for the son of

another father. His body was already cold.

But in the quiet of this Midwest home there was only peace as the father hummed the lullaby, his son resting serenely as the night marched on. The ritual was unchanging.

For now.

chapter 1

The Sky Is Falling

Simon Lynch sat alone in the small room at a square table, chair back from its edge, hands folded on his lap, his upper body swaying forward and back in a precise, measured motion, the equal of any metronome. His eyes, green and cautious, darted about the bare tabletop, focusing on no one spot for more than a second. A few blond hairs hung loose over his forehead. His lips moved quickly, incrementally, in some silent recitation.

The four walls of the room were off-white. Except for a door they seemed bare. One wasn't.

"How old is he?" Dr. Anne Jefferson asked as she watched the image on the large television monitor. The subject was fifteen feet distant in a soundproof observation room. A perfectly hidden camera was bringing the pictures to them.

"He turned sixteen two weeks ago," Dr. Chas Ohlmeyer answered. A clipboard rested on his knee. A notebook computer glowed on Anne's lap. "How can you do observations on that thing?"

"This?" Her head shook with a smile. Her smile was her most striking feature, or so her new husband had told her.

When she wasn't smiling, she was merely a classic beauty, skin the color of light chocolate and smooth as a newborn's, eyes translucent in the right light, black hair pulled into a loose ponytail because of the storm blowing in off Lake Michigan. "You still have a couch in your office, don't you?"

Ohlmeyer accepted the friendly jab. "And Freud is my idol."

Anne chuckled, then gave her attention back to the monitor. "So, Simon Lynch. You think he's a Kanner?"

Ohlmeyer's face did the equivalent of a shrug. "I'm hoping you can help in that determination. He's been coming to Thayer for only a couple months. It's taken about that long to acclimate him so he'd open up a bit. Then last week . . . well, you'll see."

She studied the young man on the screen. At first blush an untrained eye might see a case of nerves. The scene did, she had to admit, look like something out of a police drama: the interrogation room, a bland cube with one door and a light fixture in the ceiling's center, the suspect at the table, waiting for the good guy–bad guy team of cops to come in. It was not that, though, and the behavior was not a case of nerves. The reason was far more profound.

From the left of the screen the door opened. Anne noted immediately that the pace of Simon's rocking picked up a bit. A young woman entered, spoke a few comforting words to the subject, and set a box on the table before retreating. The door closed with a soft click.

"What is that?"

"A puzzle," Ohlmeyer answered. His lined face bore a subtle grin. "We've discovered that Simon likes puzzles."

Anne's fingers tapped at the condensed keyboard, recording the beginnings of her observation. Thirty seconds into the session the pace of her typing slowed, then stopped, and she leaned in close to the monitor, her eyes wide. "Oh, my."

Simon Lynch had the contents of the box, five hundred jigsaw pieces of random size and shape, spread out upon the table, none touching another. The top of the box, emblazoned with a picture of a covered bridge in a pastoral setting, he laid facedown on the floor without as much as a glance at it. The plain bottom of the box followed. Then he went about starting the puzzle.

"Chas, he is—"

"I know."

First Simon had to get all the pieces turned the same direction . . . without letting them touch. They could touch only when he placed them together. And they could go together only when the picture side of each was facedown. When the tabletop was nothing but a jumble of gray jigsaw piece backs, Simon's rocking stopped. He leaned farther forward and, eyes dancing, began interlocking the pieces. Perfectly. With nary a test fit.

"My goodness, Chas," Anne commented in a hushed, almost reverent tone. She was no longer an observer; she was a spectator.

"Amazing, isn't it?" Ohlmeyer glanced at his Rolex. *Twenty-five seconds.* Simon was a quarter of the way done, easily at the pace he'd set in previous sessions. More than two pieces a second. Dr. Chas Ohlmeyer, dean of the University of Chicago's school of psychology and director of the Lewis Thayer Center for the Developmentally Disabled, smiled fully at the brilliance he was witnessing. Not a brilliance many would ever see, nor that anyone—including him—could fully explain, but brilliance all the same.

Anne nodded to the screen. "Amazing" began to convey

her assessment of the scene. "How many times have you done this with him?"

"The puzzle? In a test situation, three. It wasn't something we planned. Simon just sort of happened."

"Come again?" Anne asked, keeping her eyes on the screen. Half the pieces had been absorbed into a lopsided triangle of gray.

"When I say 'just happened,' I mean more than just this talent you're seeing," Ohlmeyer explained. "He might never have come to us—or to anyone—if he hadn't gotten a nasty viral infection. His parents had kept him pretty much sheltered since he was about one year old. By that time it was apparent to them, and to his doctor, that there were some serious deficiencies in his development. His parents thought one thing: retarded." For a moment Ohlmeyer's expression soured, adding years to his fifty-five-year-old face. "So when they brought him to Uni for treatment of the infection a few months back, the attending—you know him: Larry Wollam—recognized the behavioral and developmental symptoms. He convinced Simon's parents to bring him to Thayer for an assessment. When we gave them the results, they kind of shrugged; they'd never heard of autism."

"You're kidding," Anne commented, glancing away from Simon's progress for just a second. When she looked back, three corners were complete.

"They're simple people," Ohlmeyer continued. "The father's a mechanic; the mother's a housewife, both in their late forties. I was the one who explained it all to them." He paused briefly. "The mother understands it more than the father, I think. He still believes that he has a retarded son."

"But he's here," Anne added as a reminder that begged more explanation.

"Yes, he is. His first day here one of the staff put a

twenty-five piecer in front of him. Real simple; a blue cow and a red pig, I don't remember exactly. Simon never touched it. The next day he took a five hundred piecer from a shelf and, well . . ."

"On his own?"

"Entirely," Ohlmeyer answered proudly. He felt pride in the progress of any patient, and in this instance it was like watching a flower blossom in the dead of winter. "The staff gave him a thousand piecer . . . nothing. Another five hundred . . . *voilà!* He does only puzzles with five hundred pieces and always after turning the pieces facedown."

"Any other abilities?" Anne inquired. The fourth and final corner was about to appear.

"Instant recognition and calculation, we're certain. We gave him a five hundred piecer with one piece removed. He started to turn the pieces over, then stopped within seconds and started rocking nervously."

"The uniform out of sorts," Anne commented. "How soon were the symptoms noticed after he was born?"

"Within months," Ohlmeyer replied with a nod. "Early infantile autism. And yes, he can communicate verbally and has since about the age of two."

The loose pieces dwindled until only one rectangle of gray paper, broken by the odd lines of a jigsaw cut, was left. Simon let a hand hover over it briefly, then returned it to his lap and started rocking easily again.

"The indications are that he's a Kanner," Anne said, confirming Ohlmeyer's suspicion that Simon Lynch probably fell into a portion of the autistic population, numbering approximately 10 percent of the total, known as the Kanner's syndrome subgroup. These individuals presented similar advanced abilities in memory, computation, and insistence on sameness in their environment. Some exhibited remarkable abilities in math, art, or music. An even smaller percentage of the autistic population showed almost unbelievable talents in certain areas. Dr. Anne Jefferson, professor of psychology at the University of Chicago, gazed in wonder at the monitor, watching a young man of remarkable—*yes*, she told herself, *maybe even that*—ability sway lazily back and forth. "Or more."

Ohlmeyer nodded. "I didn't want to predispose you."

"Ever the scientist, Chas, aren't you?" She switched off her Think Pad and closed the lid. "Have you done a right brain/left brain yet?"

"Cursory, but I think now we're going to need to do that and a full protocol. Of course I have to convince his father to allow it. The mother's on our side, but it was a major effort to get pops to let him come to Thayer three days a week. We had to work out transportation, arrange for the fees to be waived, yaditta, yaditta . . ." Ohlmeyer set his clipboard aside and took a magazine from the viewing room's desk. He rolled it tightly in one hand and pointed it in mock accusation at Anne. "You're thinking it, aren't you?"

"That he could be a savant? Aren't you?"

Ohlmeyer demurred with a tilt of his head. "Would you like to meet Simon?" He held the magazine up. "I have to give him this before he goes home."

Anne reached out, took the magazine, and uncurled it. "The *Tinkery*?" She noted the address label. "*You* are a member of the Tinker Society?"

"Is that impossible to believe?" Ohlmeyer asked with a grin. "My intelligence is up there and has been for a very long time."

She gave a friendly roll of her eyes in response and paged through the slick pages. The Tinker Society was a loose gathering of those with verifiable genius-level IQs, and this was its bimonthly publication, though an old one she could tell from the cover. "Why are you giving this to him?"

"Simon doesn't like only jigsaw puzzles, Anne. His mother told me that he's been doing crosswords, word searches, sequences, all sorts of puzzles since his early teens. That's when he found a fascination with them. Funny, though, she said he never had an overt fondness for jigsaws." Ohlmeyer boosted his shoulders in wonder and stood, taking the magazine back from Anne. "Anyway, the *Tinkery* has a puzzle section at the back. I thought I'd let him have a look at one of mine that was gathering dust. A purely unscientific exercise, I will remind you."

"Of course," Anne said with a slow nod.

"Come."

They left the viewing room and made the short trek to the observation room. Chas Ohlmeyer held Anne up there. "There's one other minor thing you should know before meeting him."

"Yes?"

"Until about a month ago he had a tendency to wet himself whenever he was around a . . . well . . . person of color."

Anne's eyes bulged.

"He grew up in a very . . . insulated environment, Anne. He's white; his parents are white; his neighborhood is white. Anyone he's seen in or near his home is likely white."

"I see."

"It hasn't happened recently, but since you will be a new face to him, well, I wanted to prepare you."

Anne giggled quietly.

"What?" Ohlmeyer inquired, his eyes narrowing.

"To think that I could scare the piss out of anybody is a bit on the laughable side, Chas."

"Anne . . . Come on." Ohlmeyer twisted the knob and let

Anne enter before he followed and closed the door behind. The pace of Simon's rocking increased, but he did not look up. "Hello, Simon."

A boyish face rose in a flash and fell as quickly. "Hello Dr. Chazzz." His voice was young and tinny, and he over-enunciated the last sound in Ohlmeyer's given name. It was intentional, but not mocking.

"Simon, I have someone I'd like you to meet. Her name is Anne. She's a doctor also."

Another glance at the face. Anne noted very fair skin this time before it retreated to ponder the nearest edge of the table. There was little color in the cheeks, maybe a hint of natural blush, and bright white teeth gleamed through a chance part in thin lips. "It's nice to meet you, Simon."

"It's nice to meet Simon," Simon said as though parroting her greeting, but he was not.

"You can call her Dr. Anne," Ohlmeyer suggested.

"I can call you Dr. Anne," came the repetition. Simon's chin rose a bit. He was now tracking the far edge of the table.

"Dr. Anne is a good friend of mine," Ohlmeyer said as a subtle assurance. And for a more important reason.

Simon wore an oversize gray sweatshirt. He reached up and then down through the loose collar and pulled out a set of ringbound three-by-five cards that hung around his neck on a lanyard. A small pen, clipped to the front card, was similarly attached by a single string to one of the rings that held the cards together. Simon pulled the pen free, clicked the top, and flipped through a precise number of cards. He stopped at one with the large title FRIENDS written across the top in blue marker. Below it were rudimentary scribbles on individual lines. Anne could make out the name DOKTR CHAZ near the top and thought immediately: *He writes phonetically . . . but without e's.*

Simon held the stubby pen close to the card in a fierce grip. He found the next empty line and wrote DOKTR AN. He now had a friend named Dr. Anne. Friends were good people who could be trusted. Only friends could tell you if another person was a friend. Father had told him that. So had Mother. And what they said was right.

Anne dipped her head a bit, eyes trying to meet Simon's. "You do puzzles very well, Simon."

His head seemed to nod between extremes of the rocking. "I like this puzzle."

"Simon, Anne is going to be working with you some days," Ohlmeyer said. "Is that all right with you?"

He inspected the FRIENDS list, then dropped the cards back down the neck of his sweatshirt. "It's all right with Simon."

"Good!" Ohlmeyer said with enthusiasm. Tone conveyed feeling more than words, he knew. "And speaking of puzzles, remember I told you I had a magazine with some good puzzles in it?"

Remember . . . He didn't. But "magazine" meant something. "I read *Ranger Rick*."

"That's a good magazine," Ohlmeyer said. "And here's a new magazine for you." He held it out. Simon accepted it with both hands and brought it to his lap. He flattened it out, pressing with both palms and ironing toward the sides, without letting his eyes settle upon it. His dry skin caressing the slick cover made a sound somewhere between a whine and a hiss. "When you get home, you can look at the puzzles."

Home . . . Simon pulled the cuff of his left sleeve up and brought the watch on his wrist very close to his face. *Big hand three ticks before the twelve. Little hand on the four.* He saw many things in that, but he knew that one of them was the time, and it was almost at the time when his mother had told him he should get in the yellow bus. He let the cuff fall and tugged at the long edges of the *Tinkery* once before tucking it under his arm. He stood, the chair screeching as it slid backward. "Dr. Chazzz, my mother said I should go now."

Déjà vu was an easy thing to experience with autistics, Ohlmeyer knew. He'd had this same exchange with Simon each afternoon when it was time to head for the bus. "You're right, Simon. It's almost four o'clock. Carolyn is waiting down the hall for you. She'll take you to the bus."

Simon reached toward his collar, then stopped. He seemed rapt in some thought.

"Simon?" Ohlmeyer inquired.

"Carolyn is my friend."

Ohlmeyer smiled, nodding. A small success. "Yes, she is."

Simon stepped around the table and took two steps toward the door; then he stopped in front of Anne, his left shoulder to her. His head came up and twisted toward her for an instant. He resumed a head-down posture and said, "My mother is a pretty lady."

"I bet she is," Anne said, accepting the roundabout compliment.

"Okay, Simon." Ohlmeyer placed a hand on the youngster's shoulder. "You had better get moving." He opened the door and guided Simon through it. He watched him until he was safely in Carolyn's hands. When Ohlmeyer turned back, Anne was resting against the table in a half sit. "You passed muster, I have to say."

"He's"—she checked "nice" before it came out—"sweet."

"He's special," Ohlmeyer added not as a correction but as a statement of additional fact. "Very special. If we can work with him and get him to explore his abilities, we might pick something up in the process." He crossed his arms, his face twisting into a teeth-gritted smile. "Something to help explain this damned disorder."

"Anything I can do, Chas, just put it to me."

"Talking to the parents might help. I want him here five days a week. He needs to be here five days."

A slow nod agreed . . . almost completely. "Just promise me something."

Some old friends never changed, Ohlmeyer recognized. "Anne . . ."

She showed a cautionary palm to her friend. "Not you, Chas, but that young man does not need to be made into a lab rat for one of these eager young Ph.D. candidates you've got lurking in the shadows. He has a life; he deserves a life. I won't be party to his exploitation."

Ohlmeyer held four fingers up. "Scout's honor."

"Wrong number, Chas," Anne commented. "Well, this has been a rather pleasant ending to the day."

"And now you get to go home to your G-man," Ohlmeyer said with a smile. "So tell me, is the Windy City keeping Art busy?"

"Well, he has a saying: 'There's bad guys wherever you go.' "

"Atrocious grammar," Ohlmeyer said, then added soberly, "But true."

Anne nodded. "Very."

The day was almost done when Art Jefferson swiveled his chair toward the window that, on a clear day, afforded him a partial view of Lake Michigan and pulled the folded note from his shirt pocket. He opened it and smiled at the five words. "Love you. Tonight, my place?"

As if it were some tryst his new bride was planning. He tucked the note away and chuckled to himself, realizing that he felt somewhat like a twenty-year-old newlywed. Well, he was the latter, but he was thirty years and change past the former, on his second and last wife—knock wood—and at a place in his life he'd hardly dreamed possible three years ago.

Recently divorced, number four in the Federal Bureau of Investigation's Los Angeles field office, handling the biggest investigation of his career, and on the edge. What had come of that combination? A good agent—a friend—with a bullet in his neck, a heart attack for himself, and a quasi demotion from command to street duty. Two years of taking stock followed, case after case, some big, most not, just plodding along until the world began to spin his way again.

Anne . . . he thought, feeling his warm cheeks rise. On a blind date, of all things, he had met her. A woman of impossibly meshed qualities. Fiercely strong and independent, vital, intelligent beyond his measure by far, and at heart she was a little girl who savored life. *Tonight, my place?*

He could mark the instant in time when the change in his life took hold. It was the moment when he realized that he loved Anne. Truly loved her beyond anything he'd felt for his first wife, in fact so different from any emotion he could remember that he'd wondered if he'd ever really loved Lois. The feeling ushered in a newness to his life, relieved him of whatever demons had haunted him. Opened new paths. The job he held now, A-SAC (assistant special agent in charge) of the Chicago field office, had come not as an offer but as a request. "I want you as my number two, Art," Bob Lomax, the SAC, had said in the call some five months earlier. The two had worked as street agents together during Art's posting to the Windy City more than a decade before.

And so he was here . . . again. With all the pieces of his

life in place, finally. Staring out his office window into the mist that shrouded Lake Michigan, his heart beating beneath Anne's note, Art Jefferson felt content, warm, and completely at home for the first time in his life.

"Your place, huh?" Art said aloud as he swung back toward his desk and locked the file drawer. He'd accomplished all he was going to this Friday. He stood from his chair and was feeding several pieces of paper into the shredder when three taps sounded on his door. Bob Lomax came in behind the knock.

"Got a minute?"

Art let the last document ride into the shredder. It came out as paper spaghetti and fell into the burn bag. "Sure. I was just finishing up. What's up?"

The SAC approached and took a seat facing Art's desk. He slid it close and laid a plain file folder on the desk. "Have a look."

Art sat and put his reading glasses on, then lifted the file's cover. A face less its eyes stared up at him from an eight-by-ten glossy. "Jesus."

"Pretty, huh?" Lomax asked the A-SAC. "Recognize who it is?"

Art's eyes, narrow and troubled, came up from the photo. "I'm supposed to recognize this?"

Lomax leaned back in the chair and scratched his scarred left cheek. He had a face more reminiscent of a boxer than a bureaucrat. "Think back. Before you transferred out west. Nineteen seventy-five or so."

Art looked back to the photo and carefully through the others. He grimaced visibly and was very glad they were in black and white. "Sorry, Bob."

"Vince Chappell," Lomax said, now rubbing his lower lip with a single finger. "Ring a bell?"

It did. Art returned to the first photo, eyes plucked, lower lip cut away and hanging in a flap over the chin, exposing the teeth like some ghoulish Halloween mask. The tip of the nose was gone, leaving a bruised pyramid of flesh less its peak.

In one picture the genitals were missing.

"Is this Vinnie?" Art asked in a hollow voice.

Lomax nodded. "He worked with us back then, doing OC investigations." OC was organized crime, always a busy assignment in Chicago.

Art closed the cover and dropped the file on his desk. The corners of several photos slid free. "My God." He covered his mouth and reclined toward the window. "What—"

"Remember when he left, where he was going?"

"CIA, wasn't it?"

"Right," Lomax confirmed. "He was assigned to the trade mission in Japan, doing whatever spooks do for them. A week ago today he was killed in an agency house north of Tokyo. He apparently took a hooker there for some fun. It turns out she wasn't a hooker." The SAC reached across the desk and took the folder. He removed two typewritten pages from behind the photos. "This is from the agency team that did a hush-hush on this. 'Victim was bound to the bed with buckled leather straps. There was evidence of damage to every pain/pressure point on the victim's body, indicating an attempt (result unknown) at information extraction.' A nice way to say 'torture,'" Lomax commented, moving to the next page. "Then this: 'Blood was evident throughout the room, and along a path leading to the shower in the adjoining bathroom. Numerous fingerprints, palm prints, and footprints (most in blood) were apparent and were collected for analysis.'" Lomax returned the report to its place in the file. "CIA sent the fingerprints to our lab in D.C. and got the results yesterday. The 'hooker' was some sick bitch named

Keiko Kimura. Ever hear of her?" Art shook his head. "The CIA brief says she's a former Japanese Red Army terrorist schooled at the finest establishments in North Korea, Libya, Iran, et cetera. A real pedigree type with a specialty in getting people to talk. In 'ninety-one she dropped from sight. She reappeared last year doing freelance work for the money."

"Not enriched by the JRA ideology, eh?" Art observed. Revolution was not the path to success for most.

"You got it," Lomax said.

Art gestured to the file. "So why do we have this?"

"We have this so I can give it to you," Lomax answered, setting the file back on the desk. "High priority, and keep that under lock and key. Assign it out to check on Vince's connections when he was here. The CIA is trying to rule in or out anything that could have compromised him. Maybe he had an old acquaintance here and said something he shouldn't have. You know the routine."

Somehow the term "routine" sounded distasteful when it pertained to someone you once worked closely with, Art thought. "I'll have it taken care of." He took the folder and locked it in his desk's file drawer. "Do we know why Kimura was put on to Vince?"

"The new round of trade talks is coming up. Vince was probably trying to get some inside intel on their strategies. Someone on the opposing team probably thought he might be privy to ours. The new gold standard, Art. Economic espionage." Lomax thought quietly, then went on. "One more thing. Somewhat related, in fact. Monday the new code gear will be up and running. NSA put it in this morning. Big damn thing. The director wants us off the Mayfly system in two weeks."

"That's a damn short time to get everybody checked out," Art said.

"That's why you're in charge of it. Monday I want you

checked out with the com clerk so you can set up a schedule to get everybody up to speed. Two weeks."

Art nodded. Lomax was very serious. "How does this relate to Vince getting killed?"

"CIA thinks Mayfly might be compromised. Everyone's been using it for five years now: us, State, CIA, Defense. If it is leaky, it could put a lot of people in jeopardy. All our office-to-office secret and top secret stuff gets transmitted using Mayfly. And worse things can happen to one of our UCs than happened to Vince if they're blown."

Worse? Art wasn't certain about that. But dead was dead, and an undercover agent losing his or her cover could easily end up that way. "All right. What's the new system?"

"It's called Kiwi. Supposed to be *the* system. Unbreakable and tamperproof."

"Hmm," Art grunted, nodding. "I heard the same thing in L.A. when Mayfly went in."

Lomax crossed his fingers and stood. "You wanna grab a beer?"

Art came around his desk and lifted his coat from the brass tree near the door. "I think my wife has plans for me tonight."

Bob Lomax raised an eyebrow and smiled. "Get lucky, number two."

Art walked Lomax back to his office and caught the elevator alone. He pressed the button for the basement garage and leaned back against the waist-high handrail. He closed his eyes and thought of Anne.

But from another part of his consciousness Vince Chappell stared at him with bloody voids where his eyes should be. Art opened his and looked straight ahead at the elevator door until it slid open. He stepped off quickly and turned right toward his car.

The school bus pulled to the curb on Vincent Street two houses past the intersection with Milford Avenue and stopped before number 2564, a two-story craftsman-style home with a fading blue exterior and pretty curtains in every window. "Sweetie, we're here," the bus driver, a pudgy redhead, called out to her last passenger. All her "kids" were "sweetie."

Simon Lynch knew that the bus had stopped, so as he did at each stop no matter who was getting off, he pulled his cards through his collar and flipped to the card that said YELLOW BUS on top. Below that he had written, with his mother prompting him: IF THE BUS STOPS AT A BLU HOUS AND TH NUMBR ON TH BLU HOUS IS 2564 GT OUT OF TH BUS AND GO INTO TH BLU HOUS MOMMY WIL B INSID TH BLU HOUS WITH HOT CHOKOLIT FOR SIMON Simon nodded to himself and returned the cards to their place, got up with Dr. Chas's magazine still under his arm, and walked to the front of the bus. "My mother says to get off here."

The driver winked and smiled at him. "Sure enough, sweetie. We'll see you Monday. Bye now."

Simon turned without acknowledging her farewell and stepped carefully off the bus, hand on the silvery rail. This was the part where he'd hurt himself sometime ago. "When" wasn't in the myriad of thoughts as his foot touched the slushy ground, but "hurt" was. His foot had gone out from beneath his body because the ground was slippery once, and he'd bumped his head hard on the step of the bus. He cried then, and he had cried when the other doctors—not Dr. Chas—stuck him with needles when Mommy took him to them. That hurt. He didn't like to hurt.

"Get going, sweetie," the driver prodded from her seat as she had every day since that first one when he'd slipped and cracked his noggin real good. Boy, the tears this one had cried then! Now each and every day he stepped off her bus, he froze at the bottom like a statue until being urged on with gentle words. "Mama's waiting."

Hot chocolate. Simon liked hot chocolate. He shuffle-stepped up the damp walkway and onto the porch. At the top step the inner door opened. "Hello, honey!"

Simon smiled giddily as the storm door swung out. "Honey is sweet!"

"Just like my Simon," Jean Lynch said. She pulled her son into a sidearm hug as she waved at the driver and led him inside. "Daddy had to work a little late tonight, so he won't be home for a wh—" She saw the magazine under his arm. "What's this?"

Simon held it out with both hands. "It has puzzles."

"That's right," Jean Lynch said. "Dr. Ohlmeyer said he was going to give you something with puzzles in it." When she said "puzzles," she playfully pinched his nose. "That's wonderful. Tell you what. You take that into the living room and look at the puzzles. I put your hot chocolate on the table next to Daddy's chair."

"I can sit in Daddy's chair," Simon said as a statement of fact. There was almost emotion in his voice, his mother thought. But then why not? Others might not be able to recognize it as well as she, but her son revered his father. Maybe in his own way, but equal to what other sons might feel.

"You're right, honey." *Oops.*

"Honey is sweet!" Simon responded.

Jean Lynch smiled. "And so is my Simon. Now go drink your hot chocolate and look at your magazine. I'll be in the kitchen. Go on." She sent him on his way with a gentle touch on his back.

Simon walked into the big living room that was at the

front of the house and went directly to his father's chair, a brown upholstered rocker with green towels draping the arms and the headrest. When he sat down, his head twisted until his nose was against the top towel. His nostrils flared, and his face lightened. It smelled of his daddy.

His body began to rock easily. His daddy's chair followed the motion in a delayed repetition.

He smelled something else. The hot chocolate, in his favorite blue mug, barely steamed where it sat. Simon laid the magazine on his lap and took the cup two-handed and put it to his lips. He drank with a loud, slurping sound in beats of three—sssoooooooop . . . sssoooooooop . . . sssoooooooop—then pulled the cup away and sighed with satisfaction, "Aaaaaahhhh." Just the way his daddy did.

He set the cup back on the coaster on the lamp table and cast his eyes to the *Tinkery*. They danced over the cover, unwilling to remain still. There were too many colors, and they bled together so that one color was not itself anymore, and then it was another color. In his mind's eye, Simon saw pictures as unbalanced, imprecise, and unsettling. A picture of a chair was not like looking at a real chair. The world reduced to two dimensions disturbed him.

Simon flipped quickly past the cover and to the pages of words and letters and numbers. He liked words and letters and numbers. Sometimes they were puzzles, and sometimes they were just words and letters and numbers. When they were just words and letters and numbers, he could look at all of them and hear what they were saying. That's what he did with all the books in the basement—

—*basement*. That meant something. Simon stopped and pulled out his cards. He found the one with STORM written on top. IF A LOUD NOYZ SKAIRS YOU AND IT GTS LOUDR AND YU KANT FIND MOMMY AND DADDY THN GO TO TH BASMNT

Simon cast his eyes upward and listened. After a few seconds he put his cards away and looked back to words and letters and numbers, their connection to the basement just a thought flitted away. He moved through the pages, sweeping them from right to left to reveal the next, capturing what was meaningful to him in furtive glances.

Through the words and letters and numbers, page after page, information filtered into his brain, filling the delicate and damaged neural matrix that guided Simon Lynch through every moment of his existence, referencing itself without conscious effort, indexing, cross-indexing, adding to the library of knowledge that had been absorbed from reading, from hearing. Squirreling it away like nuts for a time when it might be needed, though it never was . . . externally.

Internally it was a very different story, with morsels of information competing with one another in a test for prominence and validation. This occurred constantly, automatically, in streams of words and letters and numbers that occupied Simon Lynch every waking moment, rolling like a waterfall of knowledge behind his eyes as his day marched on. It was less like thinking than processing. Thinking implied choice. Simon had never known a choice in the use of his mind. It functioned beyond the primal instructions for involuntary necessities as a computer. When he woke, he was processing. When he ate, he was processing. When he did puzzles, he was processing. When his father sang to him, he was processing.

When Simon Lynch slept, he dreamed of words and letters and numbers.

He had no knowledge that this was happening, and as he flipped through the *Tinkery*, it went on, and on, and on, and continued even when he happened upon the first puzzle in the magazine. It covered an entire page. Nothing marked it overtly as a puzzle, but Simon knew that it was.

```
1839956021PFYRTKLYTE3668493216KLRMAYBPKW9865749102
6682936540368594363840575937643850504763849505847b
63840473538305645859857659575940362273021854058740
42083643849036354378302026436498362037463836538392
76354763826328393643839293764547392032764639829274
73937639823028373902092735456393203846498393746476
626238364849459050569854745638389360267364300032b3
6253453032662422293636373888121212143057846548948?
7245363784984946478490476498062202520027253243985O
7353546474745646539302374640463064035439546384056З
896759379157777777425252634350797879787979078532Чз
62432738654849463484904764662903764654945649352348
1729236437549860402484565407905965497698567350201b
73879499432943964398649864949494941964941628394028
83643840463437840458352653984504573452749457367439
32638045735373038376438490457476498505674675950739
78353903026254389450476365485490476476594647459437
73984037354785904764845057647595639027850837695047
98464846498690678403847590846498450947494904849849
6343865968690463943765944522385056559539364936З9З9
3132205629063973934639352824333499679767634398236З
7836538354383653834643846484649835280609724750723Ч
26398404363740508325743904693047494374904652849584
78363490365394363937639362920272574394723453749438
38353474950670574653783403724527629364895946485946
90221452627843940450576365484596369362920162539407
45137304329687697643964398418419688807607640642306
987438487543784785437876439869012606021060106066ЧЧ
87987587549875870554398404634543784940474354749393
7363843047454840457846539839363849464674935329490S
ATHDKTENVODGDLFOEGFDMFOFGDKDSPQSCBVVCJFDHDSGDSJYYQ
```

Simon studied the puzzle for several seconds, noting in that time that there were 1,450 numbers in the body of the puzzle and a mix of 50 numbers/letters at the beginning and 50 letters at the end. These were not part of the numbers, he saw. They told what to do with the numbers, how to split them, where to visualize breaks, the order in which they should be processed, and—he blinked quickly three times as the solution came to him—that there were three numbers of equal length—keys—that he needed to know to process the parts into a final product.

Simon had those keys, a total of 4,350 digits, in four blinks.

He used the first key to process the parts of the original number. This yielded 700,833 groups of three-digit numbers, with one nonsense digit after the 302,412th group. His brain discarded this digit.

The second key he used to extract a three-digit number from the third—103—and he processed the second key again with the 50-letter group at the end of the puzzle. This yielded yet another number, which told him how to determine which of the three-number groups to discard.

Six blinks later 700,730 of them were gone.

Simon was left with 103 3-number groups. He went back to the third key and processed it with the 50-letter group. This told him how to order the 103-number groups.

He saw them in order after four blinks.

There were 103 groups of 3 numbers left. Simon twisted his wrist and looked briefly at his watch. The time did not concern him.

Simon knew what to do next. He looked back to the 50-number/letter mix at the beginning of the puzzle. There was a shift key in this.

He saw the 103 groups in order, processed them, 087 first, shifted, and on.

The 103 groups yielded letters and numbers in a logical order.

Simon looked at the puzzle's body again. He saw a string of 103 letters and numbers.

IFYOUSOLVETHISPUZZLECALL18005551398ANDTELLTHEOPERA
TORTHATYOUHAVESOLVEDPUZZLE99YOUWILLTHENBEISSUED
APRIZE.

The string needed spaces. He saw them and read "IF YOU SOLVE THIS PUZZLE CALL 18005551398 AND TELL THE OPERATOR THAT YOU HAVE SOLVED PUZZLE 99 YOU WILL THEN BE ISSUED A PRIZE."

It had taken Simon twenty seconds to yield what he saw as an instruction not unlike those written on his cards. He stood and walked in short steps to the telephone in the far corner of the living room. His mommy had shown him how to dial 911 if something very wrong happened. (Simon understood "wrong"; he did not understand "bad.") He knew how to dial his daddy's work if something was wrong. He was supposed to push the buttons.

That was *calling* someone.

He was supposed to call someone. He lifted the phone and held it next to his face the way his mommy had shown him. It was cold plastic, and it hummed in his ear. It was supposed to do that.

Simon knew what to do next. He used a very straight finger and pressed the numbers the puzzle told him to press.

He was calling someone.

———

Leo Pedanski was mid-bite into the warm bear claw when the buzzing of the phone brought his eyes up from his linguistics text in a start. Through his thick glasses he looked at the phone. The light above line two was flashing. Recording machines and trace gear to his right began to hum.

The thirty-year-old let the sugary pastry hang in his mouth as he slid his activity log close. It was where he was to record any happenings during his thrice-weekly shift at the Puzzle Center. He looked briefly down at the nearly blank form. He'd written nothing there in six months.

"Shee-it," he said past the bear claw, then set the tasty morsel aside as line two buzzed a second time. Line two was the outside line. He could recall distinctly the last time it had shown signs of life. The previous year, just before Halloween, when some Jethro from COMSEC-T had had his wimpy subroutine busted clean. Pedanski had joyously passed the news on to the wannabe that he was no Z-man, and Pedanski should know; he *was* a Z-man.

He grabbed a pencil and noted the time quickly on his log, picked up the receiver, and, certain that all the gear was up and running, pressed the button next to line two in expectation that he was going to be able to ruin another T-boy's day. "Hi!" he said excitedly, just as he and his fellow Z-men had practiced. "You've reached the Puzzle Center." At this point Pedanski wanted to laugh. *If only they knew how close that was to the truth . . .* "You have solved one of our hardest puzzles, and having done so, you will be awarded a *two-year!* subscription to the magazine of your choice. I'll need your name and address, phone number, and the number of the puzzle you've solved." Pedanski stared at the trace gear to his front in silence. The silence persisted. "Hello?"

Stiff paper rustling, then: "I can't tell strangers my name."

What the hell . . . "Uhhh."

"You're a stranger."

Was this a kid? Pedanski wondered. It spoke like one but in an older voice. "Uh, this is the Puzzle Center. Where did you get this number?"

"I solved puzzle ninety-nine."

Pedanski snatched the glasses from his face, his gray eyes bugging. *What?* He steadied himself as best he could and swallowed before speaking. "Again, what puzzle?"

"Puzzle ninety-nine."

No. It could not be. This had to be a razz. It had to—

But it couldn't be. It was line two, and if anyone in Z was pulling this as a stunt, the boss would have his ass in a federal pen before he could spit.

It had to be a joke, and it could not be at the same time.

"Who is this?" Pedanski asked seriously.

"You're a stranger."

"Listen, I need—" Click. Dial tone. "Hello . . . dammit!" he swore as he slammed the phone into its cradle. With the hand that held it he covered his mouth. It, like the one holding the pencil, was trembling. *Oh, man, this cannot be happening. It is im-possible.*

But something had definitely happened. Something terrible. He did not know exactly what yet, but one thing was quite clear: A single phone call had just cost him and his comrades five years of work and Uncle Sam ten billion dollars.

Chicken Little would have been proud.

chapter 2

Big Dogs

G. Nicholas Kudrow paced slowly along the book-
case wall of his office, a few sheets of paper held high in one
hand, the other rubbing slow circles on his prominent chin
as he considered what he read. At the end of the bookcase
the forty-eight-year-old civil servant turned and retraced his
steps toward his mahogany desk, still reading, his tinted
glasses angled down at the object of his interest. Almost to
the next turnaround he paused, square face rising a bit in
contemplation, then lowering as the thought-walk continued.

At the end he stopped and ran a hand over his graying
brown hair, whose natural wave added an illusory inch to
his six-one frame, and looked away from the papers for the
last time. His eyes angled right, at the flexible microphone
snaking upward near the computer monitor on his desk.
"Voice," he said loudly, in a distinct tone he knew would be
recognized, then, in a more normal voice: "Intercom." His
normal voice commanded attention. An electronic beep told
him to continue. "Sharon?"

"Yes, Mr. Kudrow," a disembodied voice replied through
the speaker in the microphone's base.

"Contact Colonel Murdoch in S and inform him that I

have studied his request and that it is denied." Kudrow stood motionless, staring toward his desk.

"Understood, Mr. Kudrow."

"Intercom off." Two beeps signaled that his voice command had been heeded. Kudrow walked around his desk and sat, tossing the poorly conceived request into a large red basket. There was no need to shred what went in there.

Done with serious contemplation for the moment, Kudrow sipped lemonade from the half-full glass on his desk and flipped through a minor stack of papers. All bore the top secret designation across their top; that was why his secretary had placed them with the routine material he needed to peruse before this first day of the workweek was finished. If he'd had his druthers, he'd have had Sharon sign off on them, but the government had silly rules that only added to the work load of its truly valuable people, of whom he was certainly one, Kudrow believed without a doubt. So he moved quickly through the collection of briefs from DoD, State, and other less important entities and was only mildly perturbed when his intercom interrupted him mid-stack.

"Yes?"

"Mr. Kudrow, Mr. Folger says he's coming down." There was a distinct hesitation in Sharon's voice.

Kudrow stared silently at the speaker for a second. "He's *coming* down? Did you inform him that I am occupied?"

"He didn't give me the chance, Mr. Kudrow." She never called him sir. Military officers were "sirs." Kudrow was proudly a career civilian. "He just called, said he's coming down, and hung up. I tried to get him back on the phone, but his secretary said he just hurried out."

"Very well," Kudrow said tersely, and heard his secretary click off. Interruptions—the bane of those with purpose. G. Nicholas Kudrow was a man with purpose. And with position. Deputy director for COMSEC-Z of the National Security Agency. A position that was never publicly acknowledged as existing by those "in the know," in the same way that his domain, Department Z of the NSA's Communications Security directorate, was but a phantom operation within the world's largest intelligence-gathering organization.

But for apparitions, Kudrow and Z left an undisputable mark on the basic functions of the nation's government. He and his people were responsible for the cryptographic systems that protected the sensitive information that flowed between pieces of the United States government and its assorted agencies, departments, and bureaus. When people committed secrets to paper, or to some other storage medium, and sent it across the street or across an ocean, when imaging satellites snapped their pictures and relayed the shots to a ground station, when secure phones rang at any U.S. installation, the signals passed at each end of its transmission through something that G. Nicholas Kudrow was responsible for. In between those stations the secret was nonsensical gobbledygook.

It was Kudrow's job, his purpose, to see that this remained the status quo. To that end he was directly responsible for a budget of one hundred million dollars in discretionary funding a year, fifteen times that much in annual project money, two dozen cryptographers who dreamed up the "ultimate security," and a hundred technicians to build the physical structures—or cryptographic machines— that gave that ultimate security to select users. He had chosen the design of the building that housed Department Z, even the color of its windowless exterior—dark brown—and nearly everything else about Z had his stamp of approval on it. It was his domain, and he balanced his rule of it somewhere between father and tyrant, depending on the situation at hand.

The tyrant in him snapped eyes to the door when it opened without a knock. Brad Folger, assistant deputy director for COMSEC-Z, entered just ahead of Kudrow's secretary.

"Mr. Kudrow," Sharon said in frustrated apology, "I tried to grab him—"

"Good morning, Nick," Folger said, ignoring Sharon. Kudrow's assistant was in shirtsleeves, cuffs buttoned down smartly, but his red and blue tie was askew, fat and thin ends both showing. The lid above his right eye ticked noticeably. "Can we talk?"

This was no petty disturbance, Kudrow could tell by his assistant's appearance. "All right, Sharon." She stepped out with a poisonous glance at Folger and closed the thick door. Kudrow watched as Folger, forty but looking twenty-five, stepped close to his desk. "You should get that eye looked at."

Folger consciously tried to stem the tremor, the attempt futile. The lid shook like a flap of loose skin, covering half the eye in a perpetual jitter. "I got a call a few minutes ago. From Pedanski."

"And?"

Folger slid both hands into the pockets of his pleated gray trousers. "He wants me to bring you downstairs. He and Dean and Patel want to talk to us." Kudrow's chin rose a bit. "Nick, he sounded scared."

Kudrow's brow collapsed slowly into a series of fleshy furrows. He stood, his imposing frame against the jarring colors of the Lichtenstein that hung behind his desk. It had cost a hundred thousand dollars. "Scared?"

"I've never heard him like this," Folger said. "The guy usually doesn't take anything seriously."

But what would frighten Pedanski, or any of his animals, as Kudrow referred to the three all-stars of his team of cryptographers? He did not know. But he did know that anything involving the trio in concert required attention. They were special, after all, not only for who they were but for what they had created. "Let's go."

The Z building was but one of three dozen buildings on the grounds of the National Security Agency, which was ringed concentrically by three fences, the outer two chain link and topped with razor wire and the inner one electrified. Marines with smart-looking German shepherds walked the perimeter in an endless patrol, and from control points atop the U-shaped headquarters-operations building other marines scanned the grounds zealously for any attempt at intrusion, rifles slung for quick access. The security was meant to be oppressive, and seemed more so considering that the entire NSA complex sat *within* the boundaries of the United States Army's Fort George Meade, located halfway between Baltimore and the nation's capital.

The Z building, a hundred yards inside the triple fence and fifty yards from the nearest structure, was surrounded by its own combination of chain link, razor wire, and high voltage. Two marines guarded the single portal through the barrier at all times. They had orders to shoot any who attempted unauthorized entry into the windowless brown building known colloquially as the Chocolate Box.

They had done so twice in ten years. Neither incident had made the papers.

On the first floor of the Z building, G. Nicholas Kudrow left his office at a brisk walk with Brad Folger at his heels. He headed for the stairs to the basement and walked freely down one level.

There was no security inside the Z building. If you were in and breathing, you were supposed to be there.

At the bottom of the stairs Kudrow turned right and cruised down a hallway, passing three green doors, each opening to disheveled offices that he avoided religiously. No placards marked the spaces. At the end of the hall there was one more door. He opened it without breaking stride and entered what was called the Puzzle Center.

It looked like a college dorm at finals.

Leo Pedanski stood with a start and spilled the remnants of his soda on a layer of papers that covered one of the room's two desks. "Mr. Kudrow. Hi."

Kudrow's head twisted slowly as he surveyed the room. Dozens of empty red cans lay on the desks, on the floor next to overflowing wastebaskets, and atop equipment that had cost the taxpayers far more than they needed to pay. Stacks of paper rose to various heights almost everywhere that there was a surface to pile them. Both desks were littered with plastic wrappers. A third chair had been wedged into the room. The air smelled of sweat and junk food.

"Gentlemen," he said in greeting. Craig Dean, taller than the boss by an inch and sporting an unkempt ponytail that had seen hardly a trim in a year, rose from a cross-legged position and stood next to Pedanski, whose hair was a mess of reddish brown tangles. Vikram Patel, pudgy and balding at twenty-seven, did not trust his legs at the moment and remained on the floor, arms hugging both knees to his chest. "Scared" was a good word, Kudrow thought. "Redecorating?"

Leo Pedanski, the de facto leader of the trio by virtue of his advanced age, ran a hand hard over his head and brought the other to meet it in a grasp behind his neck. He was to be the messenger. His caffeine-filled stomach roiled loudly. "No, but, uh . . . we've got a real problem." A nervous half chuckle trailed off his words.

"It's the primary S-box," Patel said, his voice cracking. "It was weak. I knew it was weak."

Dean, a twenty-eight-year-old holder of two doctorates in theoretical mathematics and chaos theory, rotated his spindly body toward the accuser. "You damn Jethro, the primary S was mine! It was fine. It *is* fine!"

"Shut up," Pedanski said with as much authority as he could summon. It wasn't much. Their usually free-flowing, sometimes sophomoric relationship had been virtually wiped out in the span of sixty hours. All because of a single phone call.

"The primary S-box?" Kudrow inquired somewhat hopefully. "Is this about Mayfly?" He looked to Craig Dean, who stared back at him through John Lennon spectacles. It had to be about Mayfly; that's all it *could* be about. "You were doing a postmortem on Mayfly, son, weren't you? Did you find what might have compromised it?"

"Mr. Kudrow." Pedanski stepped in, drawing the boss's attention back to him. "It's not Mayfly. It's Kiwi."

Kudrow's spine straightened, his chin rising. Behind the gray tint his brown eyes flared. He heard Folger mutter, "Oh, shit," quietly behind. "What about Kiwi?"

"We ... it ..." Pedanski paused and swallowed. "Someone knows it."

"What do you mean, knows it?" Kudrow asked, more forcefully than he normally would have in dealing with the animals. They were a special grouping, one that required his fatherly touch more than a tyrannical demand for an explanation. But his paternal streak had gone AWOL for the moment.

"We got a call," Patel said between wet, teary sniffs. The twenty-seven-year-old computer engineer dragged the back of his arm across his nose and looked up to Kudrow. "Pedanski did, I mean."

Kudrow's eyes were snapping between the speakers. He

finally locked on Pedanski and took a half step forward. He took a covert deep breath to retrieve some calm. His heart rate had nearly doubled in a minute. "From the top, Mr. Pedanski. Everything."

Leo's gulp for air was plain to see before he spoke. "Okay. You know the validation protocol for Kiwi?"

"That was completed two years ago?" Kudrow responded. There was accusation in his rhetoric. "Yes."

"We did the standard stuff," Pedanski explained, though "standard" only in their world. For a full year two sets of paired Cray supercomputers, individually the most powerful pieces of computing equipment on the planet, had chewed at a piece of the digital trash produced when clear text was subjected to Kiwi.

Kiwi at that time was the most secure cryptographic system ever seen. But though the computer was the premier destroyer of crypto systems, there was one other element that had to be considered. "Including the human element test. You know, the hidden message in those puzzle sections of magazines. Three different magazines, I thin—"

"Get to it," Kudrow directed.

"The puzzles were KIWI ciphertext, and in there was a message to call the Puzzle Center. The same we've done with other systems. Minor ones, major ones." Pedanski saw the boss's nostrils flare impatiently. "So, like you said, that was all done a couple years ago. So"—the mathematician's voice went breathy for a second before he recovered—"Friday I'm doing my shift in here, and line two lights up. I figure it's some guy in T getting whacked, but when I pick it up, this ... kid, or something on the other end says he's solved puzzle ninety-nine. Ninety-nine was the Kiwi code number."

"We chose that because of Barbara Feldon," Dean said as though it would matter to Kudrow. "From *Get Smart*. She was agent—'' He wisely ended his addition to his comrade's explanation.

''Real smooth, Craig,'' Patel commented from the floor.

Pedanski took a breath and continued. ''Someone busted the ciphertext, Mr. Kudrow. Of Kiwi! I just about shit my pants. I didn't know what to do. I told the other shifts set to cover the center over the weekend to stay away, and I called in Craig and Vik right away.'' He seemed young and fragile as he looked around the room. ''We haven't slept since Friday, Mr. Kudrow. We've been going over every possible weakness in Kiwi, and we can't find anything. Not the primary S-box; that's fine. Nothing!'' He wiped a hand hard across his mouth. ''Kiwi was solid when the three of us thought it up; it was solid when we prototyped and validated it; it was solid when the gear to use it was being built and installed. But since three days ago . . . I don't know.'' His eyes glistened. ''I don't know.''

''Could someone be screwing with us, Nick?'' Folger asked quietly over his boss's shoulder. ''Someone inside or outside trying to tweak us? You know, to see how we handle a possible breach?''

Kudrow considered that and looked to Dean. Pedanski had turned away and was staring at the ceiling. ''Who knew what the clear text was in the puzzle?''

''Just the three of us,'' Dean answered. ''That was the Agent Ninety-nine thing. We were foolin' around one day and picked that for the identifier. We didn't tell anyone about it. Not even you or Mr. Folger. At least I didn't.''

''And what is that supposed to mean?'' Patel demanded.

''You two, enough!'' Pedanski glared at them, forcing them both into retreat. The anger stanched the tears he seemed ready to loose. ''Mr. Kudrow, all the Kiwi machines are going to be in and running in a few weeks.''

''Ninety-five percent are in use now, Nick,'' Folger said

softly. "FBI's the last to go on line. The embassies, DoD, CIA, they're all using it now. And we've got no fallback, Nick, not with Mayfly maybe being leaky."

Kudrow said nothing for a moment after his assistant had finished speaking. Neither did any of the animals. Instead he mentally tallied just how bad the situation could be if they were not being screwed with, as he doubted anyway. He wasn't assuaged by the result. *Disaster,* was what he thought.

"You have the call on tape?" Kudrow asked.

"Of course," Pedanski answered. "Sir, shouldn't we—"

"And the trace gear was working?"

Pedanski nodded to the boss. "The call came from Chicago."

There were two options, Kudrow quickly decided. Pull the plug on Kiwi, tell its users that it was not the unbreakable monster he'd promised it to be, and flush what he'd worked so hard for down the can. Because if Kiwi was no good, as Brad had said, there was nothing to switch to. Nothing feasible that could accommodate all the users who'd gone to Kiwi. *Ten billion dollars,* Kudrow thought. Wasted. Congress would not be happy. He would be the whipping boy, of course, sitting at a table covered by a field of green in some congressional hearing room off limits to cameras. He'd be privately destroyed by the men and women whose lives he *knew* were tangles of deceit and dishonor. And once his butt was bared . . .

G. Nicholas Kudrow had not made many friends in his long government career, but he had forced many alliances. He had not always followed the book, obeyed every law, or thought much of consequences other than how they could be avoided. He had used people, gathered information on them, held it over their heads, threatened, promised favors, persuaded, demanded.

But he had done all this in pursuit of getting the job done.

He had made the nation's communications secure and in doing so had secured his place in the future. He would have a long, quietly illustrious career, and he would someday be remembered in the texts that memorialized such things as the "Father of Kiwi." Kiwi might still be in use then. That was what he had believed. Until now.

Yes, dumping Kiwi was option one, and Kudrow knew without hesitation it was unacceptable.

Option two was the better course . . . for the country. Yes, for everyone. "I want a copy of the tape and the trace info on my desk in ten minutes."

Pedanski nodded, chewing his lower lip and digging fiercely at the carpet with the toes of his Reeboks. "But, Mr. Kudrow—"

"What?" Kudrow looked at each of the animals individually and gave his assistant a glance for surety's sake. "If someone is playing with us, gentlemen, testing us, they will not expect that we just dump the system *you* three designed. And if there is a weakness in your system, we have to find out what that is and how whoever cracked it did so. In either instance the proper course is to investigate. I will see to that." He looked over his shoulder to Folger. "Shut this room down. Assign anyone who is scheduled to work in here to other duties. Put them on the Mayfly dissection. I don't care. If that phone rings again, I don't want anyone other than a Kiwi team member answering . . . just in case. Understood?"

"Yesss," Folger replied breathily.

"You three work out a schedule to cover this place," Kudrow instructed. He thought Patel ready to complain but instead saw the small dark head fall between the worn knees of his jeans. "Understood?"

After three tentative nods Kudrow turned and left. He stopped in the hall just outside the door and slid his hands into his pockets. Brad Folger followed him out and studied the government blue carpet at his feet. The boss hadn't been able to swing a more pleasing gray sisal.

"Kiwi's all we have, Nick," Folger said once again, as though speaking of the air they breathed.

"All the more reason not to throw it away because of one phone call." Kudrow looked down the hallway, briefly at each door, then to the stairs that led up from the basement. It was the only way out. "We'll fix this."

"How?"

Kudrow began to walk toward the stairs, passing the three green doors as he did. "It won't be a problem," he answered with his back to his assistant, then disappeared up the staircase.

"So nothing?" Art Jefferson asked, looking up from the report.

"Preliminarily, no," Special Agent Denise Green answered. "That's just a quickie, remember."

"I know," Art acknowledged. "Bob said the CIA is anxious."

Green nodded and took the report back from the A-SAC. She saw him close his eyes as his glasses came off. "You knew Chappell, didn't you?"

"Briefly," Art answered. Surely not long or well enough to know some of the things the report had just told him. *To each his own*, Art usually thought, but in this case it looked as if Vince Chappell's sexual tastes had only made Keiko Kimura's job easier. "Subject acquaintances report a propensity for B & D (bondage and domination) in sexual situations." "Very briefly."

"Anything else?" Green asked.

Art glanced at his desk clock and stood in a hurry. "Nope. Gotta run. Make sure I have the full report by Friday."

"Yes, sir."

"Please, no sirs," Art said as he hurried by the youngish agent. "I'm old enough as it is."

The Chicago field office of the Federal Bureau of Investigation is located on the eleventh, twelfth, and thirteenth floors of the Federal Building on South Dearborn Street. Several blocks due west the Sears Tower rises toward the sky in stark black steps, and on late-summer afternoons when the sun is deep in the Northern Hemisphere the tower casts a shadow that leaves the west-facing bureau offices in a cooling shade.

The office Art rushed out of as winter was melting into a chilly spring had spears of bright afternoon light filling its space, but the room he arrived at one floor down from 13 a minute later knew no such measure of the day. Tucked between a conference room and file storage and, most important, just feet from the coffee and soda machines, communications was a windowless cube longer than wide, and on its door was a keypad entry system. Art fumbled mentally for the right number, mistakenly tried the one L.A. used for its com room, and knocked hard on the door after giving up. "A-SAC here."

"Just a minute." A shrill, rolling squeal came from behind the door before it opened. When it did, a pleasant but serious face looked up at Art through the opening. "Agent Jefferson," Special Agent Nelson Van Horn said in greeting. He leaned forward in a nonmotorized wheelchair, straight brown hair swept to the left, eyes dark but susceptible to a blue tint in the right light. "Memory trouble?"

Art saw the agent's face light up in jest. "All right, Nels.

I could say that thing needs some oil on the hubs, but I'm too po-lite to do so."

Van Horn wheeled back and let the A-SAC in, then closed the door. It locked and alarmed itself automatically. "Here to see the new toy?"

"That I am." Art walked deep into the com room, past fax machines, teletypes, computers, phones, and stopped just short of a three-foot-square polished metal cube that had been brought into the space through a now-patched hole in the west wall. He saw wires snaking from it, one each to the fax machines and phones, the computers, and one to a work-station that lacked a chair. Van Horn wheeled himself up to that one and reached over to pat the stainless steel cube.

"Our baby."

"It's a big damn thing," Art commented. He stepped close and touched it. His fingers tingled at the coldness of its metal surface.

"That's just the shell," Van Horn said. He rolled one wheel back so he faced the A-SAC. "That's so someone can't walk in here and take it with them. The thing weighs twelve hundred pounds, but"—he leaned conspiratorially close—"my sources say the actual works are no bigger than a shoe box. And don't worry about someone cutting into it; it's pressurized with some inert gas so that if the pressure drops, some sort of thing destroys the innards. Real James Bond stuff, eh?"

Art nodded, though he didn't understand. What mattered was that their communications were supposed to be rock solid secure now. The rest of the field office still had unsecure phones and faxes, but all sensitive communications took place in here. "So this is the Kiwi thing. As long as it works . . ."

Van Horn smiled and shook his head. He did understand

the basics of code gear—though he had no illusions about ever knowing the secrets inside the silver cube—a knowledge gained during four years at MIT and several more at Harvard. At first he'd studied computer and number theory and then, being a shrewd young fellow, decided that the brotherhood of lawyers had far too few who would be qualified to handle the cases of the burgeoning electronic frontier: piracy, electronic fraud, and the like. But somewhere along the way to a J.D. he had decided that some practical experience in the law might help, and the FBI had seemed all too eager to add to his résumé.

But a strange thing happened then. Two things actually. One, he found that he liked, truly *enjoyed* doing what a bureau man did. Two, while enjoying what he did, he caught a slug in a Philly shoot-out with some well-armed bank robbers. Scratch two bad guys and the use of his body below the waist.

So his legs didn't work? So what? The bureau had agreed, and though he didn't chase bad guys in the street anymore, he sometimes chased them in the digital realm, and was the Chicago office's com clerk, the agent responsible for the security and well-being of the crypto gear.

And Kiwi had just made his life a whole lot less stressful. "It will work," Van Horn assured the A-SAC. He pointed to a three-inch space behind the cube. "See that. Six phone lines come in. You know what comes over those? Garbage. Electronic noise. It goes through Kiwi—again, from my sources, with some sort of time-keyed three-step decryption routine, and into readable info or conversation in here. Phone, fax, or computer. Even the old teletype." He wondered when the bureau would finally get rid of that, considering that a fax was essentially the same thing. "And," he added, grabbing a blank sheet of paper from a tray next to a laser printer, "let's say that for some reason the phone lines are down, like when the Loop flooded, and we need to get a coded message out." Van Horn held up the blank paper. "We enter our message through this station and call for a loop back. The Kiwi gear encrypts the message and prints it out. On this paper you'd see nonsense, but all the operator of another Kiwi machine would have to do is enter what he sees on the paper into their station and call for a loop back decryption and . . . bingo! Out it comes, making complete sense. Slow, for sure, and it won't work for the phones, but if we have to, we could courier the message. It's a great backup when Ma Bell screws up."

Blah blah blah blah blah. Art knew Van Horn might as well have been speaking in some tongue derived from Sanskrit. "So the communications are going to be secure?"

Van Horn allowed a chuckle and nodded. "Yes, they are." He reached over and patted Kiwi again. "Trust *us*."

"Okay," Art said with resignation. He would have to succumb to the technology sooner or later. "Show me what she's got."

Several hundred miles away a phone was being answered by a man with red hair. The call was brief and to the point. A favor was needed, and the red-haired man still owed much to the person requesting the favor. When he completed this task, the debt would be nearly repaid. He hung up the phone and began to pack, confident he could make short work of things.

Not far from where the call to the red-haired man was placed, a car drove past a blue mailbox in northern Maryland

and slowed. The driver, an Asian man in a gray suit, braked the silver Lexus and noted a mark on the rounded top of the box. He parked his car and withdrew a prepared postcard from his coat. It was addressed to his mother in Kyoto, and he stepped from the vehicle to drop it in the box. As he did, he wiped off the mark.

He got back in the car and drove away at a normal speed. An hour later he had dinner with a friend in Washington, and after they had finished, that friend, another Asian man, drove to a bar in College Park, near the University of Maryland, and ordered an Asahi before going to the rest room. The stalls with doors were empty. He entered the third one and closed the door.

Someone outside the stall might have heard the squeak of screws turning or the click of the metal tissue holder coming apart. Or possibly the crackle of paper unfolding. But there was no one to listen.

A minute later the Asian man flushed the toilet, washed his hands, and dried them under an air dryer.

Back in the bar he took his beer by the neck and drew long on it, then left it half full and walked out the door. He had to get back to the office quickly. This information could not wait.

chapter 3

Children of the
Eighth Day

Jean Lynch freshened the tea in Anne's cup and set the pot back on the coffee table. She sat next to her husband, their legs touching, and took his hand in hers.

"I hope you can understand why we'd like Simon to come five days a week," Anne said after her lengthy plea/explanation. She tasted the Earl Grey and placed her cup back on the saucer on the end table to her left. An empty rocker was next to it, and a sofa across the low coffee table from her. The Lynches stared at her from it.

Martin Lynch ran slow circles over the back of his wife's hand with his thumb as he put his thoughts into words. He was talking to an educated lady and did not want to sound like the high school dropout he was. "Dr. Jefferson, we appreciate your interest in Simon. He seems to like going to the center."

"He does," Simon's mother added enthusiastically. "He even remembers bits and pieces of his day when he gets home."

Martin Lynch waited for his wife to finish. "But I don't want it to become his world." He gestured to the room and pointed upstairs. "This is his world. This room, his bedroom." He put a hand to his chest. "We are his world."

Anne knew she was losing this battle. She had sensed it from the beginning of her visit when Simon's father dispatched him to his room. The mother seemed at least receptive, but the father, well-meaning as he might be, was obviously the decision maker in this house. She might not agree with that or with him, but neither could she force a change. "I understand your concern, Mr. Lynch."

He shook his head politely. "No, you don't. Do you have children, Dr. Jefferson?"

"A girl. She's grown and in college."

"You can't understand," Martin Lynch said in a contemplative tone. "We'll never be able to say any such thing about Simon. We'll never be able to say he's all grown up and believe it. He'll never go to college. He'll never get married, have children." His wife's eyes dropped toward the floor. "He'll never be part of the normal world." He was quiet for a second, then said, "My father used to say that on the eighth day God made rogues and idiots." There was pain in Martin Lynch's eyes as the words came out. There was also acceptance. "I know my son's station in life, Dr. Jefferson. The place he needs to be most is here, in this home, with us, not—with all due respect—with you or Dr. Ohlmeyer doing tests on him. That's just the way I see it. It's the way it's going to be."

Mission not accomplished, Anne thought, scolding herself, though she wondered if there was a way to convince Martin Lynch that his son should not live his life as an island. Probably not. But she had tried. "I respect your decision, Mr. Lynch." She pulled a business card from her purse and jotted a number on the back. "I don't have cards yet, but my office extension is on the back. That's one of Dr. Ohlmeyer's cards. If you do need anything, please call. Please."

Martin Lynch took the card and dropped it in his shirt pocket while standing. "We will."

Anne looked to the stairs. "Tell Simon I said good-bye."

"I will," Jean Lynch said. They all walked toward the door.

The red-haired man was munching on pistachios when the nigger lady finally left the house on Vincent Street. He watched from the back of a rented van parked down the block as she walked to her car at the curb, and saw a man in a blue work shirt come onto the porch, but no farther. A woman stood in the doorway behind a half-open storm door.

The red-haired man didn't know who the nigger lady was, and he didn't particularly care. His focus was on the man and the woman, who turned and went back inside as their visitor drove away. He looked to the pair of driver's license photos on his lap. It was them. The Lynches. Two of the three people who resided at 2564 Vincent. The third person was a son.

The red-haired man was looking for a teenager, a boy named Simon he'd learned from medical reports on file with the father's insurance company. The son was sixteen. That was all he knew, but he would soon know more. The red-haired man was skilled at getting information.

He tucked the two photos in the inside pocket of his jacket and stepped from the van. The Lynch home was six houses away. The red-haired man walked along the sidewalk into the long shadow of his own form. It was as dark as his suit and moved out of the way when he turned up the walkway of 2564 Vincent. He made purposeful noise climbing the steps to the porch and rang the doorbell just once before Mr. Lynch appeared from inside.

"Hello."

"Martin Lynch?" the red-haired man asked in greeting.

"Yes."

He removed a black wallet from his inside pocket and flipped it open. A badge shone at Martin Lynch. "I'm Detective Burrell, Chicago Police." It was a lie, but the red-haired man had no trouble with that. He was after the truth, not its keeper. "Can I have a word with you?"

Martin Lynch blinked nervously and reached for the storm door latch. "Sure. Come inside."

The red-haired man smiled and entered. He noted a dining room to the left, a staircase and an arched opening directly ahead, and a living room to the right. A woman came through the arched opening. She smiled at him, then saw her husband's face and the expression faded.

"This is—"

"Detective Burrell, Chicago Police." The red-haired man finished the introduction and shook the wife's hand. He heard water running in the kitchen.

"Is something wrong?" Jean Lynch asked. Her husband closed the door and stood next to her.

"Not exactly," the red-haired man said. "But I do need to ask you a few questions."

Martin Lynch nodded. "About?"

The red-haired man produced a small notebook and clicked open a pen. "Are you familiar with a Dr. Lawrence Wollam?"

Jean Lynch's eyes narrowed. "He treated our son a few months back. Why?"

"Well, Dr. Wollam has been accused of some inappropriate behavior, I'm afraid to say." He saw the wife's eyes go wide. *Perfect.* "These accusations all center on one day, the day your son was seen by Dr. Wollam."

"What did he do?" Martin Lynch asked with a rising

voice, then turned to his wife. "Weren't you with Simon when he saw the doctor?"

"Almost all the time."

"Listen, folks," the red-haired man said in a calming voice. "So far we've found nothing to back up the accusations. The other patients he saw that day have said nothing happened. But we have to check with everybody. Now you say your son was with Dr. Wollam alone for a while?"

"A short while," Jean Lynch answered. Her husband's eyes burned at her. "For a few minutes. That's all."

The red-haired man nodded and recorded her response in his notebook. "Okay. I'd like to talk to your son. Just to ask him a few questions about the visit."

Jean Lynch's eyes dipped briefly. "Our son is autistic."

"Autistic? Is that like retarded?" the red-haired man asked, just as a cop would. He knew better. *Autistic?* The medical report in the insurance company's computer hadn't mentioned that, but that was just a report. He hadn't delved into the complete medical history. Just an opening to the son, that was all he'd been looking for. But autistic? That would fit—*Spoke like a child, but with an older voice*—or would it?

"He doesn't function like normal people," Martin Lynch said.

The red-haired man slowly nodded. "But he can talk? He could answer questions, right?"

Martin looked to his wife. "You'd better get back to dinner. I'll take the detective up to Simon."

"Uh, it's better in these situations if we talk to the person alone," the red-haired man explained. He had to be alone with the kid. Had to. "That's standard."

Martin Lynch disagreed with a shake of his head. "Simon won't talk to you without his mother or me there. He doesn't know you."

The red-haired man considered further protest but

thought better of it at this point. *Get the information . . . period.* He had to get to the kid. "All right. As long as you let him say whatever he has to say."

That admonition seemed strange to Martin Lynch, but then cops thought differently from ordinary people, he believed. "Let's go."

Jean Lynch watched them ascend the steps, then returned to the kitchen and her Hungarian goulash. It was her son's favorite.

Simon sat in a chair at his desk with a pad of graph paper before him. His right hand held a pencil, and with that he was tracing over the pale blue lines that dissected the paper, scoring graphite channels down one column vertically, over one horizontally at the bottom, then up again covering the adjacent line. When he was done, every vertical line on the page would be covered.

Six sheets had already been completed. They were stacked neatly beneath the desk lamp.

When the door opened, Simon did not look up. His body did begin to rock.

Martin Lynch brought the red-haired man fully into his son's room and closed the door. Simon did not like open doors. "Simon."

The blond head bobbed up and swung briefly toward the voice.

"There's someone here who wants to talk to you." Martin Lynch walked to his son's bed and patted the white comforter. "Come sit over here."

Simon carefully placed the pencil along the top edge of the paper and walked toward the bed. He stopped a few feet short. The red-haired man was in his way.

Martin Lynch noticed his son shuffle-step back a bit.

"Hello, Simon," the red-haired man said. He said no

more when he saw the father caution him with a wave. The gesture urged him to give the kid room.

"Simon, it's all right. Come over by Daddy and sit down."

The big black shoes moved away, and Simon scooted by and sat where his daddy told him to. His hands balled on his lap, and he again set to rocking.

"Simon, this is Mr. Burrell," Martin Lynch said as he squatted and put a hand on his son's knee. "He wants to ask you some questions. Is that all right?"

Simon did not answer.

"I'll be right here," Martin Lynch assured his son.

Between the rocks Simon's head bobbed twice.

"Okay." Martin Lynch stood and backed away a few steps so he could lean against the wall.

The red-haired man smiled big and bounced low into a squat as the father had. He tried to look the kid in the eyes but was thwarted by their constant motion and the low angle of his head. "How ya doin'?" he asked as though a longtime friend. Simon knew that he was not and did not answer.

Behind the red-haired man, Martin Lynch observed cautiously. His son did not like this man.

The red-haired man covertly swept the room with just his eyes. On the bedstand beneath a lamp he saw a magazine. He recognized the title. He picked it up and casually paged through it. "Do you like to read?"

Simon's rocking increased.

The red-haired man skimmed through the *Tinkery* and stopped at the first page of the puzzle section. "Do you like puzzles?"

Simon's head tipped up toward his daddy and then fell again. His thumbs began to work hard against the skin of his hands. Martin Lynch stopped leaning and stepped forward.

The red-haired man tilted his head to look beneath the angled young head. "Do you like puzzles?"

"Hey." Martin Lynch tapped firmly on the red-haired man's shoulder. "What are you doing?"

"Just trying to make him comfortable, Mr. Lynch." *Get the information . . . period.*

"Up," Martin Lynch said, and the red-haired man stood and faced him. "He's not comfortable. That's the problem."

"I guess so," the red-haired man said. He chewed at his lower lip and added a nod, then laid the magazine on Simon's lap. He seemed sorry.

"He's not going to talk to you," Martin Lynch said.

"Well, maybe we should just talk, you and the missus and I, downstairs," the red-haired man suggested. . . . *period.*

Martin Lynch nodded and looked to his son. "I'll be back up in a few minutes, Simon."

Simon rocked quietly as his daddy and the stranger left his room. Footsteps tapped on the stairs after the door closed. The box spring squeaked beneath his motion. A truck passed the house. At this time Simon knew it would be the truck that delivered milk to the market on the corner. A man named Mr. Toricel—

Tsewp-Tsewp. Tsewp-Tsewp-Tsewp. THUMP. THUMP. Simon's rocking stilled at the sound of breaking glass. Mommy must have dropped a plate. She had done that before. On the day they ate turkey and mashed potat—

Footsteps rose on the staircase. Heavy feet.

Simon began rocking again. Daddy walked softly.

The door eased open and stayed open. The red-haired man walked into Simon's room alone. Simon smelled something strange. Like smoke.

"Hi again, Simon," the red-haired man said as he neared the kid. He reached into his pocket and removed a folded piece of paper. "I wanted to talk a little bit more about the puzzles." He stood directly in front of the kid. With a gloved hand he took a fistful of hair and lifted the kid's head until his face was visible. "You know it's rude not to look at someone when they're talking to you."

Simon's lower lip turned to jelly, but he did not cry. His eyes darted about in search of something familiar. They locked on the picture of his old dog, Ranger, on the wall by the window. Ranger had died when—

"Look at *me*, kid." The red-haired man shook Simon's head sharply.

"You're a stranger."

"Nah." The red-haired man put his face very close to Simon's. "I'm your friend."

Daddy hadn't told him that.

"I just want to talk about some puzzles. You'll tell a friend about puzzles, won't you?"

This man was a stranger. He was not a friend.

The red-haired man backed off but kept hold of Simon's hair. He unfolded the paper in his other hand and held it in front of Simon's face.

It was covered in letters and numbers.

There were 50 numbers and letters mixed together at the beginning and 50 letters at the end. In between were 1,450 numbers.

"What do you see, kid?"

Simon's eyes flitted over the numbers and letters. He blinked several times.

"What does it say?"

Simon knew this kind of puzzle. It was not hard. "I know kiwi."

The red-haired man pulled the paper away. "Right." He stuffed the paper in his coat pocket and aimed Simon's face toward the magazine on his lap. "There's a puzzle like that in there. Remember that?" He lifted the head again with a tug. "How'd you figure it out, kid?" His other hand was now unoccupied. He drew it back, palm flat under black leather. "How?"

Martin Lynch lay in a spreading pool of his own blood when his son's cry echoed down to the kitchen. With a great draw of air he forced his head up and looked around. His wife lay where the two walls of cabinets met. Her dress clung to the front of her body, soaked dark. A line of red trickled from the center of her forehead over one cheek.

He shot us, Martin Lynch realized. He did not remember its happening, but he knew. He should have sensed it coming, as Simon had—

"Thimon," Martin Lynch said in a weak, wet voice. Blood spurted from his mouth as he did. He rolled to his side, sat against the stove, and looked down. There was a dime-size hole in his work shirt, just right of the pocket. The blue cotton had turned red. He touched a hand to a fiery spot above his left eye. One finger found a wet depression that stung tremendously.

Martin Lynch was suddenly nauseated and vomited onto his legs. *My God, I'm shot . . . In the head and in the chest . . . I'm going to die. . . .* He looked again to his wife. She was still. *He killed my Jean. . . .*

A slap from above snapped Martin Lynch's throbbing head upward. Simon winced loudly.

"Not my thon," Martin Lynch said. He let anger fill him, let it overcome the pain, the sickness, the sorrow, let it lift him from the floor, let it guide him step by step through his wife's blood out the kitchen and into the den.

The red-haired man's hand was cocked for a third blow when a crashing sound rose from the first floor. He let go of Simon's head and drew his weapon. A slender blued tube extended from the barrel.

"You stay—" The red-haired man caught his folly. *Like you're going anywhere, kid.* "I've got some unfinished business downstairs. Be right back."

Holding the silenced Walther PPK in a relaxed forward stance, he left the upstairs bedroom and advanced with care down the stairs, measuring each step, easing his feet lightly to the treads below. Near the bottom he crouched and scanned the front room. Nothing. The front door was still closed, and nothing seemed amiss here. He continued, coming upright at floor level and checking both left and right; left farther into the living room, and right toward the kitchen. He saw the mother's legs through the arched opening, but not the—

"Bastard," Martin Lynch said from behind the red-haired man. He had gone into the den through the archway directly across from the kitchen and had come out through the opening to the living room. In the den was a china hutch. Resting atop it had been a .38-caliber revolver. Martin Lynch now held it in his right hand.

He shot the red-haired man six times in the back before collapsing himself. His last thought was of his son and what would become of him, and before the world went dark, Martin Lynch dropped the revolver and reached into his shirt pocket.

BOOM! BOOM! BOOM! BOOM! BOOM! BOOM!

Simon's body shuddered at the loud noise. It seemed to echo, going on, and on, and on. His ears rang almost painfully.

It scared him. The loud noise scared him.

He knew what to do.

With his face stinging and one eye swollen almost shut, Simon pulled his cards from beneath his sweatshirt. He flipped through them to the one titled STORM. IF A LOUD NOYZ SKAIRS YU AND IT GTS LOUDR AND YU KANT FIND MOMMY AND DADDY THN GO TO TH BASMNT

Simon replaced the cards and put the magazine that lay on his lap under his arm and walked out of his bedroom. His eyes scanned the carpet at his feet. One hurt very bad. He did not cry.

The ringing in his ears crescendoed. Simon held the banister in his right hand and went down the steps as quickly as he could. He stopped there and searched the living room with one watery eye. He was not crying. "Mommy. Daddy."

No answer came. Simon took a step, then stopped. There was something at his feet. It was the man who had shown him the puzzle. The man who had hit him. "Mommy. Daddy."

Nothing, and the sound in his head now deepened, gaining bass, thundering in time to the throbbing around his eye. Mommy and Daddy were not answering. He had to get to the basement. The man on the floor was in the way.

Simon's feet shuffled in place for a moment. Then he lifted one over the man, and the other. He walked past the kitchen and stopped one last time as the avalanche of noise grew. "Mommy. Daddy."

They were not here. If they were here, they would come. Simon knew what to do.

He walked quickly to the door to the basement, opened it, and closed it behind. His footsteps were light on the stairs as he descended.

chapter 4

The Friend Card

The silver Volvo 940 eased into the minor stream rushing down the gutter and stopped curbside in front of the Federal Building. Art opened the door and stepped across the waterway to enter the warm interior of the wedding present he'd given his wife. She accelerated into a break in the traffic and began the trek to the JFK Expressway.

"Thanks for the lift, babe," Art said as he opened the front of his overcoat. Hot air washed over him from the vents.

"It's no problem," Anne replied tepidly, her eyes straight ahead, thumb tapping rhythmically on the steering wheel. The stereo was off. Her husband leaned over and kissed her cheek.

"My car took a crap this afternoon," Art explained. Six months old and the bureau Chevy Caprice Classic had thrown a rod! "And can you believe there wasn't one damn spare in pool?" Budget cuts were wonderful things, he was thinking when he realized Anne wasn't commenting. He turned attention to her and saw her "I'm not pleased with myself" face. Had it been her "I'm not pleased with you" face, she'd be looking at him or at whoever was deserving of it. Instead she stared blankly at the brake lights ahead, but

Art knew she was really looking inside. "Something wrong, babe?"

Anne straightened and let out part of a breath she felt she'd been holding for almost an hour now. "Have you ever tried your damnedest to make something happen, but it just wouldn't?"

Every day, Art thought, but he knew that wasn't what she needed to hear. "Sometimes."

"Well, I had one of those sometimes this afternoon." She frowned and shook her head and even considered giving the steering wheel a good thump with the heel of her hand, but didn't.

"Is this about that kid you told me about?" Art asked. Of course the Bulls had been on in the background when she was telling him in mild shouts from the kitchen of their home in Evanston, about an hour from the city on a good traffic day.

"Simon," Anne said, irritation beneath the word. "The autistic young man?"

"I remember," Art said.

Anne relaxed a bit. "Sorry."

Art rubbed her leg through the blue skirt. "Forget it. Go on."

"His"—she retracted the invective she almost let slip— "father refuses to—" The ringing of a cell phone interrupted her complaint.

"Yours," Art said.

Anne fished the compact flip phone from her purse with one hand and answered it after the third ring. "Hello . . . Yes, this is she— What?"

Art watched his wife lean forward to the steering wheel, almost as if she needed the support. "Babe?"

"When did this . . ." She pulled the Volvo hurriedly to

the curb to a symphony of angry horns and closed her eyes. "How did you get my number?"

Art saw her nod a few times; then she clicked off and practically dived toward him across the center console. "Babe, what is it?"

Anne pulled him very close, as tight as she could, and silently cursed herself for the thoughts she'd almost expressed toward Simon's parents. "It's . . . Simon," she managed to say between sobs, then pulled back from Art and tried to regain her composure. She put both hands very properly on the steering wheel and said, "I've got to get to him."

"What is it?" Art almost begged as his wife screeched back into traffic and doubled back toward the Eisenhower Expressway.

The Cadillac limousine was an hour outside Tokyo when the youngish man facing Keiko finished reading her report on what the American had revealed. He looked at her and set the twelve pages on the seat next to him. "Again, you have done fine work. Mr. Chappell knew even more about the Americans' position on tariff limits than we anticipated."

Keiko stared back at him through dark glasses. She was reclined in the leather seat, facing the direction of travel and had counted two trains passing the car on the right at a very great speed. She wore tight black jeans and a black blazer over a white T-shirt. Her hair hung loose. One hand lay across her stomach. The other picked quietly at a seam in the upholstery.

"Mr. Kimodo will be pleased," Mitsuo Heiji said, his expression cooling a bit before continuing. "But he is concerned with your . . . method."

Keiko looked right, past the train tracks to the farmland

beyond. In the far distance the morning sky was gray and threatening. The rain was going to come. "Are we going to turn back soon?" she asked the window, ignoring the question.

Heiji did not answer immediately. With her attention on something outside the car he let his eyes wander over her body. She was thirty, and those years showed somewhat in the serious cast of her face, but her body could have belonged to a teenager. He might have chanced a proposition once, but not after seeing what remained of Carlton Kerr, the first American she'd handled some months before. Heiji had laid eyes upon the body before seeing to its disposal at a highway construction site. It was difficult to think of the man that way with his tongue torn out and one knee bent forward at an impossible angle. That this ... woman had done that frightened Heiji more than a bit. If only she were tame, his thoughts might be of pleasure.

"Heiji, don't imagine yourself with me," Keiko said without looking to him. "Imagination is the second most dangerous thing a man has."

Heiji snickered a bit, nervously. He had been too obvious in his musings. "The second, is it?"

"Yes."

"What is the first?"

"A heartbeat," she answered while turning back to face him. A bulge rolled down his throat.

"Again, I must convey that your methods are of concern to Mr. Kimodo."

"I got what he wanted," Keiko said with quiet authority. Twelve pages of drivel that the American had offered quite freely after she'd crushed one of his testicles in her hand; the second she popped between her teeth just prior to gutting him alive, during the course of which he'd had the sense to die. Twelve pages of *words.* Trade policy decisions. Commerce Department needs. Tasks ahead and information desired by his superiors. *Words.* To Kimodo the business tycoon they were gold, but Keiko knew she'd felt the American's true worth spill over her naked body in a spout from his open belly. She had come soon after that.

"But the remnants of your . . . success are quite graphic," Heiji persisted, choosing his words haltingly at times, but with care. "These things are not public, of course, but to anger the Americans with a . . . distasteful display of one of their own is not wise." He felt her stare harden and added quickly, "In Mr. Kimodo's eyes. Perhaps it would be wise to conclude your . . . sessions as you did with Mr. Hashimoto last year. You succeeded then and left no . . . untidiness."

There was no need to leave Yoshihiro Hashimoto, the son of one of Kimodo's business rivals, in any state other than dead and slightly damaged. He was not of the taste Keiko desired in playthings. Those had to be, if the gods were smiling, Americans. Ever since defiling that American in the Bekaa Valley for her onetime Hezbollah comrades, that kind was all she could think of. All she wanted. "I do my job in the manner I see fit. Please inform Mr. Kimodo of that. Now, when are we turning back?"

Heiji collected himself and removed an envelope from inside his coat. "In a moment." He handed it across to Keiko. Her nails were short and painted blue, he noticed when she took it from him. "Mr. Kimodo requires your assistance in a new matter."

So soon . . . Keiko thought longingly. "Go on."

"The particulars are in the envelope, but Mr. Kimodo requires that you travel to America. An individual there may be able to provide some very valuable information. Concerning their top code."

"Top code?" Keiko probed. "What is that?"

"The particulars are in writing."

Keiko let her fingers caress the coarse package. Some things were so much better spoken than coldly read. "An individual?"

Heiji hesitated briefly when a flash of pity ran through him. "A young man. It is in writing, and you will have a contact in America."

A young man. That was an enticingly large spectrum. "America, you say."

"Our trusted ally," Heiji commented. He noticed Keiko shift slightly where she sat. It was almost as though she were squirming.

Keiko heard Kimodo's lackey speak, but she was looking out the window again, watching the first sheets of gray begin to fall upon the fields in the distance, wanting to think of the crops and the farmers and anything other than the one thought that kept repeating in her head: *young man, young man, young man, young man.* They would meet soon, she knew, but soon always seemed an eternity.

Then again, with deprivation her hunger would rise to glorious heights, and it would be all the sweeter a sacrifice that quenched it.

"A young man, you say?" She just had to hear it one more time.

Heiji nodded and noticed that Keiko recrossed her legs very, very slowly. "Yes, a young man."

The limousine exited and reentered the motorway heading back to Tokyo. Keiko chewed quietly, impatiently at her lower lip the entire way.

Anne parked the Volvo at a hasty angle on Milford just short of the police line that held a neighborhood of gawkers at bay.

She ran to the nearest Chicago police officer with Art at her side. Though it wasn't his territory, he held his bureau shield high out front for the city cop to see.

"I'm Dr. Jefferson," Anne said.

The patrolman saw the authority backing up the lady and let her through. A minute later Anne trotted up the steps of 2564 Vincent for the second time in a few hours. A police lieutenant stopped her and Art there.

"You're Dr. Jefferson?" Lieutenant Jerry Miklovich asked. He noted the FBI shield now clipped to the belt of the man with her.

"Yes, where's—"

"And you're?"

"Art Jefferson, assistant special agent in charge."

"Right, you just—"

"Where is Simon?" Anne demanded loudly.

Miklovich was quiet for a second. "He's all right, but he seems to be in shock or some—"

"He's autistic," Anne said.

Miklovich nodded slowly, knowingly. "Is that like retarded?"

Anne didn't have the time to educate the lawman. "Something like that. Where is he?"

"He's in the basement. We can't coax him out. Like I told you on the phone, the father had this business card with your number on the back. We called . . . uh, Jewish name—"

"Ohlmeyer," Anne said. *Take me to him. Hurry.*

"Right, and he wasn't in. His office gave us your name and number, and well, it was on the back of the card too, so we got in touch with you." Miklovich spit to the side of the porch. Two of his lab people walked past into the house. "So you're this kid's doctor."

"One of them. Can I please see him?"

"If you can get him out of the basement, great. This kid

may have seen what happened in there. I didn't want to mess him up any more than he already looks."

Anne bent dumbly forward. "Are you finished?"

Miklovich looked at Art. "It's a mess in there." Then back to Anne. "Lots of blood."

"I won't touch anything," Anne said.

"Nah, I just don't want you to get sick," Miklovich admitted.

"She won't," Art said, his hand on Anne's shoulder.

Miklovich chewed at something in his mouth and spit off the porch again. "All right. Follow right behind me."

Art brought up the rear, keeping one hand on his wife's back. He was an old hat at messy crime scenes. She wasn't. He kept his thumb moving in circles between her shoulder blades, reassuring her as the tactless lieutenant led them through the living room, right at the stairs—*one man down, shot in the back,* Art noted—*left into a den—a body there, on its side, at least one obvious wound, a medium-frame Smith on the rug*—and toward the kitchen—*one female down, head shot, fully clothed, broken glass on the floor*—and right down a hall to an open door. One patrolman guarded it. Darkness descended from the opening.

Miklovich turned toward the lady. Her face quivered briefly. "You okay?"

Anne nodded.

"He's down there. I've got someone down there just keeping an eye on him."

Anne nodded again and forced the grisly images she'd just walked past from her thoughts . . . for now.

"Do you want me to go down with you?" Art asked.

Another nod. Art eased her forward with a guiding hand and followed her down the stairs. The dimmest light shined from a yellowed fixture over a collection of boxes. Books poked into view from the top ones.

The cop at the bottom made way for them and then re-treated upstairs at a wave from the lieutenant.

In the far corner of the small basement, in shadows that fell from towers of brown, bellied cardboard boxes, Simon Lynch stood silently swaying. His arms were held tightly to his body against the chill. Something was tucked under his arm.

The preceding moments faded away when Anne saw her young patient. He was the most alone being in the universe at the moment, she knew. "Simon. It's Dr. Anne."

The sway leaned into a step forward. Jaundiced light painted one side of his form.

"It's Dr. Anne." She slid out of her coat and eased one stride toward him. "Dr. Anne. Remember?"

Simon touched his cards through the sweatshirt. "Dr. Anne is my friend."

Anne nodded, her eyes wet, a smile beneath them. "Yes, I'm your friend." *You have no one, Simon. No one. No relatives. No one. You're only sixteen. Social Services might help you. Some court somewhere, maybe. But what kind of help is that?*

Simon took another metronomic step forward before halting. His head rose in a flash, eyes flitting over the man behind Dr. Anne.

"It's okay, Simon." Anne reached back and brought Art next to her. She immediately noticed that the young man didn't wet himself. *So far, so good.* Then she saw the rising bruise on the left side of his fair face. It sickened her, but a mark such as that would fade. Would ones less noticeable? she wondered, and knew that *that* had to be her primary concern.

"Hello, Simon," Art said, feeling uncomfortable offering a greeting to someone whose parents had just been brutally killed. He felt Anne's grip on his hand tighten. It was her "You're doing fine" touch. "It's nice to meet you."

"It's nice to meet Simon." He did not close the scant distance to Dr. Anne.

"Simon, Art is my . . . very good friend." Anne waited for a reaction, hoped that he would make the connection himself. A few seconds passed before Simon pulled his cards out and turned to the one marked FRIENDS. Then he waited, pen in hand.

"What's he doing?" Art asked.

"Tell him your name," Anne prompted.

Art hesitated for an awkward few seconds, then said, "My name is Art, Simon."

"Dr. Anne is my friend." The pen clicked and hovered over the card. "There was a loud noise."

"I know," Art said. He felt himself drawn to Simon and took a step closer.

Simon's eyes flashed over him. Then, with the pen gripped intensely in his right hand, he wrote ART in the space below DOKTR AN.

"What does that mean?" Art asked, looking back to Anne. She was smiling over tears.

"It means he trusts you."

chapter 5

The Bell Curve

G. Nicholas Kudrow usually paused only long enough at his secretary's desk to grab the morning's briefs, but her look this day stopped him cold.

"Mr. Folger is in there," Sharon said, her expression hinting at the futile battle that had been fought and lost not long before.

"So he is," Kudrow said, seeming not very surprised as he took the briefs in hand and entered his office.

Brad Folger, in an uncharacteristic three-piece gray number, sat in a chair facing Kudrow's neat desk, his back to the door, the Lichtenstein staring down at him. "What time did they wake you up?"

Kudrow let the door close of its own accord and walked around his assistant. He placed his briefs where he would remember them in a few minutes and set his briefcase aside his desk. He did not sit. "At four this morning. And you?"

"I've been fucking awake since two!" Folger swore, his crossed legs and folded hands incongruous with the rage on his tired face.

Kudrow adjusted his glasses and moved his chair close before sitting. "You managed a shave."

"A shave . . ." Folger's posture loosened now, and he slid close to the desk, leaning toward Kudrow. "Are you fucking brain-dead?"

"Watch it," Kudrow snapped.

Folger fell back in mock apology. "Oh, pardon *moi*. I forgot, I wasn't the one who brought Mike Bell in."

"This wasn't the plan."

"You bring *Bell* in and you expected a plan to be followed?" Folger challenged.

"He fitted the requirements. I didn't know his weaknesses like you did."

"Exactly why I was called in at two!"

"Ease up, Bradley," Kudrow suggested with a coolness that hinted at waning patience.

"You knew he'd be linked to me," Folger said.

"They came to my house," Kudrow informed his deputy.

"Poor fucking Nick," Folger said, standing angrily and showing Kudrow his back as he seethed.

Kudrow sensed the tantrum was over and let his deputy's emotion simmer away while he began perusing the morning briefs.

Folger turned back to the sound of shuffling paper. "Nick, why didn't you ask me about Bell? You knew I was the one that had him booted when I was in O."

Nothing interesting from the stations in the Caribbean. "You answered your own question, Brad. What would you have told me?"

"Just what you think."

"Next question." Some tidbits, interestingly enough, from Chile. Traffic from the Russian Antarctic station to home. Ozone measurements. *Surprise, the hole isn't that big on their instruments either.*

"Wonderful," Folger commented through a dry throat. He felt parched and as if he'd stepped from the real world to some horrid parallel universe created a few days earlier by one stupid phone call. "So what did they ask you?"

"They asked me about you," Kudrow said, hiding the pleasure, and power, he felt in doing so. He saved Europe for later. No one could figure that continent out before noon.

"Wonderful," Folger repeated. He began pacing in the path worn by Kudrow.

"At least he died with his screw up," Kudrow said. "And I can assure you things will be quite different now."

Folger slowed, his feet taking a second to catch up with his brain, which had been frozen mid-thought by the statement. "Things? What things? You're not going on with this?"

"If you will recall, Brad, as a deputy director I have authority to initiate investigations as needed to ensure the security of our product." Kudrow noted the incredulous, gaping stare directed at him. "Or are you too frazzled to remember that? Do you need the day to recompose yourself?"

"You're going to do it."

"*We* are going to find out what we can about this kid who made the call. Right now we don't know much, not even if your old O buddy learned anything before he died."

My old O buddy. Folger looked away.

"All we know for sure is that the kid is staying with his doctor."

"Why does he need a doctor?" Folger asked, the timbre sucked from his voice, replaced by a tired hollowness.

"He's autistic." Kudrow nodded when his assistant looked his way. "An interesting spin, wouldn't you say?"

Folger chuckled weakly and rubbed his eyes. "An interesting spin. Yeah, that's the way to look at it."

Kudrow folded his hands slowly on his desk. "Maybe you need more than a day, Brad."

Folger felt the threat slide by. His concern was elsewhere.

"You know, Nick, if they know who Bell is or was, this will go beyond the local police."

"It already has."

"I'm not talking about our security."

Kudrow let his assistant's worry die slowly without response. "The beauty of a rogue is that it explains itself eventually."

"You hope," Folger said.

Kudrow said nothing and returned to the morning briefs. Somewhere during the silence Folger left his office. When the door clicked shut, G. Nicholas Kudrow's eyes came up and fixed on it for a long time.

Friday, noon, and Art Jefferson was already exhausted. He pressed his hands against his face and yawned hard. When he pulled them away, Lomax was standing in the doorway, mild smile twisted by the prominent scar on his cheek.

"You could scare children, you know."

Lomax nodded and came in. "Only when I need to." He plopped into the small couch across the office. "You look as whipped as I feel."

"The nights have been rough."

"How's he doing?"

Art shrugged. "I don't know. You ask him and he just repeats the question. All I know for sure is that he hardly sleeps. He stands and rocks most of the night until he's so tired he drops off."

"That's a hell of a thing to deal with," Lomax observed. "Sometimes I wonder if God dreamed these things up on a bad day."

"That would explain it."

Lomax moved from the couch to a chair near the desk. "How's Anne holding up?"

Art breathed deeply. "She's doing it somehow. The university gave her some time so she could deal with Simon. That helps."

Lomax agreed with a slow nod that had "preface" written all over it.

"What?" Art asked.

"I have to give you a case. It could get fairly involved."

Art eased back and did a few neck rolls. "All right."

"This is quiet. You only use resources if absolutely necessary."

Interested now, Art straightened in his chair. "Resources."

"Other personnel in the office. You don't go outside under any circumstances."

"A one-man show, is what you're saying."

"Yes. The file's in your vault on the system. The reference name is Roma."

"You want to give me a quick synopsis?" Art probed.

"It has to do with your houseguest."

"Simon?"

Lomax nodded. "NCIC got a DoD hit on the fingerprints of the guy who killed Simon's parents. Not even a category hit. The prints were a hospital set taken when the guy was wounded in Grenada." The National Crime Information Center had links to fingerprint files of other government entities, and in this instance at least, the system worked perfectly.

"Who was he?"

"The name was Mike Bell. He was Marine Recon and apparently did work for about a dozen government agencies after that."

"Work?" Art questioned. "We're not talking nine to five."

"We're talking nine millimeter," Lomax confirmed.

"I doubt that's in his records."

"Look at the holes," Lomax suggested. "Holes are where things happen."

"Was he working for anyone when this happened?"

Lomax shook his head. "It doesn't look like it. He was excused from his last position over a year ago."

"What position?"

"He was doing 'training activities' at Fort Meade," Lomax answered doubtfully.

"A marine training at an Army base?" Art wondered with equal doubt.

"Meade is a big place," Lomax said as a reminder. From the look on the A-SAC's face he saw that he got it.

"I'll take a look at that hole."

Lomax pushed himself up from the chair and arched a crick from his back. "Chicago PD is backing off until we have a chance to look at it."

"There's no family to demand answers," Art said. He felt the sadness of that fact.

Lomax thought quietly for a moment, then asked, "Do you think he might talk about it?"

"I don't know."

Lomax nodded without pressing the point. "Let me know what you find."

"Will do," Art assured the SAC, and called up his personal "vault" on the computer system as Lomax left. After entering his password, graphical icon folders dotted the screen. He noticed the new one right away and double clicked on it.

A vapid, coarse face stared back at him a second later, red hair atop and a crooked cleft in the chin. Art looked long at it, not even bothering with the written information yet. He studied the eyes, the lines of age, the crook of the mouth. On the generous monitor, the face was as large as his. Mike Bell could have been sitting two feet from him.

"So, what did you want with Simon's family?"

The answer did not come, but Art did not expect it yet. The dead did not come right out and answer. You had to drag it out of them. And it only made it easier if you already hated them.

"Do you have anything to declare?" the youthful customs inspector at the Vancouver, B.C., International Airport inquired of the oddly exotic Asian woman as she set her purse on the inspection table before him.

Keiko Kimura smiled behind dark glasses and beneath a silky blond wig. "Only that you're cute."

The inspector, mindful of the plainclothes Royal Canadian Mounted Police officer standing a few feet away, suppressed a smile and dutifully examined the woman's passport. "Miss Jiang, you are coming from Hong Kong?"

Keiko nodded. The glasses hid her eyes, and she doubted that the scrumptious young man would notice the difference between Japanese and Chinese features. Oh, if only that dreadful Canadian lilt didn't taint his speech, he might pass for American. But that really did not matter. America was not far away. A short drive. So close.

The inspector took a quick look in Miss Jiang's purse and handed her passport back. "Enjoy your stay in Canada."

"I will," Keiko said, and left the customs area with an exaggerated wiggle in her walk. The inspector admired her until she disappeared into the terminal.

chapter 6

Blood Tears

It was called the guest room, but in reality the only guest who had ever used it was Anne's twenty-year-old daughter, Jennifer, when she stole a free weekend once from her studies at Stanford. Now Simon occupied it, sitting on the bed, legs barely touching the floor, his thin frame tilting to and fro.

In the open doorway, leaning against the jamb, Art stood watching the young man, thinking, wondering.

"You should come to bed," Anne said, coming up from behind and sliding her arms around Art's waist, feeling him breathe beneath her touch. "He'll fall asleep eventually."

Art nodded absently and crossed his arms over hers. In one hand a sheet of paper was rolled into a white tube, which he tapped against his bare chest. "He misses them."

"His world is out of sorts, Art. Miss probably isn't something he comprehends."

Simon rocked gently, silently, hands folded on his legs. His eyes danced over something, over nothing, over a bare space in the corner.

"He misses them," Art repeated.

Anne cocked her eyes toward Art's face and planted a

soft kiss on his cheek. He could still surprise her, the rugged, stubborn G-man. "Come to bed. Soon."

Art nodded and felt Anne's hands ease away. A moment later, when the door to their bedroom down the hall clicked shut, Art opened the rolled paper and looked at it. It had been taken off Mike Bell's body at the Lynch house, folded in his coat pocket. Of all the other information in the Roma file, the fake Chicago PD credentials, the copies of Lynch family medical records found in Bell's van, their driver's license photos, this one page stood out because it had no apparent meaning. It was a hole, and Art knew Lomax's words to be quite true when it came to investigations. Looking at the holes would give texture, sometimes form, to the surrounding landscape of inquiry.

But this was a hole like no other, a hole of numbers and letters, covering one entire sheet of paper. Art looked from it to Simon as his fingers curled it again into a tube.

What happened in that house, kid? Art wondered, knowing that soon he would have to pose that question outright. Maybe Simon would answer, maybe not, but beyond that there was the paramount question that Art knew he would have to give satisfaction to. The question whose response more often than not generated more questions. Art resisted the urge to crush the flimsy roll of paper and loosed the query upon himself. *Why? Why to this family? To this kid?*

Thousands of miles west, in a club on the expansive Seattle waterfront, a Willamette University student squeezed through a crush of people at the bar and ordered a Sharp's from the bartender. His elbow innocently brushed the bare arm of a pretty woman on his right.

"Excuse me."

Keiko Kimura, black hair sculpted into a French braid that narrowed as it crept down her back, looked at the young man through small, round blue-tinted specs. She smiled, her eyes traveling down to his arms, over biceps that did not deserve to be hidden by sleeves, past the casually rolled-up cuffs just below the elbows, to forearms that might have been chiseled from marble by a Roman artisan.

And then to the hands. The perfect fingers spread on the bar, thumbs prominent, nails clean and tailored.

When she looked back to the young man's face, Keiko could almost *feel* the resistance of the nails as they came free of the flesh that anchored them, could *hear* the slender bones of the hand snapping, could imagine the screams. Screams, probably no, she decided, but she could imagine. The agony. The ecstasy.

The young man smiled at her. That was a mistake. It would not be his last.

"I'm Suzy," Keiko said, leaning closer to the prey she had just claimed.

The closet door creaked open in the dark, and the man with red hair stepped out, holding a knife, the dangerous end toward Art.

Guess, he taunted. *Guess*.

The upper half of Art's body sprang up in bed, tugging at the sheets and waking Anne. She rolled toward him and put a hand on his back.

"What is it?"

Art wiped at his face and batted his eyes. "A dream."

"Good or—" Anne's inquiry stopped abruptly, and she sat up next to Art, ear tuned to the door. "Do you hear something?"

The blurred image of Mike Bell fading, Art opened his eyes fully and listened. There was something. He nodded and pulled the covers off his legs.

"What is that?"

Art stood and could tell that, behind, Anne was doing the same. His instinct was to take his weapon from the night-stand, but something about the sound quashed that.

Anne came around the bed, gathering her robe. "You hear it, right?"

A low, broken buzzing . . . no, humming, almost melodic in its fracture. Art stepped toward the door and eased it open. When he did, the sound defined itself. It wafted through the open door to the guest room, a tortured repetition that made their hearts sink in unison.

"Daddy's gonna sing. Daddy's gonna sing. Daddy's gonna sing."

Anne started past, but Art held her back. "Let me."

"Art."

He didn't know why he was about to say what he was about to say, but he nonetheless knew that it was right. For some reason. "I should do this."

If she thought she'd been surprised earlier, Anne was doubly so now. Not by the words her husband spoke but by the calm surety with which he spoke them. Before she could react, with either shock or approval, or a combination of both, Art was through the door and moving toward the guest room.

The lyrical repetition continued, even after Art pushed the door slowly open and saw Simon standing in the empty corner of the room he'd earlier stared endlessly at. Standing, hands folded together, rocking gently, and singing as though the song would make itself come true.

Art stepped into the room and said, "Simon."

The singing ended, fading away on the word "Daddy." The rocking increased as Simon stood, silently now, in the barren corner of the room.

A few steps closer, until he was right at Simon's side, and Art lowered to a crouch, looking up into the downcast face. The eyes flitted over his for the briefest of instants before finding haven in the inanimate anonymity of the rug.

"Did Daddy sing to you?" Art asked, notching his voice down somewhere below its normal commanding tone.

"Daddy's gonna sing," Simon said, the melody gone from the words.

Art nodded slowly. "What did Daddy sing?"

Simon's head tilted away and came back as a yawn swept over it.

"You look tired," Art said.

"Simon is tired." Another yawn now, manufactured this time, a gesture to please.

"Do you want to go to sleep now?" Art asked, his hands coming to rest on his knees. Without reply to the question, Simon reached with his hand and gripped the fingers of Art's right hand. He looked long at the small white hand before standing and leading Simon back to bed. He guided him under the covers and pulled the bedding up snugly over the exhausted body. Simon looked away, head sideways on the pillow, eyes dancing as the lids closed over them, and Art realized that for the first time since his grandmother had lain dying in her bed, he had tucked someone in.

He watched Simon for a long time before he turned for the door. When he did, he saw Anne standing there, watching him with wonder. He was embarrassed.

It was the first time she had seen him cry.

chapter 7

Process of Elimination

The lone door to the Chocolate Box swung open into the brilliant light of the early spring day, patches of snow still on the ground, and uniformed marines staring seriously from their perimeter posts at Brad Folger. After a moment he saw their eyes track in another direction and followed the lead.

Kudrow walked slowly along the gravel bed that ringed the Chocolate Box just inside the inner fence. He knew he'd be causing havoc in the security center right then, trampling the buried motion sensors as he was, but he honestly didn't give a damn. He needed air. He needed to walk in the open. He needed to think.

He did not, however, need Folger.

Granite pebbles grinding beneath expensive shoes brought Kudrow's walk to a halt. He looked up and stared through the several layers of wire toward the woods beyond still more wire, letting Folger come to him. When his assistant was alongside, he said, "I take it you've heard."

White mist flared from Folger's nostrils. "Nick, end this now, before we all end up in prison."

"I'm tiring of your resistance, Bradley," Kudrow said, as

if referring to an annoyance that could be driven off with the swat of his hand.

"Nick, the kid is with his doctor, who is married to a ranking FBI agent, who just happens to be running the investigation of Bell!" Folger glanced toward the marines, but they were out of earshot.

"I'll note your concern."

"Goddammit, Nick!" Folger swore, loud enough now that two marines did look, briefly, before turning discreetly away.

Kudrow snatched his glasses off and snapped his head toward Folger. His small, myopic eyes glared at the shorter, younger man, saying much before the words came. "Bradley, I don't have to say to you what I can say to you. Do I?"

Folger's eyes fled first, then his face, looking off to the same woods that Kudrow had gazed at. He breathed deeply, haltingly, and felt almost like laughing, but nothing was funny. Everything, however, was quite absurd and quite awful. "I never thought you'd do this to me."

"I've done nothing," Kudrow said in warning, then replaced his glasses.

Folger nodded. "Yeah."

"I hope I don't have to."

Now Folger did chuckle, at himself, for being so damn naive as to believe that G. Nicholas Kudrow had once saved his ass out of pure humanity. One mistake. One lousy mistake.

"You find this amusing?" Kudrow asked, mildly perplexed.

"Fucking hilarious, Nick," Folger answered through a pained grin. "You're good. You know that?"

Kudrow again looked off toward the trees and thought of whitetail season, the crack of the rifle, the taste of venison.

"You kept it real close, right up to the chest, making me feel like you weren't even looking." Folger swallowed hard. "You kept that card to play later. Right?"

"Stop worrying," Kudrow said with irritation. "You think you've sinned?" His head shook slightly. He knew real sinners. "You're a saint, Bradley."

A saint. Folger was certain the authorities wouldn't characterize him as such if Kudrow played his ace. "You have all the cards, Nick. The whole fucking deck. Who else do you own . . . or rent as needed?"

Kudrow told himself that when this was all over, when the next season opened, he was going to go into the field and bring down a magnificent buck with just one shot. Dead on. A clean kill. "You don't want to know what I know, Bradley. You might wonder what we work so hard for."

"Yeah," Folger agreed with offhand sarcasm. "Yeah. That'd be a shame."

A venison tenderloin sizzling on the grill. Kudrow could hear it, could smell it. But he could not see it. All his mind's eye could manage to conjure at the moment was the face of the FBI agent he'd seen in a photograph transmitted from one of the field teams. A black man, a serious, hard-looking man, with careful eyes and determination cut into the jaw-line.

A smart man.

An uncompromising man.

"He'll have to be removed," Kudrow said to the distant tree line.

"As in 'gotten rid of, done away with, eliminated,' " Folger observed. "You suggest it like it's no harder than lighting a cigar. Do you really think it's that easy?"

"Removal through less than lethal means," Kudrow explained. "It is possible. Quite possible."

"And how is that?"

Kudrow had been considering how it might be done before Folger's interruption, and there was one, and only one, course to follow to that end.

"I'm going to run it by Rothchild," Kudrow said. He looked at his assistant to measure his response. Folger had one hand over his quivering right eye, the other cast toward the ground. Without a word he showed Kudrow his back and walked away.

Conrad Cabral, in thirty years on the Seattle Police Department, sixteen of those working homicide, could not remember seeing an arm bent at the angle it had been on the body of this male. At least they were reasonably sure it was a male. No genitalia had been found as yet, and the face was no help, chopped and even bitten as it was. There were no breasts, but then the chest had been opened with a rough X cut from each armpit to the opposite hipbone, making certain determination doubtful until the medical examiner got a look.

But the damn arm. As the police photographer's strobe pulsed, Cabral stared at the limb from his vantage point aside the queen-size bed in room 1312 of the downtown Seattle Hilton. It was the only one of the four limbs not bound, and it was twisted around at least once, wrinkling the skin and underlying tissue near the shoulder. The distorted hand at its end was shoved into the bloody cavity opened across the sternum, as if reaching in for something.

"Three Stooges," Cabral said aloud, drawing the attention of his partner, Zack Norris, scratching notes a few feet behind.

"Huh?"

Cabral turned back to Norris. "The arm. Moe used to grab

Curly's arm and twist it around and around until you'd figure it would look like that."

"I thought he twisted Shemp's arm," the photographer interjected.

Cabral thought. "Coulda been Shemp, I guess."

Norris put his notebook away. "You ever see one like this?"

"Nope."

An evidence technician exited the bathroom, stepping over a pronounced blood trail. Norris looked his way and asked, "You find the dick?"

The evidence technician shook his head and held up a clear bag that contained bloody towels. "Just these. Someone cleaned up. Showered and all. Even dried their hair. Long and black."

"Have the toilet pulled and the plumbing checked," Cabral directed. "It could be stuck in the pipes."

Norris came around the bed, his eyes sweeping the walls spattered with red, marveling at the amount of blood both there and on the bedding. "The mattress acted like a sponge."

Cabral nodded and thought quietly as the photographer burned through two more rolls. "Zack, does this look like some fun gone bad?"

"It looks like something *bad* gone bad."

Rage, mutilation, revelry in the corpse, positioning of the body after death (*God, please, after death*, Cabral hoped). It was a textbook serial murder, the most important word being "serial" in this case. "This wasn't the first time."

"Nope," Norris agreed, pulling his notebook again, ready for his partner's direction.

"Run the method through NCIC," Cabral instructed as he bent forward to examine the feet. The toenails were gone. "Be real specific."

· Norris made a few notations. He would take care of the paperwork and fax the request to the National Crime Information Center as soon as they got back to the office. And considering the nature of the homicide, it was likely there'd be a quick "hit" if any at all. Some killers left their signatures at crime scenes, and some crime scenes were signatures in themselves. Norris was betting on the latter.

"Give me that desk receipt," Cabral said, and Norris fished it out of a pocket and handed it over.

"Susan Pu," Cabral said, reading from the credit card impression.

"Long black hair," Norris offered.

Cabral passed the receipt back, impatience welling. "Go do the NCIC paperwork now."

"Right now?"

Cabral looked at the body. "Yep."

chapter 8

The Fixmeister

Sixty feet below the headquarters-operations building of the National Security Agency, in an office lost amid a vast subterranean labyrinth, a man who did not exist sat before several computer terminals and schemed as the need arose. That was his job.

Those few who had access to him called him Rothchild.

He was a man of unimpressive features, slightly below average in height, slightly above in weight, and somewhere shy of forty in years. His thinning hair was a dark brown, and he favored gray slacks and button-up long-sleeve shirts, but no tie. Ties were out. He had nightmares about being hanged from a creaking gallows while magpies stared at his swinging body. The thought of anything looped around his neck brought on cold sweats. Yes, ties were definitely out.

He had no driver's license, no Social Security card, no recorded fingerprints, no information of any kind pertaining to him stored anywhere in any file cabinet or electronic data bank. No pictures, no birth certificate, no medical or dental records. He was not married, had no children, subscribed to no magazines or newspapers, did not enter the Publishers Clearing House Sweepstakes. Once each month an envelope with two hundred fifty-dollar bills was delivered to his office, his "salary." If he needed more, he knew how to get it. He lived in a modest apartment for which he paid the rent in a money order each month. Gas and electricity were paid for by the landlord.

He did have a phone, but not from traditional sources.

Rothchild had not "been" anything traditional for seven years. Not since G. Nicholas Kudrow had had him killed.

Of course death, like existence, was little more than the manipulation of information. One could become dead at any time and continue breathing. It was simply a matter of ability and, sometimes, resources. Death certificates could appear from laser printers and be affixed with official signatures that would never be questioned. Accident reports in the computer system of a large police department could be "corrected." Rothchild, in his previous life, had once gone boating on the Chesapeake and never returned. Lost at sea, another inexperienced sailor swallowed by the waters. That was what the records said, and records didn't lie.

And so Rothchild was now just Rothchild, either last name or first, employee of no agency, department, or entity. Rothchild existed as vapor and performed as a tool, taken out when something needed fixing. And something again needed fixing.

There was no knock before the door opened. Kudrow entered quickly, with some haste, Rothchild noted, and planted himself a few feet away, hands folded behind his back. The room was dim, the light of the displays washing it a pale blue and bringing a near black tint to the deputy director of COMSEC-Z's glasses. Rothchild sipped from a can of Pepsi and swiveled his chair toward Kudrow.

"It's Jefferson, isn't it?" Rothchild asked with full confidence that he was right.

"I suppose I shouldn't be surprised," Kudrow said, his voice controlled to the point of flatness. Rothchild was the only man he feared.

Rothchild grinned and whipped his eyes briefly at one of the displays. "The President did her doggy style last night. Wanna see?"

Kudrow shook his head. The Secret Service might have looked politely away, but not Rothchild. That he could look at all was no mystery. Wires especially were not mysterious. If something, be it an innocent phone call or the most intimate of digitized video imagery, traveled over a wire, or as a radio signal between stations, anywhere on the planet, Rothchild could intercept it. Uncle Sam had made sure that he could without even knowing that he was. Only Kiwi vexed Rothchild, a small favor Kudrow was grateful for.

"You know, her body came back real fine after that baby," Rothchild commented, wanting Kudrow, the ever-faithful husband and father, just to sneak a peek, just one peek, so that he might seem human. But the offer found no takers. Rothchild cocked his head with mild regret, set the Pepsi aside, and pointed himself back to his main display. "So, what do we need to do with Special Agent Art Jefferson?"

Kudrow stepped behind Rothchild as his fingers began to work the keyboard. Information, the basics at first, concerning Art Jefferson scrolled on the screen. "He needs to be separated from a young man."

"Simon Lynch," Rothchild said. "Autistic. You know, I met an autistic guy once in a class. The prof brought him in. He could play the piano, the sax, French horn, violin. You name it, he could play it. But he never finished a song. Just couldn't do it. Vivaldi or 'Mary Had a Little Lamb.' Couldn't finish. Strangest damn thing. That and the way his tongue hung out of his mouth like some limp dog dick."

"What can you do with Jefferson?" Kudrow asked, forcing away the mental image generated by Rothchild's crass description.

"I only have the basics so far," Rothchild explained, his eyes darting left and right over the data draining down the screen. "Phone numbers, medical history, bank balances, blah-blah-blah. I'll need more to work something up."

"When?"

Rothchild thought, squinting at the screen, the data reflected as bright raindrops on his glassy blue eyes. "I'll let you know."

"It needs to happen soon."

Rothchild looked up at Kudrow, the big man, the powerful man, and smiled. "I'll let you know."

Kudrow turned away first and swore he could feel Rothchild's eyes on his back even when the door had closed behind and he was walking down the hall.

chapter 9

Mr. Tag and the Red Rocker

Six people stood some distance from the grave site, five of them watching as two men with shovels began heaping dirt into the twin rectangles cut in the grass. Simon Lynch was the only one not to look, his attention snatched by the squared-off peaks of the Chicago skyline.

Art, one arm around Anne while both eyes kept watch over Simon, asked her, "What's he doing?"

Both Anne and Chas Ohlmeyer looked and smiled in knowing unison. Simon's head was cocked sideways, his eyes peering through blond strands, his posture otherwise remarkably steady, no rocking and arms folded across his chest.

"Something's caught his fancy," Anne said.

Nita Ohlmeyer leaned close to Anne. "Maybe a squirrel. In the trees."

Art's face reflected several emotions as he watched, something that was not lost on Chas Ohlmeyer. "Why don't you go ask him?"

"Me?" Art reacted. "He doesn't respond to me."

"Hogwash," Anne said quietly, then in almost a whisper, "I saw you. Remember?"

A few seconds drifted by until Art gave in—to his own urge as much as to Chas's suggestion—and went to Simon.

Reverend Charles Lewis, his heart heavy for the boy after speaking over his parents' caskets, watched with some measure of satisfaction. "I'd say Simon Lynch is lucky to have you and Art, Anne. It was more than decent of you to arrange this."

"They had no family," Anne said. "They didn't go to church." She glanced off toward Simon, then came back to the pastor of the church she and Art had started attending soon after arriving in Chicago. "People don't come into this world alone. They shouldn't leave it that way."

Ohlmeyer caught Anne's eye with a familiar tilt of his head. "You paid for this, didn't you?"

Anne said nothing, and that was enough of a confirmation for Ohlmeyer. He touched Anne's back gently, then walked off toward the cars with his wife.

"Anne, if there is anything more you need . . ." Lewis hugged her. Then he too was gone, leaving Anne almost alone, gravediggers to her rear, Art and Simon to her front, tiny against the downtown skyline.

She stood where she was, leaving them be.

"Do you like the buildings?" Art asked, his hands loose in his pockets, one fiddling with change and the other trying not to do so with the house keys.

"Black is up," Simon said. Then he squatted low and cocked his head as close the ground as he could to get the lowest possible vantage point. "Up more."

Art's eyes shifted curiously from Simon to the skyline and back again several times before the meaning behind the words became clear. "The tower, you mean. The tall black building?"

"Up, up, *up!*" Simon shouted, giddiness flavoring the exclamation.

Art chuckled and gave the Sears Tower a good once-over. "Yeah, she's up there. You're right about that."

One of Simon's hands reached toward the black monolith, and a single finger poked at it, stabbing into the air, trying to touch it. Hunched to the ground as he was, the childlike pleasure in the effort was obvious.

But sadness surrounded Simon like an aura, touching those who were his link to the horrid reality that had become his. Art, closest at the moment, was caught in the pull of the emotions. After a moment he could take no more, damned if he was going to cry again, funeral or no funeral.

He put his hand out and said, "Simon, time to go home."

Simon rose almost too quickly, and Art had to steady him, grabbing his hand firmly. Then the mild green eyes came up and danced around the knot in Art's tie. "Two-five-six-four Vincent. A blue house. Mommy has hot chocolate."

Art said nothing, knowing there was nothing to say, then led Simon back to Anne, who took his other hand. They walked to the car together.

A half hour later, slowed in Monday traffic heading north from the city on the Edens Expressway, Art Jefferson yawned deeply.

"You've got to get some more sleep," Anne said, knowing she should have made the statement inclusive of herself. The nights had been extremely rough on them both. But Art had to get up every morning and put in a full day at the office. Anne felt quite guilty that Chas had been so generous with the university's leave policy. Guilty but still thankful. "Worrying about him falling asleep won't do either of you any good."

Art tapped the Volvo's brakes and forced an easy breath as a car on his ass came *very* close.

"You had the same dream last night," Anne probed. "Didn't you?"

Art glanced low in the rearview. Simon was staring off toward a refrigerated truck, shiny white, passing on the left. "Not with him around."

"What can be so bad about a dream that—"

"Anne . . ." Art gave her *that* look, and she understood. She was pressing, being "earnest," as she would put it. "Anyway, you're right. There's got to be some way to get him to go to sleep before three in the morning."

Her hand found his knee and rubbed reassuringly. "We'll find it."

The wave of cars ahead sped up, and the refrigerated truck moved right, taking a space that had opened in front of the Volvo. Art shook his head, adding a breathy sigh when he saw the small inspection door, about as big as a license plate, flapping freely open in one of the truck's twin rear doors. "A lot of ice cream is going to waste."

Anne nodded. "I could use a sundae."

"Me too," Art agreed, but his thoughts swerved back to more important matters with little hesitation. "I guess it's hard knowing only one place for sixteen years and then out of nowhere you're in some stranger's house. Especially for him."

"We're not strangers, remember," Anne said, tapping her chest.

"That's right," Art concurred. "He's got it in writing."

The lightness of the moment, the freedom of a jesting observation opened a space in Anne's thoughts for a possibility more concrete. Something that might, just *might*, bring some measure of peace to Simon and to their nights. "Babe, you have the key to his house, right?"

"Yeah."

"You *can* go in," Anne continued.

"Yes...?" Art confirmed warily, knowing that tone. "Why?"

"You should take him," Anne said. "Tonight. Not where there might be, you know..." Her mouth spelled B-L-O-O-D. "To his room. Let him see that it's there, that it's okay. Maybe he has a pillow or something that he can bring back. We got him out of there so fast last week that there was no time to think of taking anything other than some underwear and clothes. Let him show you what he's attached to."

Art hardly had to think about it at all before deciding that she was on the mark. "You'll come too, right?"

Anne shook her head and smiled. "Get past it, G-man. You don't need me there. He likes you. And you're good with him."

"Come on," Art protested, though his heart wasn't in it. "I've never even had kids."

"I'd say that was a waste from what I've seen."

Traffic slowed again, bringing Art close to the truck ahead and the tailgater right up on his ass. But nary a curse was uttered, though a few were carefully *thought* in higher decibels.

"I'll have sundaes waiting when you get back," Anne said.

"Wonderful," Art said as traffic began to inch forward. "I get to get back into this."

Lying on his stomach on a grossly inadequate pad of some variety, a former marine named Georgie burned through the last roll of thirty-six exposures and came to a cross-legged sit in the back of the truck now yards ahead of the silver Volvo. He lifted a radio to his mouth in the dark and empty box of the truck, light entering only in spurts as the inspection portal slammed open and shut.

"Done," Georgie said.

In the cab Ralph, a once-promising Green Beret officer who'd had the misfortune of riding in a humvee that hit a mine in the Kuwaiti theater of operations, pressed the gas pedal with his titanium and Kevlar right foot and brought a radio up from the seat. "Four rolls?"

"Four rolls," Georgie replied, pressing a button on the camera that began rewinding the film. "The kid ain't photogenic."

"I doubt that matters."

Georgie peeked through the inspection portal a final time and squeezed the transmit key hard. "The guy driving is going to be out of the way before we grab the kid, right?"

"You weren't told to take any more of him, right?" Ralph responded with a confirmatory question.

Georgie popped the canister of film out as the rewind motor stopped. "I sure as hell hope he's gone."

"Why?"

"The guy's eyes never stop moving. I doubt he'd go quietly."

Ralph changed lanes right and caught a glance of the driver in the truck's side view mirror. His eyes checked the lanes, his head moved, all while he talked, and drove. Ralph brought the radio up a final time as he peeled off toward the exit. "It's supposed to be taken care of."

Before Rothchild was Rothchild, he was a man named Kirby Gant, but even Kirby Gant was known by another name. A more prominent name. One feared and respected by the denizens of cyberspace and the heads of corporate computer security alike. Once he was known as Mr. Tag.

Mr. Tag was a cyberspace resident, a net surfer of the highest and most dangerous order, a computer age equivalent to Jesse James or Attila the Hun, though it was joked that even those criminals and savages knew some limits. Mr. Tag knew no limits, be they legal or moral.

He trafficked in digitized child pornography and shut down regional telephone-switching systems at will. He played havoc with computer systems from Japan to South Africa. When Hurricane Miranda was twenty-four hours from landfall in the Florida Keys, Mr. Tag tweaked the National Hurricane Center's computer to erase its data every ten minutes. He raided New York stockbrokerages and had millions of dollars transferred to accounts he had electronically created, then directed the computers of the banks holding those accounts to disburse cash in steady streams from ATMs in Minnesota, much to the delight of the fortunate few to be in the vicinity.

He lived on the run, the feds always on his heels, half wanting to lock him up for twenty years, the others wanting to talk shop with him and learn how he did it. One bank offered him a quarter million dollars if he would turn himself in and help it make its system secure. Later, when he thought about it, he realized it would have gotten off cheap, considering he'd placed an order in its name for three hundred million dollars in municipal bonds, a mess that had cost the bank more than a million just to fix.

Yes, Mr. Tag was a fugitive, a criminal, a hacker, a danger, and he loved every second of his existence. So, when the cuffs were finally on him and he'd spent a few weeks in federal detention, the offer relayed to him through a soft-spoken government attorney seemed attractive. And when he met G. Nicholas Kudrow while out on a suddenly agreed-to bail, the offer became irresistible.

Do what you do best, but for us now. And without risk.

And so, after a tragic accident on the Chesapeake, with Mr. Tag's body written off as food for the fish, Rothchild came into being. Doing what he did best from a smallish office deep in the earth beneath the most secure installation on the planet. Phone lines came in; phone lines went out. Fiber optic cables snaked in, and out. Satellite up and down links were wired in.

All to a place that, like Rothchild, did not exist. No records. No mess. No worry.

Hacker heaven.

And in that heaven Rothchild stared at a screen and dreamed of a way to ruin Special Agent Art Jefferson of the Federal Bureau of Investigation's Chicago field office. Dreamed and plotted, culling useful tidbits from the seemingly endless streams of data pouring through the display.

At one spot he suddenly paused the scroll, a disbelieving glint lifting from his eyes. "You used a credit card? What a fool." With a few keystrokes he cross-referenced that with a check Jefferson's former wife, Lois, had written to a private detective several months earlier, when she had put him on her husband's trail. An obvious case of cold sheets. "Jefferson, Jefferson. Who was she?" Rothchild scanned the credit card info from the motel. "And only once. Well, you weren't that bad a boy." *Especially considering what your ex was doing back then*, Rothchild thought. Phone records gave her away. "Dumb and trusting, Jefferson. You should have checked the phone bill. Called a number or two. Man, she was burning up beds all over L.A."

But an affair, or dozens of them, as titillating as they might be, were far too mundane to be of use in what Rothchild needed to craft. "The demise of a man," he said aloud as the information once again flashed by. "The end of a career."

Career. Rothchild froze the display. "Career. Wait a minute."

For several minutes he swam through the digitized information until he had what he wanted, something that had whizzed by hours before but now took on new meaning. A newspaper article about some mobster's beating a federal rap, and in particular the portion where the U.S. attorney had none-too-kind words for the man of the night. "Oooh, I am thinking, I am thinking. . . ."

Rothchild's eyes glazed over for a long while, nothing in the room moving except the air through the vents. His mind worked, taking that which had happened and twisting it into a picture he wanted to see. Into a false reality, but one nonetheless as real as his own false existence.

At some point his cheeks bulged above a grin, and his eyes narrowed. He had it. The picture. Whole. "Oh, Special Agent Jefferson, have I got a surprise for you."

Art guided Simon through the living room of 2564 Vincent, leaving the lights off, and led him up the stairs, where he finally turned a light on in Simon's room.

The young man took a tentative step in, then another, and finally went to his bed and sat on the edge. His face angled toward a corner of his room, a corner where a large red rocking chair sat in pained stillness.

"Daddy's gonna sing," Simon said. Then his jittery gaze shifted to the floor near his feet.

From where he stood just inside the doorway, Art brought his hands free of the pockets that provided the implements of nervous distraction. He clasped them first in front, then crossed his arms, finally tucked his thumbs in his front waistband. Glancing down and picturing the image, he thought, *An Armani cowboy*, and gave up, letting his hands back where they wanted to be, with the change and the keys that provided relief.

A minor relief.

And why did he need relief?

What is the matter with you? Art demanded of himself as he watched Simon begin to rock slowly where he sat on the bed. *He's the one who lost his parents. What's your problem?*

But he knew what his problem was. It was a lingering remnant of the old Art, pre–heart attack, pre–new life. A trait that was part of his successes and part of his failures. He was sure there was a gene in his makeup just for it.

You want to fix it. You want to make it right for him.

Simon stood and went to the chair, but he did not sit. Instead he touched the wooden arm. After a moment he pulled out his cards and flipped through them, searching, it appeared to Art, for an explanation, an answer. *You and me both, kid.*

"Daddy . . ."

Art walked to where Simon stood and put a hand on his shoulder. The cards disappeared back beneath a pullover sweater.

"Where did Daddy sing to you?"

Simon caressed the worn arm of the rocker. It moved eagerly beneath his touch.

Art watched the motion and thought how soothing it was, remembering his grandmother rocking him when he was young. He wondered quietly, equating it with Simon's seemingly furtive motions, the rocking, the swaying, wishing he knew if he found comfort in it.

"Do you want to sit?" Art asked. The rocker moved, old wood moaning softly against the hardwood floor.

"Daddy's gonna sing," Simon repeated.

Art eyed the chair thoughtfully. "Did Daddy sit here? And sing to you?"

Simon reached over and took Art's left hand in his and squeezed hard. "Daddy sits in the chair and sings."

The skin, cold and soft, churned a pang in Art's gut, and he said, "What did Daddy sing, Simon?"

Simon let go of Art's hand and backed away, once again sitting on the edge of his bed, downcast face toward the rocker.

Dammit, what is it? Art swore internally. *I don't know what he wants! He's sitting here just like at our house, except there it's an empty corner. Here it's a—*

Anne heard the garage door open, her cue to get the sundaes from the freezer and top them with whipped cream and a drizzle of glorious chocolate. As the door from the garage to the house opened, she decided that she wouldn't tell Art that she had sneaked a few spoonfuls of Hersheys earlier. To test it, of course.

"Well, my men, how did it—" Surprise screwed onto Anne's face at what came in the door, Simon in the lead, followed by Art, and a big red rocking chair in a stretcher carry between them. "What is that?"

Two hours later Art came to bed after turning the lights out in the guest room.

"Is he?" Anne asked hopefully, rolling toward her husband.

"He's under the covers, and it's not even midnight," Art said, sliding into bed and turning off the light on his nightstand. Moonlight filtered through the curtains, shining off their skin as Art pulled Anne close. "Staring at that rocker."

They held each other tightly, Anne letting one finger trace random patterns through the hair on his chest. "It's something familiar to him. Comforting, you know. What's his name in *Peanuts* always has his blanket. Pigpen, or Schroder. I can never remember. But it's the same thing." She kissed his chest and said, "You did good, G-man."

Art said nothing back. When Anne rose on one elbow, she saw that he was fast asleep.

chapter 10

The Spark

Leo Pedanski had no sooner come into the Puzzle Center than Craig Dean was on his feet. The taller man's hair, usually in a ponytail that at least made one wonder if he'd washed it recently, hung loose and dirty, strands and clumps going every which way. His eyes were open but glassy. He snatched his jacket from a cluttered table and pushed his lanky arms through the sleeves.

"Where's Vik?" Dean asked, his voice hoarse. He coughed and spit into a used coffee cup.

Pedanski came no farther into the room. He'd never seen Dean look *this* bad. "Man, you look absolutely toasted."

"Yeah." Dean agreed through a yawn. He looked quickly around and tested three soda cans resting near the main console. He chose the one with the most heft and downed the remnants with a fast gulp. "So where's Vik? He's supposed to relieve me."

"We switched," Pedanski said, coming past Dean, his nose twitching. "Man, take a shower, Craig."

Dean sneered at his illustrious leader. "Yeah, like fucking when do I have time for hygiene?"

"Ease up, man," Pedanski said. He checked the activity log. "Anything?"

"What does the log say?" Dean asked sarcastically as he headed for the door, haste in his step.

"Where are you going?" Pedanski asked innocently.

"Fucking home, Leo," Dean answered brusquely. "Where else would I go?"

Just one step into Art Jefferson's office and Lomax knew that something was different about his number two. "You get lucky last night?"

"No, I got some sleep," Art said. Lomax took a seat and swung his feet onto the visitor side of Art's desk.

"How's the Bell investigation coming?"

"Slow," Art replied. He took a sip from his coffee mug and made a silent offer to Lomax.

"No, thanks. Red-tape trouble?"

Art set the mug down. "More like red armor."

Lomax thought for a few seconds. "We could shake things up a little. Get the U.S. attorney in on this."

"Breem?" Art's head shook. "Give me a little more time, Bob. I've got other approaches to try."

"Have you talked to Simon yet?"

"About the night? No, not yet." Art stood from his chair, stretched, and leaned against the window ledge. "I know I need to, but I don't know if he'll be able to give us anything of use."

Lomax accepted Art's estimation with a facial shrug made uneven by his scar. "Well, how would you like some interesting news on another front?" The SAC made a stabbing motion in the air.

"Kimura?"

Lomax nodded. "Seattle PD found a body all cut up. They ran it through NCIC. Kimura came up as a possible. Prints confirmed it. Exact matches to the ones found with Vince Chappell."

"Here? In the States?"

"Go figure," Lomax said as he stood. "Glad it's not yours to figure out."

"Glad indeed," Art confirmed.

Rothchild, as usual, had his ducks in a row, Kudrow thought, but some fairly substantial ducks they were.

"There are some problems with your plan."

Rothchild frowned doubtfully. "Where?"

"I can't arrange a disappearance."

"Ah, gun-shy after Mike Bell's graceful entry into the picture." Rothchild paused. "Or exit, I should say."

"My people can surveil, and when the time comes, they can take. But no killing."

A pouty smile came to Rothchild's face. "Who said you had to arrange it?"

The power behind that statement became slowly apparent to Kudrow.

Rothchild leaned far back in his chair, content, pleased with himself. "Do you think Alexander Graham Bell had any idea what he was creating?"

Did your parents? Kudrow wondered alternately. "All right."

"Good."

"And the banks?"

Rothchild smirked. "Their security is vapor."

"Jefferson's files?" Kudrow pressed.

"Do you know who designed the FBI's computer fire walls?" Rothchild pointed straight up. "This is a two-hour project, Mr. Kudrow. You say 'go,' and this time tomorrow

Special Agent Jefferson's world will start atumblin' down around him."

He had come through, as expected, and Kudrow felt almost sorry for Art Jefferson. He was an innocent, but an innocent in the way of a higher purpose. A purpose Kudrow was going to achieve, no matter what.

"Go."

In his office, with the small hand of his German-made wall clock sweeping toward the eight, G. Nicholas Kudrow picked up the last stack of briefs he had to peruse and initial before he could take leave of the Chocolate Box for the night. He scanned the cover summary of each, some from State, some from DoD, and some from the CIA. Anything and everything remotely related to the work done by Z had to be looked at and judged unworthy of further concern by Kudrow.

The State briefs, relating to communications failures in Asia, he signed off on first.

The DoDs, one a report of a relay satellite in need of repair were dispatched with next.

Those from Langley he began, signing off each as he read, before the third in a stack of five made him stop and take a closer look.

Kimura? She was in the country, if the Seattle Police Department and NCIC were to be believed. But why? Why would her Japanese controllers risk sending her here? They already had Mayfly, Kudrow was almost certain. One dead CIA agent and a handful of other mishaps was proof enough of that. So why have her come to the States?

Her own initiative, Kudrow theorized. Her fetish for, as one analyst put it, "fatal sex Yankees." No. No way. Her controllers would never have allowed it. She was an asset to them, a sick asset, to be sure, but a master at getting information out of the unwilling.

Kudrow leaned forward, elbows on the desk, one hand scratching his head while the other held the report close. After a moment he looked off toward a wall of plaques and photos. *You have Mayfly. What could you want that you would send her—*

And in that instant, in one flash that brought Kudrow slowly back in his chair, he knew. He had the answer, not only to the question he had been asking but to one plaguing him now for some time. "You're here for Kiwi," he said to the empty confines of his office, then smiled and added, "And how did you know it was available?"

He continued smiling as he lifted the phone.

"Section Chief Willis."

"This is Kudrow. I need you to redirect some surveillance resources from our young friend."

A pause as Willis shuffled some paper. "To where?"

Kudrow told him as he gladly signed off on the last of the CIA briefs.

chapter 11

Deep Water

Two taps, timid almost, sounded on Brad Folger's door.

"Come on in."

Leo Pedanski pushed the door inward, letting light from Folger's secretary's office flood into his own darkened work area. "Mr. Folger?"

A lamp at the end of a short couch came on, revealing Folger stretched out in repose, his hand coming back from the switch to a bottle of Jack Daniel's on the floor. He lifted the bottle to his lips and took a short draw of the smoky brown liquid.

Leo Pedanski closed the door and took a few steps toward the assistant deputy director. "Mr. Folger, are you okay?"

Folger pulled himself into more of a sitting position against the arm of the couch and chuckled before taking another quick drink. "You ever make a mistake, Pedanski?"

"A mistake?" Pedanski said, puzzled.

"Yeah, like you do something that was wrong, and you almost get caught, and you wish to God you'd never put yourself in the situation that allowed it to happen. A mistake. You know."

Pedanski eyed Folger carefully. An odd expression flavored his appearance, as if he were afraid, but not afraid. "Sure. A mistake. I've made mistakes."

Folger nodded. The bottle of Jack Daniel's hung loosely in his hand. A splash of the liquid dribbled onto the carpet. "My advice, Pedanski, you fess up to them when you make them. Don't let nobody save your ass." The bottle came up for a long swallow this time. Folger said nothing for a moment, then pushed himself up on the couch and put the bottle aside. He sniffled and looked to Pedanski, casually, as if the normal course of events were that he should offer some drunken advice to a subordinate. "So, enough about me. What can I do for you?"

Pedanski could only manage a slack-jawed stare for a few seconds, then said, "Um, it's, uh, Craig."

"Dean?" Folger asked, eyes squinting in the weak light.

"Yes. Something's up with him. I mean, we're all screwed up by what's going on. The schedule. Kiwi. Everything. But he—I don't know. He's not himself. This is beating up on him worse than the rest of us, I guess."

"Ah, well—"

"Maybe he needs a break," Pedanski suggested.

Folger shook his head. "It's a nice thought."

Pedanski understood. He was asking the wrong person. The right person would have said no anyway. "Yeah. Well . . ." He glanced at the bottle. It was a third gone. "Well, I gotta get back downstairs and fill Vik in before I split."

Folger looked away and nodded.

"You're all right . . . right?" Pedanski checked one more time.

Brad Folger again chuckled. "I can neither confirm nor deny the truthfulness of your inquiry."

A quizzical cock tilted Pedanski's head. "What?"

"Nothing," Folger said, resignation in his voice. "Just practicing."

It was either very late or very early, depending on one's nocturnal perspective, when Craig Dean parked his five-year-old Toyota pickup in a lot at the Walter Reed Army Medical Center in Washington, D.C., and jogged across Sixteenth Street to Rock Creek Park. He stayed north of the golf course and followed Rock Creek south, thankful for the lights of the night maintenance workers patching the remnants of winter's wear on the greens.

He continued south, taking the foot trail past Military Road, where he turned right, lest he end up smack-dab in front of the Park Police Headquarters, and followed a branch of the trail toward the horse center. He stopped somewhat short of the facility, right where a crumpled beer can lay to the right of the path.

"In here," a voice said, startling Dean when he knew he shouldn't be. *The fatigue,* he told himself. It was getting to him. The hours at work, the time spent setting up this latest endeavor, and the worry.

"Where?" Dean asked the darkness among the trees.

A few branches shook. Dean stepped between the shrubs and followed a man in dark clothing deeper into the foliage. Beneath a barren tree the Asian man turned to face Dean.

"Your contact is here."

Dean looked around, surprised to the point of horror. "Here?"

"Not here, you fool. Here. In the country."

"Oh. I wrote down the information."

The Asian man's expression soured. He held out his hand, waiting for Dean to put the information in it. When he did, the Asian folded it twice and ripped the paper into slender shreds.

"What—"

The Asian man grabbed Dean by the shirt, bunching the material in one fist and shaking the remains of the paper in the other. "Never write something down! Never!"

He had a good eight inches on the Asian man, but there was no doubt in Craig Dean's mind who would win a fight. "Sorry."

The strips of paper became a wad in the Asian man's hand, which he dropped in a pocket as he released his grip on Dean. "Saturday morning, ten o'clock. Here. There is a bench on the path by Miller Cabin. Your contact will be there."

"How will I know him?"

"*She* will know you," the Asian man answered with a correction. "You tell her what she wants to know then."

Dean nodded. "Yeah. Ten. Got it."

The Asian man gestured with a toss of his head for Dean to leave. He backed toward the path, watching as the Asian turned and waded into the black foliage with hardly a sound.

"Fucking ninja," Dean commented. Once on the path he walked faster than he had on the way in.

"Smile," Georgie said from a hastily chosen position a hundred feet west of the trail, just off the footpath from the planetarium. Through the long lens of his camera Craig Dean jogged north toward the path along Military Road. The shutter clicked softly, repeatedly, until the film ran out.

Several minutes later Ralph approached from the south, a small bag in hand. "I stepped in horseshit."

"Good," Georgie said. "How close did you get?"

Ralph opened the bag and removed a cassette. "Close enough."

The respite lasted but a single night.

Art heard it first, around two, restless mumbling now instead of the broken melody, and when he sat up in bed, Anne was still out like a light. *Someone should sleep*, he thought, and gingerly got out of bed and went to the guest room.

The light by the bed was on, and Simon sat on the edge of the mattress, covers folded haphazardly down. The red rocker had been for naught, Art was thinking when he saw something on Simon's lap. It was a magazine, the one Simon had with him the day Anne and he coaxed him out of the basement.

Art sat next to Simon on the bed. "What are you reading?"

"Simon is reading puzzles."

"Puzzles," Art said softly, bending his neck to see under Simon's mop. As he did, he glanced at the page the magazine was open to. Then the glance became a look, and the look a stare of near disbelief. The page, covered by a jumble of numbers and letters, was familiar. Shockingly familiar. "Can I look at that?"

A single rock forward; then the magazine slid toward Art. Simon's head twisted away.

Art lifted the magazine, took a look at the cover to get the title, then focused on the page in question. As he did, he realized it was more than familiar; it was nearly identical to the sheet found on Mike Bell's body. A twin, except maybe for the specific numbers and letters. The format was the same.

He handed the magazine back to Simon and asked, "Can you do this puzzle?"

Simon blinked several times, in a series of spurts, and said, "If you solve this puzzle call one-eight-zero-zero-five-five-five-one-three-nine-eight and tell the operator that you have solved puzzle ninety-nine you will then be issued a prize."

What? Art touched the page. "This says all that?"

"The puzzle says all that."

What the hell kind of puzzle is this? Art asked himself, wondering next if there might be a similar message on the paper recovered from Mike Bell. "Wait here, Simon. I want to show you something."

Simon watched the big feet walk away. Art was his friend. If Art told him to wait, he would. Simon knew to listen to friends.

Back a minute later, Art leaned his briefcase against the dresser and removed a sheet of paper from the hard copy of the Roma file. He sat again next to Simon and laid the paper on the young man's lap, covering one jumble of numbers and letters with another. "Is this a puzzle, Simon?"

The green eyes played over it, blinking, looking, blinking, until it made sense. Until it became words. Three words.

"Does this puzzle say something?" Art gently pressed.

Simon began to rock. His cheek stung, and he remembered heavy footsteps. And a man with red hair. A stranger.

"What does it say?" Art asked once again, putting a hand on Simon's back.

Eyes opened, and Simon saw it. Just as he had before the man with red hair hit him. "I know kiwi."

For a few seconds the statement brushed Art, tickling his intellect, and then the connection was made. To an hour spent with Nels in the com room, to one of Bell's past employers. A time and an entity that should mean little to him, except for their relationship to the kid sitting next to him and what he had just said.

"Again, Simon. What does it say?"

"I know kiwi," Simon repeated. A friend had asked him to do so.

Art straightened where he sat and rubbed Simon's back. *Scratch one hole*, Art said to himself. But he knew he'd done more than fill a hole. He'd created a mountain.

The time had come to rewrite a small portion of one man's history, and Rothchild silently thanked Bell and Marconi for making it all possible. Smiling at the computer screen, he reached forward and pressed the Enter key.

What happened next took less than five minutes, and it would have taken less time had not the completion of some changes been required for others to begin. Over phone lines and through the air, from sixty feet beneath the headquarters-operations building, millions of bits of digital instructions flowed to hundreds of computers in several countries.

All the systems resisted the unexpected intrusion, demanding proper authorization, just as they did with any communication.

It took just milliseconds for their security to be breached.

The first changes, actually creations, were in overseas banks, and here was where Rothchild believed he'd done his best work. Next came alterations to the records in U.S. banks, and then credit bureaus, and phone records, and on, and on, and on. It was all automatic, scripted in advance. All Rothchild had to do was watch the progress meter on his screen climb toward 100 percent.

Beauty, he thought to himself.

"You nervous?" Calvin Pachetta, behind the wheel of the motionless blue Chrysler, asked the man seated to his right.

Maurice "Big Mo" Tucek shook his head and lit a cigarette, his first in three years.

Calvin looked back out the windshield, toward the black Lincoln parked in front of Mama Josie's Ristorante. "Who you figure is setting this up?"

Big Mo, a hundred pounds lighter than the last time he'd seen Calvin, rolled down his window a bit and spit the smoke through the crack. "Somebody with connections."

A slow nod moved Calvin's puggish head. "Where they got you?"

"I ain't supposed to say."

Another nod. "Me neither. But it's nice. Good schools too." Calvin tapped thick thumbs impatiently on the steering wheel. "I'm Buddy Burns," he said almost proudly, a smile lifting his cheeks. "What name did they give you?"

"I ain't supposed to say," Big Mo said once again.

"Right." Calvin agreed. "Me neither."

Someone about Fiorello's size came out of Mama Josie's but then passed the Lincoln and continued on.

"You know, I kinda think it's the guys who made us rat," Calvin theorized.

"When did that truck hit you?" Big Mo asked sarcastically. "Of course it's the feds. Who else would know where we lived, huh?"

"But why didn't they just say so?" Calvin asked, truly at a loss.

"Look, Calvin, we sold our souls when we ratted. We are owned. They know we'll do whatever they want 'cause they know we're more afraid of our old buddies than them."

Calvin considered that, then said, "The guy threatened me. Said it would be real easy to let slip where me and Loretta and the kids are now."

"Yeah, well, we do this, and everything is right as rain," Big Mo said, puffing deeply on his smoke. As he let it out, he saw what they'd been waiting for and tossed the cigarette through the crack and into the gutter. "Here he comes."

"He's alone."

"You ever remember Kermit keeping a sidekick?"

"He never needed one," Calvin recalled, then added with some regret, "Until now."

"You know how to get to Calumet Harbor?"

"I told you before, yeah." Calvin started the car.

Big Mo took a gun from an envelope between his legs and screwed a silencer to the threaded muzzle. "This is nuts," he said quietly, then louder, "Let's fucking get this done."

The phone on G. Nicholas Kudrow's nightstand rang at three. He snatched it up during the first ring. He had not been able to sleep. "Yes."

"It's the Giraffe," Section Chief Willis reported.

"Your people are certain?" Kudrow's wife stirred, but a gentle hand on her hip stilled her.

"They have a tape. And pictures."

The expectation that had kept him awake drained suddenly away. Kudrow could feel the tiredness filling the void it left. "Good. I want it tomorrow."

"Yes, sir."

Kudrow laid the handset in its cradle and let his head sink into the soft down pillow. He was asleep in two minutes, eyes dancing in REM sleep not long after that, a smile lasting through it all.

Big Mo, feet wide against the motion of the boat, ripped the duct tape from Kermit Fiorello's eyes first, then from his mouth. The sun was almost up, blue haze to the east, and the lights of Chicago across the water to the west. The cabin cruiser's motor was silent after a half-hour run into deep water. Calvin was vomiting over the side.

"What in the name of holy fuck is going on?" Fiorello yelled, competing with the cawing of an early flight of gulls on final approach to the stockyards. More duct tape held his hands and arms together behind, and his legs were similarly bound at the ankles. He sat on a padded bench at the rear of the boat. After a second to orient himself, he looked right at Big Mo. "You look like someone."

"My hair used to be reddish," Big Mo said. Calvin, wearing a puffy orange life preserver, finished his heaves and came aft from the pilot deck.

Fiorello squinted, studying the face, his eyes going wide after a minute. "Holy son of bitch! Mo? Big Mo? Is that fucking you?"

Big Mo smiled and confirmed it with a nod. He respectfully crossed his hands in front. One held the silenced pistol.

Fiorello winced suddenly and rolled his neck. "Shit. My fucking head."

"Sorry I had to bop you, Mr. Fiorello," Calvin said.

Fiorello knew that voice without question. "I don't fucking . . . Calvin? You too." He looked skyward in disbelief. "This boat must be sinking 'cause the rats are on deck."

Calvin, offended, stepped back.

"Look," Big Mo said, "I didn't have to take the tape off."

"Then why did you?" Fiorello demanded defiantly. "You wanted to show me your pretty new hair?"

Big Mo glanced down, then back to Fiorello. "No, I wanted to ask you a question, and I thought it rude to do so with you not being able to see who's doing the asking."

"A question!" Fiorello blew a breath hard past his lips. "You bring me into the middle of— Where are we?"

"Lake Michigan," Calvin answered.

"The middle of fucking Lake Michigan to ask me a question. Okay. Ask away."

Big Mo crossed his arms over his chest, the pistol pointing toward Indiana. "I was wondering if you wanted me to shoot you in the head before we throw you in or if you just wanted to drown."

Calvin shuddered when Big Mo said "drown."

Fiorello could say nothing. He looked to his feet. Not only did duct tape circle his ankles, but so did a length of yellow nylon rope, which snaked over the deck to a pair of anchors and a half dozen cinder blocks all tied together. "You're nuts."

Big Mo looked to Calvin. "I guess that's a no on the shooting."

Calvin nodded and dragged the weighty conglomeration to the side, lifted it over the deck rail, and let go.

"No!"

The slack on the line was gone before Fiorello could finish his scream. His feet snapped away from the bench and were pulled toward the rail, dragging the rest of his pudgy frame, which stuck on the rail.

Calvin reached down and gave gravity a little help, lifting Fiorello over the edge. He screamed once more before a splash and a sucking *whoosh* drowned him out. Calvin brushed his hands against each other and looked to Big Mo.

"I kinda wanted to shoot him," Big Mo admitted, then motioned for Calvin to take them back in.

chapter 12

Missing Links

Nelson Van Horn looked long at the piece of paper the A-SAC handed him before his eyes came up. "Where did you get this?"

"Do you know what it is?" Art responded with his own question. Behind him one of the com room's secure fax machines began to spit pages.

"It's Kiwi ciphertext."

Art handed a photocopy of the page from the *Tinkery* to Van Horn. "And this? Is this in Kiwi also?"

Van Horn needed just a quick scan to confirm that it was. He nodded and asked again, "Where did you get this?"

"Nels, I can't tell you that right now. But I need to find out something."

"What?"

"What's in these?" Art said, seeking the information as confirmation of, well, the impossible made real. "Can you do that loop back thing you told me about last week?"

"Sure, but—"

"Nels, this is damn important. And sensitive."

No shit, Van Horn thought, looking at the pair of ciphertext pages. For all he knew they could be things not intended to be seen. Intelligence of the highest order. And to have someone hand him two pages of ciphertext—*Kiwi ciphertext!*—and want to know what was in them, well . . .

But it wasn't just someone. It was the A-SAC. It was Jefferson. No one came straighter than Jefferson.

"All right," Van Horn said. "It'll just take a minute."

A quarter to five, the sun red and low in the west. Keiko Kimura stood on the balcony of her second-floor room at the Belle View Inn and watched a fishing boat lumber in the distance. She could not see the setting sun, but its shimmer was quite plain, and quite beautiful, on the wide waters of the Potomac.

She was in America.

The hunger roiled impatiently within. One college boy could not quench the desire.

But she had to resist the temptation to seek out another just yet. There was the one she had been promised. The one she had to work her magic on.

And only that one.

America, a smorgasbord of her favorite flavors. She ached at thought of what she would miss once she was gone. Her desires denied.

Being *here*, experiencing *here*, only to leave. *Torture*, she thought. *It is torture.*

A stale bagel sat on the desk of Angelo Breem, United States attorney, a bite-size chunk missing and a fly picking at the rest. Breem rolled up a brief and swung it at the insect. He made contact and batted it across his office. It landed on the floor by the door and was squashed when an excited assistant

United States attorney Janice Powach came in.

"A knock would be nice," Breem commented, turning his attention quickly back to the work on his desk.

Powach approached, a devilish, satisfied grin on her face. She stood right at the edge of Breem's desk, red skirt pressed against it, and said nothing.

After a second Breem knew he had to ask. It was a familiar game and would have grown tiring long ago if the legs beneath the skirt weren't wrapped around him on occasion. "Yes, Janice?"

"We got a transfer hit on one of Fiorello's accounts," Powach said. "One hundred thousand from a stateside account to an overseas account."

"Mm-hmm," Breem grunted, but did not look up. Fiorello had ceased being interesting, becoming more a reminder of that damn Jefferson.

Powach leaned forward on the desk, and now he looked up. She had on a white blouse, the loose one. "Don't you want to know who got the money?"

"Okay," Breem said, his eyes moving from her face to her neck and to the cleavage she was so innocently letting him admire. "Who?"

"The name is Anne Preston," Powach said, and when Breem did not react or lift his eyes, she put a hand under his chin and lifted.

"Preston. Who's that?"

"Her name isn't Preston anymore," Powach explained. "It's Jefferson."

Breem's eyelids batted fast, and he pulled slowly back, settling into his chair. "Anne *Jefferson*?"

"His pretty new wife," Powach confirmed, standing now, the inviting curve of her body drawing no interest from her boss.

"His wife!" Breem commented incredulously. "Son of a bitch."

"Was it okay not to knock?" Powach asked playfully. Breem was staring past her.

"He used his wife," Breem said, a gleeful smile forming. "Jefferson, Jefferson, Jefferson. I have you." A fist came down hard on the meaningless work of the day. "I have you!"

As he was leaving for the day, Craig Dean didn't notice the contrast of the shiny black Chrysler LHS parked next to his aging Toyota, but he jumped when his name was called through an open window.

The shudder faded, and Dean turned and bent to look through the passenger window of the LHS. Mr. Kudrow sat on the opposite side, behind the wheel. "Mr. Kudrow."

"Long day, Dean?"

Keys jingled nervously in Dean's hand. "Yeah. Well, you know."

Kudrow nodded. "Get in."

Eyes that had been fatigued slits ballooned. "I . . . was heading home."

Kudrow looked forward through the windshield, away from Dean. "It's about Mayfly, son. There may have been a leak."

A wet bulge rolled down Dean's narrow throat. He told himself to stay cool, that it was all right, that, after all, he was the one doing the postmortem on Mayfly, and that he had been really careful with the money and they'd never find it, so there was no way he could be accused of anything. *Be cool. Be cool.* It was probably something simple anyway. Maybe a crypto clerk that quit sometime ago; they were always leaving. Or the British. There had been that initial suspicion of someone in their structure, since they used Mayfly too. *Cool, calm, easy.*

Dean opened the door and got in, the comfortable leather accepting his wiry frame. Kudrow locked the door from his side and rolled the window up.

"We have to talk about it," Kudrow said, then started the car.

"Where are we going?" Dean asked, nervous eyes on the ignition.

"We can't talk here. You'll understand."

The LHS pulled out of its space and moved through the workers' lot, passing two guardposts where barrier gates sank into the pavement and allowed the car to move on a serpentine path between concrete planters. Dean forced his gaze straight ahead, glancing only once or twice toward Kudrow once they were off the base and on the highway, heading northwest. Hands at ten and two, Kudrow never even tickled the speed limit.

They meandered on interstates and state routes until just outside a place called Sunshine, Kudrow said, "We're being followed."

Dean looked cautiously over his left shoulder out the tinted rear window, but all he could see were headlights that appeared no different from any other. "Where? Why would anyone follow us?"

A rural intersection came fast upon them, and Kudrow hardly slowed when he turned the LHS right, heading now for the Patuxent River State Park. "Because we're about to save your life," Kudrow said, looking briefly at his passenger. "I'm disappointed in you, son."

The bulge that had rolled down his throat now seemed minuscule to what Dean fought to keep down. He slid a hand onto the armrest built into the door, searching for the door release.

"It won't open unless I want it to," Kudrow said, flicking a switch quickly once to demonstrate. "Good old American ingenuity." He turned left onto a narrow, rutted access road that snaked into the trees. "But you're more familiar with how our Japanese friends work, aren't you, son?"

"I—" *Cool, cool, oh, shit, no . . .*

The LHS bounced, and Kudrow slowed to match the road's condition, the headlights sweeping the desolate path ahead. Dean looked out the back window again.

"They'll wait at the road," Kudrow said. "To make sure we're not disturbed while we talk."

"Mr. Kudrow, I don't know what you're talking about," Dean said, not pleading yet, even though the urge to was almost overpowering. Apologize, express remorse. Come clean. No. Not yet. *He has nothing. Noth—*

The microcassette player Kudrow pulled from inside his jacket brought an abrupt end to Dean's self-reassurance. "Are you aware how far surveillance technology has come?"

Dean stared at the silvery player, the brand name almost bringing a smile to his pained face.

"Rock Creek Park, not far from the planetarium," Kudrow said to freshen Dean's memory and lower his resistance. His thumb hovered over the Play button as he spun the wheel with his free hand, guiding the car into a circular bald spot in the forest, a turnaround for construction vehicles that maintained the park's network of primitive interior roads. As the car stopped, Kudrow looked hard at Dean and asked, "Would you like to hear what you said to Mr. Atsako last night?"

The young eyes, tired, defeated, looked away.

"Or see the pictures?" Kudrow challenged him further.

Dean had no reason to consider the option at any length and shook his head. Kudrow slid the player back inside his jacket and flipped a switch on his armrest. The latches clicked. "Get out."

Dean hesitated.

"Your new life begins tonight, Mr. Dean," Kudrow said in a calm yet firm voice. *Reassuring,* he thought with some satisfaction. "Your treachery has cost a great deal. Both in dollars and in some lives." He noted that Dean actually flinched at that. It was a touching but futile flash of human- ity. "And that was from Mayfly. If you had succeeded in giving your friends someone who might have broken Kiwi, well . . . the consequences would be unimaginable."

Silence held Dean. What could he say? Should he tell Ku- drow that money had been his motivation. *Money?* Cash. A growing bundle stashed, of all places, in a shed behind his brother's farmhouse in Iowa. Nothing he could say could change what he'd done. He was suddenly sorry beyond words and fought to hold back the tears.

"So now what happens?" Kudrow continued. "I'll tell you. You and I will get out into the fresh air, and we will have a talk. You will tell me everything. Everything about what you've done and what you are still to do. About this contact you are supposed to meet Saturday. About what you were going to tell her."

A sniffle got past Dean's resistance. He dragged his coat sleeve across his nose and nodded.

"And then, Mr. Dean, you will be gone." The young, now-red eyes turned worried and locked on Kudrow's. "A new identity, son. Your Japanese friends won't be too happy with you for failing. And certain people on our side either, if things should get out."

"No jail?" Dean asked weakly.

Kudrow shook his head in complete truth. "No jail."

Dean could hardly believe it. He'd always expected that

if he were caught, it would mean a long time, if not life, in a solitary cell in a federal institution somewhere. Not a new start. He couldn't finger his emotion right then. Relief was closest he could come, but that was not strong enough. "I'll give the money back."

"That goes without saying. Now . . ." Kudrow opened his door. "Shall we have our talk?"

Dean followed Kudrow to the clearing in front of the car. They stood facing each other, talking for almost an hour, the deputy director asking frequent questions and the youthful cryptographer answering every one to the best of his ability. Dean never became boastful of what he had been able to accomplish, but the atmosphere was actually becoming cordial.

He was quite surprised, then, when Kudrow removed a pistol from the pocket of his overcoat and pointed it at him.

Kudrow said nothing at first, watching instead as Dean took a half step backward and utter shock hardened his expression. "I have to thank you for your cooperation," Kudrow said, then lowered the pistol a bit and shot Dean in the left knee.

"*Shit! Ahh!*" Dean collapsed on his right side and pulled his shattered joint to his chest with both hands over the wound. Blood trickled between the fingers and spilled onto the ground.

"But I've never trusted the Hollywood depiction of moments like these. I've always figured that a person who has a gun pointed at them and knows they're going to die would fight to survive, rush their would-be executioner." Dean pushed with his good leg, scooting his body toward the trees, frightened eyes wide and watching Kudrow follow. "I would."

"Don't, Mr. Kudrow!" Dean pleaded, a wave of pain twisting his face into a wincing mask of agony.

"I come here often to walk," Kudrow told Dean. "There's a crevice about a hundred feet into the woods. That way. A few shovels of dirt and some dead wood tossed in, and no one will find your body." Kudrow pointed the pistol at Dean's face, his finger on the trigger, feeling the steel, bringing another hand up to steady the weapon, breathing, breathing, breathing. . . .

"There was no one following us," Dean said through the pain, as if it were some timely, salient point to make.

Kudrow shook his head no and squeezed the trigger four times.

When he was able to lower the pistol more than a minute later, he was surprised, utterly astonished at how easy killing a man had been.

Five men sat around a poker table, cigar smoke wafting upward into a fan whose wasted motion only served to circulate the fumes for later inhalation. Each man held five cards, and each had chips before him, some in neat stacks, some in tilted and fallen piles. One man, the dealer at the moment, had far more chips than any other player. And he was smiling, teeth clenched on a stogie.

Two players folded, then a third after examining his hand long and hard. That left the dealer just one challenger.

"I'm waiting," the dealer said jauntily. The others at the weekly game knew him as Mr. Pritchard.

The challenger, setting his cigar in a flat metal ashtray, tossed two blue chips into the pot as a door opened behind Mr. Pritchard. A young man entered and leaned close to Pritchard's right ear. "There may be a situation developing."

"In a minute, Sanders," Pritchard said, and the young man retreated out of the room. "Is that a call?"

The challenger nodded and laid his hand on the table.

Three queens and two fours stared into the whirling, smoke-shrouded fan blades. "And you?"

Pritchard's smile never waned as he laid a pair of eights on the felt.

"That's it?" the challenger said, shock turning to laughter an instant later. "You stupid son of a bitch."

"Had you going, didn't I?" Pritchard said as the challenger scooped up his winnings.

"You get joy in bluffing, don't you, Pritchard?" one of the men asked.

Pritchard left his trash cards on the table and stood, blowing smoke toward the fan. "I'd rather have four aces. Now, if you'll excuse me for a moment."

His cigar clamped firmly in one side of his jaw, Pritchard left the smoky room and found Sanders waiting in the hall. "Go ahead."

"A situation may be developing," Sanders repeated.

"You said that. Where? And what's the involvement?"

"It's coming from inside, and it involves an extreme innocent," Sanders elaborated.

Pritchard removed his cigar. "An *extreme* innocent?"

Sanders nodded. He knew what that characterization would mean to Mr. Pritchard, what weight it would carry.

"You'll watch the situation closely and let me know," Pritchard said.

"If we wait, sir, it may be too late," Sanders said, every bit of seriousness he could manage thrown into his tone.

Pritchard met him with his own brand of seriousness, a stare that had melted the toughest of men where they stood. "Nothing, Sanders, I repeat, nothing, is worth rushing into. Nothing."

Sanders swallowed and accepted the dressing down with a deferring nod. "Yes, sir."

The cigar found its way back between Pritchard's surprisingly white teeth. "Extreme innocent, you say?"

"Yes."

Pritchard considered that through two puffs. "In the morning, Sanders. Get the particulars to me. I'll bring it up with the boys."

A somewhat reinflated Sanders nodded crisply. "Yes, sir."

The young man hurried off down the hall. Pritchard watched him, admiring the eagerness, thanking whoever was up there that people like Sanders had chosen his side of the fence to play on. There were enough on the other side already.

chapter 13

Pebbles

Art Jefferson came into the kitchen Friday morning, eyes tired, wanting coffee and answers. The former was waiting for him on the counter, along with a granola bar for breakfast. In search of the latter he sat in the nook across from his wife, who stared out the window at dawn breaking over the garden.

"Is he still asleep?"

Anne nodded and sipped at her own steaming cup of coffee, caffeinated, unlike his, though that hadn't kicked in yet.

"I need to ask you something," Art said, and Anne turned his way. He felt awful having to probe when she was in her robe and barely awake, but he had no choice. "Do you think Simon remembers what happened that night? Enough to tell me if I asked him?"

Hands wrapped around the warming mug, Anne's mind worked behind quiet eyes, through the mental gears, coming up to speed. "Art, have you looked at his cards?"

"His cards? Not really. But what—"

"He doesn't use *E*'s. In anything he writes he doesn't use the letter *E*. The most common letter in the alphabet. Do you know why?"

He'd asked a tired woman a question, and he was getting what he deserved. "No, why?"

"I don't know. If you ask Simon, he can't explain it, but it still is part of how he functions." Anne sipped slowly and set the mug down. "Not everything can be explained. Don't expect too much." She might have said, "Don't push too hard," but what she had seen develop between Art and Simon made that unnecessary.

It wasn't how Art wanted to start the morning. But less than hopeful had more wiggle room than hopeless. "I've got to try. For his sake."

Anne was about to take the mug in hand again when the tone of Art's statement struck her. "I don't like the way you said that."

"It's nothing."

"Liar."

Art took her hand and kissed the back of it. "Babe, you're the doctor. Give me some pointers. I'm used to questioning bad guys and not giving a damn about their feelings."

"Make him comfortable."

"The rocker only worked for a night," Art reminded her. "What's comforting to him?"

She kissed his hand now. "I think you know."

It took him a minute to realize she was as usual right.

Far later than usual Brad Folger arrived at his office in the Chocolate Box and learned that he was needed immediately in Kudrow's office. He told his secretary to let the boss know he was on his way, then went in his office and downed two shots of whiskey behind closed doors.

A few minutes later, feeling bolder, if not better, he entered Kudrow's office without knocking and sat on the couch, far too casually for his own good.

"Glad you could join us today," Kudrow said, swinging his chair to face his assistant. "How was breakfast?"

"What, Rothchild have my office wired too?" Folger gave the room a mock visual inspection. "How about yours?"

For now Kudrow would let the insubordination pass. For now. When all was again right with the world, Bradley Folger would be promoted out of Z on Kudrow's recommendation. A nice, cushy spot somewhere in S, probably, overseeing security reviews. Or maybe T-Com. Somewhere, anywhere, just no longer here.

And after that, a car swerving out of control as he crossed the street one day. Who knew what could happen when one started his or her day?

But for the moment Folger would have to join the team. "Brad, you'll be replacing Dean in the Puzzle Center until this affair is cleared up."

Still pressed into the cushions, Folger became instantly less cocky. "Why?"

"Craig Dean is no longer with us."

Folger began to sit forward. "Why?"

"Our Mr. Dean was selling the store out from under us, Bradley. He gave away Mayfly, and he was about to do the same with Kiwi."

"What the hell are you talking about?"

"A leak," Kudrow said. "Dean was it."

"Bull," Folger said, coming to his feet and pacing once in front of Kudrow's desk before facing the man, taking on the appearance of an animal that wanted to fight but knew better. "I don't believe it."

"I'll make the tapes and photos available to you if you require proof. And aside from those he admitted it to me last night."

Five feet separated Folger from his supervisor. He wondered if the contempt could be felt at that distance. He fervently hoped so.

"He was about to give Kiwi away whole," Kudrow said, making a minor effort to convince Folger.

"He doesn't know Kiwi whole. None of them does." Folger gestured to a Picasso reproduction to the right of the Lichtenstein. "You're the only one who has it whole, in that safe."

"He had an idea who might."

"And just who was he going to . . ." Folger's words trailed off. "*Had?*"

Kudrow brought his hands together, fingertips touching, just below his chin. "You know, it wasn't that difficult. I was surprised."

Folger's jaw went slack, his mouth suddenly as dry as cotton. "Nick, what have you done—"

"Do you know what the real lesson from all this is, Bradley?" Kudrow mused. "It's that people can be manipulated just like the machines Rothchild plays havoc with. Dean taught me that. He was a willing participant in his own demise until just before the end, and he didn't even know it. You tell a machine what to believe, like Rothchild does, and it believes it. And people believe the machines. If you give a person something to believe in, he will, even if it's a lie."

Folger backed toward the door. "Oh, dear God, what have you done?"

"People and machines, Bradley," Kudrow observed. "The similarities are striking."

The thick, soundproof door stopped Folger, or he would have kept backing until his eyes could no longer see Kudrow. Then he would have run. But never, never now would he turn his back on this man.

"Are Mary and the children prepared to live without

you?" Kudrow inquired, then added before Folger could respond, "Or will they visit you in prison? What is the going sentence for running down an old woman when you're drunk, Bradley?"

"So . . . it's an outright threat now."

"It's manipulation," Kudrow corrected Folger to his own preference. "I made that unfortunate accident go away, Bradley. If it comes back, you will be on your own."

The devil was calling in his chits, Folger saw. And what else would the new prince of darkness do? "Who else are you going to kill, Nick? Simon Lynch, once you have your hands on him?"

"Me? No. We need to know some things from him, and oddly enough, thanks to Dean we'll have the means to get what we need. Beyond that . . ."

All Folger could do was shake his head and ask himself over and over again how this had all happened. How had it come to this?

"Now, Brad, Patel has had a long night. He's stayed over into your shift." Kudrow picked up a file folder from his desk. "If you don't mind, I have some reading to do."

Folger watched Kudrow sit and go about his reading as if all were as it should be. He slid to the side and opened the door, backing out, surprising Kudrow's secretary by hurrying past like a runner out of the starting blocks.

Already Breem was visualizing the larger office, the Georgetown residence, black-tie events, but a question from Deputy United States Marshal Peter Kasvakis interrupted his pleasant interlude.

"All right, Breem," Kasvakis said. "Why us? Why use my warrant service teams? You could have Lomax call him into his office, and that's it. No guns, no nighttime raid."

Breem's head shook slowly from side to side. "I'm not taking any more chances on bureau weak knees." The image of Jefferson's stalking away down the courthouse steps burned in Breem's head. "He goes down at home, with the missus."

What some sons of bitches would do to make a name for themselves, Kasvakis thought with distaste. He looked again at the arrest warrant signed just hours before by Judge Kinmont, flipping through the pages. "I can't believe this. Jefferson is cleaner than any cop I've ever known."

"Well, he just got dirty," Breem countered.

The deputy U.S. marshal slid the warrant back to Breem. "And Fiorello?"

"You get him too. As soon as Jefferson has the cuffs on."

Kasvakis shook his head once and left the office without another word. Passing the secretary's desk, he gave the wall a solid punch and went off to make preparations for two warrant services that night.

Glasses off and set aside on the date blotter, Kudrow rubbed at his eyes and listened to Rothchild relate the latest information.

"Very good," he said, and hung up the phone with Rothchild making some wisecrack at the other end. The day before he would not have done that, but the day before he had feared Rothchild. That was no more.

Kudrow slipped his glasses on and placed an internal call.

"Section Chief Willis."

"Have the surveillance teams back off," Kudrow directed. "Something will be happening this evening, and I want no exposure. Understood?"

"Yes."

And that was it, Kudrow thought. The end was in sight.

His mistake, though, was forgetting that with the culmination of most things, others quite easily began without warning, and in this case it wasn't a true end at all by which circumstances could be measured. No, G. Nicholas Kudrow had ended nothing. He had done little more than toss a pebble onto a glassy pond, defining the center from which ripples were already spreading.

chapter 14

The Song and the Dance

Breem was impressed with the facade of the old brownstone and the window boxes expectant of spring. He spit into one and pounded on the door, ignoring the brass knocker. When it opened, an ugly man stared out at him.

"Agent Lomax," Breem said in greeting.

Bob Lomax, in sweats and a pullover sweater, gave Breem a cursory glance but seemed more intrigued by the man standing next to him. "Pete?"

Kasvakis tipped his head in a joyless greeting.

Past both Breem and Kasvakis, Lomax now saw the familiar dark vans, windows tinted. He knew what was inside or, rather, who was inside. But why were they here? "What's going on?"

From inside his coat Breem removed the warrant, folded in half lengthwise, and passed it to Lomax. "I think you'll want to come with us."

The surveillance teams were gone as ordered by Kudrow, pulled back to locations sufficiently far from the neighborhood where Art and Anne Jefferson lived that there would be no chance of errant contact with the authorities closing in on the area.

The sun had long since set. It was getting late. The streets were quiet. Just a lady walking her dog, a diminutive Westie, enjoying the crisp night, circling the block repeatedly.

Each time around, she took special interest in the two-story Tudor with the Volvo in the driveway. It was usually in the garage, she was aware.

On one particular trip past she slowed, making mental notes, and after she had turned the corner at the end of the block, she came back no more.

In the captain's chair behind the driver's seat of a van following those carrying the warrant service teams, Bob Lomax finished reading the warrant. When he looked up, Breem was smiling at him from the passenger seat.

"Where'd you get this crap?" Lomax demanded angrily.

"Bank records don't lie, Bob."

"Someone is lying because this just ain't true. Art Jefferson would no more get into bed with Kermit Fiorello than I would. Or you."

Why was it so hard for them to accept it? Breem wondered. Did the bureau boys think they were all beyond reproach, that they were genetically incapable of selling out? *Well, sorry to rain on the parade, Lomax, but I have your man cold, in the bag.*

"This is not right," Lomax said, collapsing back against the resistance of the high-backed chair, swiveling it left and right, his heels digging into the carpet. "No way."

"Your cooperation here is expected," Breem said, eyeing the warrant. "He *is* one of your people."

"Are you enjoying this?" Lomax asked, satisfied that he knew the answer beyond what Breem might say.

"I'm doing what I have to do."

"Making your name?"

Breem quieted, then said, "Jefferson has a weapon and a shield. You'll take those."

Out the side window streetlights blazed by as whitish streaks. Lomax stared at them until his eyes hurt, and then he simply closed them.

This time only Mr. Pritchard smoked, savoring a cigar that was nearing the end of its life. It glowed brightly with each breath, a fat stub poking from between his teeth.

And as he smoked, he read, eyes scanning the message given him just a minute before by Sanders, who had promptly and properly retreated from the room. When Pritchard was done reading, he passed the message to a man on his right, Mr. Bellows, and with serious, contemplative eyes watched it progress around the table.

Bellows passed it to Muncy, who passed it to Yost, who passed it to Pike. Pike read it twice and laid it on the bare table they circled. All eyes tracked to Pritchard.

"This is not good," Pritchard said, choosing an understatement over the actuality.

"And the expected result of this . . . glitch?" Yost inquired of the group.

"He's an honorable man by all accounts," Pike said. They'd read much concerning the parties that day.

"He's not our concern," Pritchard said coldly. "We have an innocent to think about. How does this affect our efforts there?"

Silence ebbed from man to man, broken only by Muncy's

throat clearing, a wet, raspy product of the cancer assaulting his esophagus.

"It complicates anything we do tenfold," Yost observed. There were no disagreements.

"So," Bellows began, looking to Pritchard, "the question becomes, do we intervene?"

"The situation has changed since we agreed to step in this morning," Pike said.

"An extreme innocent is involved," Pritchard reminded the boys.

Muncy leaned forward, coughed into his hand, and said, "And if something goes wrong, what about the next innocent? And the next one?"

Pike agreed with a nod. "Will we be in a position to help them?"

"I think," Bellows began thoughtfully, sitting back, "that it all depends on one man. How he reacts."

"To them or to us?" Pike asked.

"To us," Yost said. "Do you doubt how he'll react to them?"

After a moment's contemplation Pike shook his head.

"Well, how do we determine one man's reaction to something he has no knowledge of?" Pritchard asked the boys.

"He is an honorable man," Yost observed, adopting Pike's earlier point.

"Meaning?" Pritchard probed.

"He has to understand the big picture," Yost explained. It was difficult to suggest what came next. "If it is presented to him."

"Presented?" Pike challenged.

"That is not the way to do these things," Muncy said. "It is not the way. It's dangerous."

"Extremely dangerous." Bellows had to agree.

Pritchard, though, was silent. After a moment the boys looked to him.

"You're not considering this?" Pike inquired cautiously.

"It's too early to say yes or no," Pritchard responded. "How the next few hours play out will affect any decision on that point."

Pike shot a derisive look Yost's way before getting up from the table. He walked toward the door, saying directly to Pritchard on his way out, "One innocent we can't save is not worth risking everything we've worked for."

No response seemed appropriate, and Pritchard simply watched Pike leave, followed by the others, none of whom had any comments to add. They knew the decision was in his hands, and like Pike, they had a fair idea what that decision was going to be.

Alone in the room Pritchard pressed the stub of his smoldering cigar into an ashtray and leaned back in the chair to stare at the ceiling. It would have been so damn easy if it weren't for Jefferson. He was a good person in the wrong place at the wrong time.

What Pritchard needed was someone who didn't care. What he had on his hands was the FBI's equivalent of Gandhi.

Gandhi with a gun.

A little before ten in the evening a dark van cruised past the Jefferson house in Evanston, Illinois, and glided to a stop at the opposite curb, lights out and no screeching tires. A second, similar van was doing the same one house shy of the two-story Tudor. The side doors of each opened quickly, but quietly, and seven men in black exited, fourteen in all moving stealthily to positions around the house.

Four went down the side walkway, scaling a fence to

cover the house from the rear and sides. The remaining ten huddled in front of the garage, weapons ready. One man held a Kevlar riot shield. Another gripped a small battering ram. Ten seconds after their comrades went over the side fence, the entry team made their move.

In a union choreographed through countless sessions, both practice and real, they moved in one line from the garage to the front steps, guns tracking to every window. The man in the lead pried the storm door open and held it as the man with the ram came up the steps, his implement already swinging, and knocked the simple wood door in with only one hit.

Anne's head was twisting toward the front door from her spot on the living room couch, alerted by the pop of the storm door's latch, when she saw the jamb around the dead bolt explode into splinters. She screamed and stood, thinking, *Dial nine-one-one, dial nine-one-one,* but there was no time for her body to react to the mental directions.

"U.S. Marshals! Get down! Down! You! Down! On the floor!"

Anne froze at the sight of men with guns invading her home. For the oddest instant she thought it might be some of Art's friends from the office playing a joke, but the absurdity of that coupled with a faceless man shoving her to the carpet, foot on her back, gun at her head, made it very clear this was no joke.

"What is going—"

"Shut up!" a deputy U.S. marshal ordered, pulling her hands behind and cuffing them as the rest of the team fanned out through the house, clearing room after room, checking closets and the attic, the basement, the garage, and under the beds.

Within two minutes it was clear that there was no one

else in the house. One minute after that Angelo Breem entered behind Peter Kasvakis and Bob Lomax.

Anne, straining to look up from a forced position face-down on the rug, saw her husband's boss right away. *"Bob!"*

Lomax looked at Anne, embarrassed, and went to her, giving the man standing over her a sharp look that matched the scar. "Get her off the floor."

The deputy U.S. marshal looked to Kasvakis, who nodded, and with Lomax on one arm they helped her into a chair.

"Bob, what is happening?"

One of the entry team trotted down from the second floor and went to Kasvakis. "He's not here."

Anne, disoriented, angry, scared, and more than a bit sore, looked away before Lomax could answer her question and said toward Kasvakis and Breem, "What are you doing in my house?"

Lomax crouched in front of Anne, his hands on her shoulders. "Anne, where is Art?"

"Art? Art?" She looked at anyone with a face, shock everywhere on hers. "You're here for Art?"

Breem stepped closer and said to the man guarding her, "Mirandize her."

Getting a nod from his boss, the man did.

"Anne," Lomax said when the rights had been read, "something needs to be cleared up."

"Where is your husband?" Breem asked.

Anne tried to focus her attention, but too many things were happening at once. Plus, with the disorientation and fear fading, her anger had room to grow, and when it reached critical mass, it had its own questions. "Who are you?"

"I'm United States Attorney Angelo Breem. Now, where is your husband?"

"Why do you want to know?" Anne demanded, remembering the name and some choice characterizations her husband had made about the man.

"Because I have a warrant for his arrest as well as yours."

Arrest? Art, arrested? And . . . me? She needed a familiar face and turned to Lomax. "Bob?"

"Anne, something has happened. I don't know how to explain it, but I know Art can."

Breem rolled his eyes. "Your husband? Where is he?"

"Why are you here to arrest him?"

"Stop playing stupid," Breem said.

Lomax stood. "Watch it, Breem."

"No, you watch it, Agent Lomax. I have a warrant, I have one suspect from this residence. Now I want the other." He stepped right up to Anne now and glared at her. "I want your husband. Where is he?"

Anne started to say something, then stopped and swallowed. The conversation over the breakfast table flashed in her head, Art saying nothing was up and her knowing it was a lie. Did this have something to do with that? She thought hard, in silence, the thin man who said he was the U.S. attorney waiting for his answer.

For the second time that week Art Jefferson took Simon Lynch back to the house where his parents had been murdered and up to the room that not long before had been a large part of his physical world.

The first thing Simon did was go to the corner where the red rocker had been and fix an unsteady gaze on the empty space.

"We took that back with us the other night," Art said, lowering himself onto the bed behind where Simon stood. "Remember?"

Simon studied the floor, the corner, the walls where they came together, even glancing at the ceiling, but it was not there. The red rocker was supposed to be in the corner. It was in the corner in the room at Art and Dr. Anne's house. It was not here. Simon chewed his lip and fretted over the inconsistency.

"Simon, come here." Art patted the bed next to him, picking the same spot as the previous night.

Simon did as his friend asked.

Art leaned casually forward, elbows on his knees, and did not try to force eye contact with Simon. On his lap were the *Tinkery* and the paper taken off Mike Bell. It could have been a repeat of their earlier visit. Art hoped it would not be.

"Do you remember the man with red hair?" Art asked.

"The man with red hair," Simon parroted partially, and began to rock.

All right, was that nerves making him do that, or was it because of the simile Art had seen with the rocker? Art did not know that, but he knew he hated with every fiber of his being the condition that afflicted this kid.

"Simon, did the man with red hair hit you?"

Simon's head swung right, then came back. "The man with red hair hit me."

Art considered the answer and its repetitious nature. After a moment he asked, as a test, "Simon, did the man with red hair sing to you?"

A pleasing silence followed.

Okay. So he hit you. That could have angered Art without end, but he would not let it. There were more important—

"Daddy's gonna sing," Simon said.

Oh, shit. You had to ask him about singing. Would this ever end? Art wondered. Did he still believe his mommy and daddy were around, just AWOL for some unexplained reason? If he did, it was torture to let it go on.

"Simon, Daddy's not going to sing to you. He's not here."

That triggered something in Simon, and he pulled his cards out and flipped through, choosing the one at the very back. IF DADDY IS NOT AT HOM AND CANNOT SING TO SIMON THN GO TO TH TOP DRSSR DRAWR AND TAK OUT TH TAP TO LISTN TO.

Art leaned over enough to read the card for himself, mentally adding the *E*'s where needed. *A tape . . .*

Simon was up and at the dresser before Art's revelation had run its course. He came back and sat next to Art, a black plastic cassette cradled in both hands.

"Daddy's gonna sing."

Well, it wasn't an answer Art had been looking for, but he was damn glad to have stumbled upon it. It meant sleep for him and Anne, and more important, it meant a measure of peace for Simon.

But first there were more questions.

Art took the cassette and put the *Tinkery* in Simon's hands, open to the Kiwi page, as he was thinking of it now. "When you saw this, what did you do?"

Simon saw the puzzle, and the words inside the letters and numbers, and Mommy was in the kitchen, and he got up from Daddy's chair, and . . .

"I know how to call someone."

"Did you call the number in here?"

The number. Number. Simon's brain played with that for a moment. There were so many possibilities with any number. But his friend Art was asking about calling. Calling. Pressing the buttons with numbers on them. That was calling. Calling had numbers.

"I called that number."

Okay. Okay. "Where were you when you called?"

"Mommy was making dinner, and I had hot chocolate."

Not the exact answer, but something nonetheless, telling Art that Jean Lynch was alive when her son called this number. This was all before Mike Bell came into their lives.

"You were downstairs," Art said.

"Downstairs."

There was only one phone downstairs, Art knew. In the living room. About ten feet from a dark stain on the floor.

He had no choice and carefully led Simon down the stairs and into the darkened living room, keeping himself between the kid and the horrific marks on the hardwood floor.

At the table where the phone rested, Simon stood and stared at the device. Art picked up the phone. It was still connected, the dial tone humming. He put the phone to Simon's ear and held the *Tinkery* where the moonlight could hit the Kiwi page. "Can you see the number, Simon?"

Simon saw the number and the words. Together they told him to do something, just like before. He straightened a single finger and began to press numbers on the phone. He was calling someone. Again.

Art bent forward and kept his ear close to the handset, listening for an answer. It came after one ring.

"Hi," a voice answered with strained enthusiasm. "You've reached the Puzzle Center—"

Before Simon could respond or the person at the other end go on, Art took the handset and put it to the side of his face. "I'm calling about puzzle ninety-nine."

Silence, mostly, from the other end. Art thought maybe a muffled quick breath also.

"Hello," Art said.

"Uh . . ."

"Who is this?" Art asked.

"Uh . . . You . . . *puzzle ninety-nine?*"

A little too surprised, Art thought. *Okay. Let's shake 'em up.* "This is Special Agent Art Jefferson, FBI. Who am I speaking to?"

Click.

Art kept the phone to his ear, listening as the dial tone followed, and hung up after a moment.

Well, well, well. He asked himself where that call might have been answered. Placing Bell and Kiwi into the equation, he could easily hazard a guess.

"We called someone," Simon said.

Art looked to him, putting a big hand on the bony shoulder. "We sure did."

The sound erupting suddenly in the dead quiet of the Lynch's living room sent a short-lived shudder through Art. He took the ringing cell phone from inside his jacket.

"Jefferson."

"Art. It's Bob."

Squeezing Simon's shoulder softly, Art said, "What's up?"

The pause before Lomax answered was oddly uncharacteristic, and Art picked up on it instantly.

"You'd better come home, Art."

Come home . . . Anne! "Bob, what is it? Is Anne all right? What's wrong?"

"Anne's . . . all right. But, Art, there's . . . a problem."

"A problem?" What the hell was Lomax talking about? "Are you at my house?"

"Yes, along with Breem and a dozen or so of Pete Kasvakis's fellas."

"What!" Art reacted.

"Just come home. We'll straighten this out."

"Straighten what out? Dammit, Bob, put Anne on. I want to talk to her."

There was a muffled discussion at the other end, which

Art could not make out through the hand that was obviously covering the mouthpiece. Then . . .

"Art? Babe?"

"Anne? What's going on?"

"Art, there are a bunch of men here. With guns. They broke in and said they have warrants to arrest us."

Art's hand slid off Simon's shoulder and balled into a fist at his side. "Arrest us. You included?"

"They have handcuffs on me right now."

Instinct drew Art's gaze to the rough oval of dried blood a few feet distant, then to the body of the phone on the table, and finally to Simon, who stood in blissful silence, rocking ever so slightly next to him.

"Breem is there?"

"Yes. Art, what is going on?"

Jaw muscles flexed, and Art said as calmly as he could, "Put Bob back on."

More muffled talk, then: "Art, where are you?"

"What is this, Bob? What am I supposed to have done that Breem would want to arrest me and Anne?"

"Art, they found bank accounts. One overseas with Anne's maiden name on it and full of money from one of Fiorello's accounts."

"That's bullshit."

"I know it is. But there's more, Art. A lot of stuff that makes you look guilty just because it exists."

"It doesn't exist."

"I know, but I've seen the account records. They're there."

"Then someone put them there," Art said, invoking the defense of those with no defense. A setup.

"Where are you?"

Art looked around the room. It seemed suddenly smaller

than a few minutes earlier. *Why set me up?*

The fist thumping against his leg brushed the small arm next to him, and a hand came to his, wiggling its way between the clenched fingers, relaxing them, until it was comfortably in his palm.

The *Tinkery* blazed white in the moonlight where it lay on the phone table.

Simon squeezed his hand.

Lomax pressed the question.

This is the Puzzle Center . . .

Mike Bell hit Simon. Mike Bell had a page of Kiwi ciphertext reading "I know kiwi."

Simon can decipher Kiwi.

Mike Bell once worked for the NSA.

The NSA developed Kiwi.

Kiwi is unbreakable.

Simon knows Kiwi.

They wanted Simon.

They still want Simon.

Art's brain waded through the pieces. Placed together, it was a clear picture. He knew that neither he nor Anne had done anything wrong. It had to be a setup. And who would want to set him up, to get him out of the way?

Who wanted Simon?

"Bob, this isn't what it looks like," Art said. He knew, though, that if he said any more, he'd sound like a man with guilt at his core. The unbelievable could not explain the impossible. It had to be made believable first.

"Where are you?"

"I'm sorry, Bob." *Oh, God, Anne . . . How can I let her—* "I can't tell you."

"Art."

"Tell Anne everything will be all right. I'll figure this out."

"Art! Don't do it this way."

"Bob, if you believe me, follow your own advice. Look at the holes. This is a big one, and you know it."

"Art."

The line clicked off.

"Well?" Breem asked.

Lomax hung his head. When it came up, he threw the U.S. attorney's cell phone at the wall, breaking a vase in the process.

"Hey!" Breem protested angrily.

Lomax afforded him just a brief glance, then said to Anne, "Sorry about the vase."

One of Kasvakis's men came hurriedly in, interrupting the heated moment. "We got a cell hit."

Kasvakis and Breem looked at the slip of paper the deputy marshal held out.

Anne caught Lomax's eye. "Bob, is Simon all right?"

"Simon?" Breem asked. "Who's Simon?"

"That's the Lynch kid," Kasvakis recalled aloud, turning to Breem and adding, "His parents were killed last week." The U.S. attorney's blank stare requested more information. Kasvakis gave it with an edge. "Chrissakes, Breem, don't you read the intel attached to your warrants? Under 'Occupants'?"

Breem looked to Anne. "This Simon is with your husband?" Then to Lomax: "Now he has a hostage."

"Art is running the investigation of his parents' murder," Lomax explained.

"Was," Breem corrected.

The deputy marshal who brought word of the cell hit now had the warrant out and was flipping through the attached information. "Hey, look at this."

Kasvakis did first, Breem joined him a second later, peeling his eyes from Anne and Lomax.

"The cell hit," the deputy marshal said, pointing. "The repeater that bounced the call is here. And look where the Lynch house is."

Breem looked instantly at Kasvakis. "Get there. Fast."

"We're an hour away."

"Get someone there! *Now!*"

With an apologetic glance at Lomax, Kasvakis left through the front door.

"Bob?" Anne said, her eyes pleading, for an answer, for a solution, for anything that would end this.

"Anne—"

But Breem cut him off, saying to the deputy marshal guarding her, "Get her out of here."

The man helped Anne to her feet, carefully, gently, lest the FBI agent with the scar lay one on him the way he looked he wished he could. Anne's eyes trailed back toward Lomax as she was led out of her house.

"So help me, Breem, if anything happens to her . . ."

The threat from the Chicago SAC amused Breem. "You're in no position to make threats."

Lomax took two steps forward, making Breem back up one until his back was against the wall under the stairs. "I'm not the one you'll have to worry about."

Breem felt Lomax's hot breath on his face. Then the bigger man turned for the door. "He's finished, Lomax!"

With a slight, confident shake of his head, Lomax said, mostly to himself as he trotted down the steps from the porch, "Not by a long shot."

The sheer curtains that hung in the front windows of the Lynch household glowed in the bath of pale lunar light. At one window that looked out onto the porch, the curtain moved aside.

Art stared out into the street, at the Volvo parked at the curb. He wasn't a praying man, but his eyes angled up as he asked, "God, what am I going to do?"

From behind Simon said, "God is up, up, up!"

"Yeah. Yeah, he is."

But they were there, feet on the ground, and in the worst spot Art figured he'd ever been in. Others had been tight, but he'd always been a good guy in those.

You are still a good guy.

The one-line pep talk, true as it might be, brought little comfort. Someone had painted him as a bad guy, and he had to make that right, and he had to see that whoever was doing this didn't succeed. Didn't get what he wanted. Didn't get Simon.

And then there was Anne, the mere thought of her in handcuffs twisting a knot in his gut.

Not now. Focus. She's strong. She'll understand. He looked to Simon, who was sitting in a big chair next to the window, his face sideways against the headrest. *Anne would do the same thing.*

Art put his hand out to Simon, and a second later the little hand was in it.

The knot in his stomach disappeared. There would be time for anger. Plenty of time, he assured himself, and for sure there would be targets for it.

But later. For now he had to think. Like the professional he was. And like others he had come to know.

The Chicago Police Department cruiser closest to 2564 Vincent approached the house with its lights blacked out just minutes after the dispatch center put out the call. The passenger officer had his gun out before his partner stopped two houses away. They both saw the silver Volvo parked in front.

The driver, after opening his door and taking cover in its V, lifted his radio from its place on his belt. "The car's here. Where's our backup?"

A minute later the first backup arrived from the opposite direction, then three more cars within five minutes. In ten minutes there were thirty officers on the scene, and they had a perimeter set up around the house.

After trying to make phone contact for twenty minutes, the senior officer on the scene ordered his men to approach the house. Receiving no resistance, they entered through an open back door and checked the house from top to bottom. It was empty.

So was, they discovered, the garage.

He hadn't hot-wired a car in fifteen years, but considering Martin Lynch's Ford pickup was about that old, Art was able to get it to turn over with only a few shocks to his fingertips.

With the tank halfway between E and F, he drove slowly away from the area, knowing he would have to find someplace for them to stay for the night. Knowing that he could not use his credit cards, or his ATM card, or go to a friend, or, he was beginning to believe, lift a phone from its cradle. Maybe he was being paranoid, but someone with power had decided that his life was expendable. All because of the kid sitting close to him on the truck's bench seat.

Simon laid his head on Art's shoulder, twisting his nose toward the seat back. He sniffed. "Daddy," he said.

Art patted Simon's leg and noticed that Martin Lynch had done one thing to bring his aged vehicle into the future. A radio poked from the center of the dash. In it, a tape player.

Art took the cassette from his pocket and slid it in. It began to play.

"Wander boy, wander far ..."

Simon snuggled closer to Art.

"Wander to the farthest star ..."

Art drove on, the song playing, tearing holes in his heart, but putting Simon fast asleep in nothing flat.

chapter 15

Offers, Favors, and Worries

Precisely at ten in the morning, G. Nicholas Kudrow crossed the Beach Drive bridge over Rock Creek on foot and turned left toward Miller Cabin and a gathering of benches nearby. The sun was out and stealing the bite from the morning chill, and as he strolled, he could see that a woman seated on one bench was staring at the rising ball of yellow, sunglasses black against her brown face.

When he was close enough, he saw that her nails were painted blue.

Keiko Kimura looked briefly at the stranger as he took a seat on the bench adjacent to hers, the sculpted metal armrests of each separating them. An older man, she saw, at least older than she, with features so plain that they could become agonizingly boring in short order. And the eyes. She didn't care for the eyes at all. Even through the tint of his glasses she could see that they were little more than immature olives lost among folds of pale skin.

He was not the man she was waiting for, thankfully, but he smiled at her. A prelude, she just knew, to some banal comment offered as a friendly greeting, leading to a one-sided conversation she would escape from only when her American contact arrived.

Her young American contact, long hair, economical frame, and all accessories included. And off limits.

But she could fantasize. That, no silly alliance of convenience could deny her.

"A beautiful morning," Kudrow said, eyes admiring the mare of a Park Police officer slow-trotting aside the horse trail.

Keiko angled her face away from the man, hoping he would get the hint. That want died as he stood from his bench and moved himself to hers.

"He's not coming, I have to tell you," Kudrow said, smiling as the eyes behind the glasses twitched his way.

"You have me mixed up with someone," Keiko said, the hand that had been under her purse sliding covertly in to grasp the straight razor.

Kudrow watched the horse and rider speed to a slow gallop and disappear through the trees. "No, Miss Kimura, I have exactly the person I want."

The razor unfolded into blade and handle as Keiko now looked directly at the man. She would bring it backhanded across his throat, cutting the windpipe and preventing any scream. It would be messy, and a certain attention grabber, but it would give her time to run.

The movement within the brown leather bag was subtle, but not subtle enough that Kudrow would miss it. "If you have a weapon, I would urge you not to use it. I am not a policeman."

Lines appeared on Keiko's brow.

"I'm not here to arrest you or even to stop you," Kudrow explained cordially. "Just to inform you of a change."

Holding the black bone handle firmly, Keiko played dumb. "Change?"

"In your employment."

The lines became wrinkles, and the wrinkles deep furrows that arched down toward the bridge of Keiko's nose, creating a demonish mask in concert with the black shades over her eyes.

"I understand that you must be quite surprised by this, and you must have many questions, so let me put the situation to you as simply as I can. You no longer work for Mr. Atsako or for whomever he works for . . . most likely Kimodo, if my information is correct. They are part of your past. Now, Miss Kimura, you work for me."

After a slash across the throat, Keiko decided, a few strokes to lay vertical scars on the man's face would be appropriate, right below the eyes and stretching down to the jawline, creating permanent clown tears for this overconfident pig. No one . . . no one . . . told her whom she worked for.

"You got some crazy ideas," Keiko observed. Joggers and walkers were passing in steady streams, leaving little opportunity for a clean break once the shiny blade was out. She would bide her time, keep him talking until an opening appeared.

"No, not at all," Kudrow countered. "You see, I need the same job done that I know you were sent here to do. The difference is, your previous employer was, unless I am mistaken, going to compensate you in purely monetary means. I, Miss Kimura, can give you that—and something no one else in the world can give you. I, Miss Kimura, can give you your dreams."

My dreams? Unless he was some sort of god with an endless supply of pretties to offer, she thought not. But as his head dipped knowingly, and she saw over the gray lenses to the small eyes, she sensed in his gaze that he at least understood her dreams. *But how could—*

"America, Miss Kimura," Kudrow said, gesturing with

his head to a teenage boy gliding past on skates. "Your favorite flavor, if what I've read in the past twenty-four hours is to be believed."

Keiko's fingers caressed the bone handle, eyes following the passing boy, then coming back to Kudrow. "What have you read?"

"Oh, psychological profiles, from CIA-retained psychologists mostly. Reports of your activities, your background."

Who was this man? Keiko wondered. To ask would be to care, and she did not care who he was. She was, however, intrigued by what he seemed to be saying.

"So many like that boy, Miss Kimura," Kudrow observed with a wistful sigh. "Imagine being able to satisfy your most urgent desire whenever you choose . . . within limits, of course. Say, twice a month. No worry, no risk. Simply have your fun and disappear, then emerge later in a different place with a different name and no record following you. No fingerprints. No police."

Was he offering— "How can such a thing be done?"

"Ah, I have your interest, I see." Kudrow nodded, pleased. "Such a thing can be done. I have ordered it done before. The world is a vast net of wires, Miss Kimura, and they all lead to one place."

Now she had to ask. Now she cared. "Who are you?"

"Do you know how simple it would have been to have you arrested?" Kudrow inquired of her, for the purpose of suggestion only. "Instead I offer you what you crave. And all you need to do is what you were going to do in any case."

"The young American?"

Kudrow nodded. "With one addition. He now has a protector who must be removed in order to get to him."

Removed? Just killed? Where was the fun in that?

"Then"—Kudrow pulled an envelope from his pocket

and emptied the several sheets of folded paper inside onto Keiko's lap. His fingerprints were not on those, just on the envelope, which he promptly tucked away—"you get what I need from Simon."

"Simon?" Keiko flattened the paper and scanned the first page.

"Simon Lynch," Kudrow said.

Sixteen, five-seven, 130 pounds, blond . . . *blond* . . . hair, green eyes, and . . . "Autistic?"

"A challenge, Miss Kimura. No?"

A challenge? Who the fuck cared about a challenge? Keiko knew what "autistic" meant. It didn't necessarily mean stupid. But it did suggest one thing to her that made an already attractive young man simply irresistible. He was likely a virgin.

A virgin . . . Keiko fought a tremor that wanted to ripple through her hands. *A virgin* . . . Could it be much better than that? Could it?

Thinking about that, she looked up from the paper as another perky teenage boy jogged by, running shorts bobbing with the motion of his stride, rising and falling where his thighs became . . .

Oh, this place . . .

"A fine life, Miss Kimura. That is what I am offering. Money. Freedom." Kudrow paused, searching for the right word. "Pets."

Keiko folded the papers, focusing on the inconsequential task, controlling her breathing, telling herself that no, this was not a dream, that she was in America, and someone had just offered to make her dreams come true. Someone who knew what her dreams were. Someone who understood.

"The decision is made, Miss Kimura," Kudrow said with a friendly firmness. "You can accept it, or you can kill me with the straight razor in your purse." The black sunglasses angled his way, bug eyes considering a prey that surprised a would-be predator as a male mantis might if he pulled a gun on his mate after copulation and changed the dynamic of the relationship. "Our sources are quite thorough."

Keiko reached into her purse, felt the cold handle carved from some unfortunate animal's leg bone, snapped the razor shut, and placed her hand, empty, on her lap with the other. "I guess I accept."

"Good." Kudrow might have offered his hand, but this was an agreement that needed no handshake, and he honestly had no desire to touch the woman. "Now, some details we need to discuss."

Nelson Van Horn heard the beep of the keypad outside the com room's door and looked up to see Denise Green enter. She leaned back against the door as it closed, head shaking.

"Can you believe it?"

"No," Van Horn said. "I can't."

"Jefferson?" Green asked the air. "I don't know—"

"Why are you here?" Van Horn asked. "Aren't you off Saturdays this month?"

Green nodded. "There's a lot of Saturdays here today. I think people just wanted to be here, to be around each other."

Van Horn nodded. He understood perfectly.

"I was just working something for him," Green said.

Van Horn recalled his own recent involvement with the A-SAC and how he'd been asked not to mention what was discussed with anyone. Unusual only in that confidentiality was requested at all. That was a given in the job.

"He seemed normal, just Jefferson," Green commented.

"Yeah," Van Horn said. But had he been acting normal? And if not, why not? And, still gnawing at Van Horn, the question of just where the A-SAC had laid his hands on the Kiwi ciphertext.

And the biggest question of them all: Should he tell Lomax about it?

"I've got a lot of stuff to take care of, Denise."

"Sure. I just wanted to say hi. If you want to grab a bite for lunch, I'll still be around."

"Okay."

The door beeped as it closed and locked. Van Horn wheeled himself back from the main terminal and let his head flop back, eyes to the ceiling, mind working through the pros and cons of breaking his trust with the A-SAC. With a man wanted by his and every law enforcement agency in the land.

He found that no answer offered itself up for easy selection.

Lunch that day would have to wait.

Kudrow was back in his office an hour after finishing with Keiko Kimura and on the phone with Section Chief Willis.

"Cover his family, friends, everyone close to him, and move out from there," Kudrow instructed.

This time the usually affirming Willis did not reply with a snappy "Yes sir." "Our resources are not limitless."

Surprised, Kudrow squeezed the handset. "I don't care what your resources are. Get more if you have to." He waited, wondering if there would be any further hint of reluctance, if there would be any need for him to mention Willis's unfortunate dalliance with the wife of a Czech diplomat.

She wasn't a spy, but the mere act itself suggested all that needed to be suggested. "Are you clear on that?"

"Yes, sir," Willis answered in a resigned monotone.

Kudrow hung up without another word. None was required. Willis had confirmed that he still knew who was in charge. Of everything.

At seventy-six Pooks Underhill was the dean of dominoes at the daily gathering in Palmer Park on Chicago's South Side. He was the master. The king. A slammer of the highest caliber. When it came to the spotted black rectangles, everyone knew he was the best.

And everyone knew he cheated.

"Got you, you old son of an old mother," Pooks taunted, knees coming up to be slapped and a smile that lacked a fair number of teeth opening a hole in his dark brown leathery face. "Got you! Got you!"

People played him to find out how he cheated, to solve the mysteries of mysteries.

Pooks's opponent, a thick man some twenty years his junior, hung his head as the revelry continued across the picnic table.

The mystery would remain just that.

Suddenly, in the midst of the joy, Pooks leaned on the table, laughing over, face serious, one eye cocked oddly askew of the other, and his hand out. "Five. Come on, you owe me five."

The opponent handed it over, and Pooks got the requisite backslaps from the onlookers as the defeated slinked away. But with one hand on his back there came a whisper in his ear.

"Hey, Pooks, some kid wants to talk to you," Jersey

Chuck said, pointing back toward a group of trees ringing three overturned garbage cans. Birds picked at the spilled trash. A jittery white boy stared at the birds.

"Who's that?" Pooks asked.

"How the hell should I know? He scared the shit out of me as I was comin' over. Who you think knocked those cans over?"

Pooks's old eyes squinted at the kid. "I don't know him."

"Well, he asked for you," Jersey Chuck said.

Pooks stood up from the bench, made sure he had his winnings safely stashed in his pocket, and walked over to the kid. "Who are you? What you want with me?"

Simon turned, his wandering gaze flashing over the man who might be a friend. He held his cards at chest level. "Simon is looking for Pooks Underhill."

"Are you Simon?" Pooks asked, bending to get a look at the kid's face. He found it to be an impossible endeavor. "Shit, boy, you the damn squirreliest boy I've ever seen."

"Simon is looking for Pooks Underhill," Simon repeated, following the instructions on the top card.

"Well, squirrel boy, if you is Simon, then you found the Pooks."

The top card was flipped back. "An old friend wants to see you."

"An old—" The kid turned and began walking toward a pickup truck in the lot. "Where you going?"

Simon stopped halfway to the truck, flipped another card, and made a "this way" windmilling motion with one arm.

"Shit," Pooks said. If this wasn't the strangest damn thing, he didn't know what was. "An old friend, you say. Well, let's see."

By the time Pooks got to the pickup, Simon had already climbed in. Pooks stopped at the passenger door, peeking in gingerly at first past the squirrely kid to the person behind the wheel.

"Well, *son* of a *son* of someone else's bitch!" Pooks's few sallow teeth showed through another smile as he almost crawled through the open window, poking his hand past Simon.

"Good to see you, Pooks," Art said, shaking the old con man's hand.

"Son of a—shee-it." Pooks looked to Simon. "He ain't yours . . ."

Art shook his head and checked the area around the lot once again. "Pooks, listen, I need some help."

"I watchez the television, mister," Pooks offered. "I should say you do."

"I didn't do anything," Art said, thinking how absurd it was that he was professing his innocence to Pooks Underhill, a man he'd busted for running a credit card fraud ring almost twenty years before. Simply *having* to do so churned an uncomfortable warmth in his stomach.

"Hell, you think I thought you'd do anything that ain't A one hundred percent over the top and through the woods straight! No way." Pooks's head shook in wide sweeps, the skin of his narrow face sliding over each cheek with the motion. "You's the man, Jefferson."

"And you are the Pooks," Art said.

Again Pooks's attention turned to Simon. "So who is he?"

"Someone I'm protecting."

Pooks bent his body into the truck and tried as he had outside to get a good look at the kid's face. "He don't like looking, or what?" he asked, pulling back.

"Long story," Art said. "Pooks, listen, I need some help."

"Going to Mexico?" Pooks wondered conspiratorially. "Canada? Africa?"

"No, I just need some help until I can clear all this up. A place to stay. A different car. Maybe, if you know who might have access to them, some credit cards. The basic fugitive package."

Pooks laughed without restraint. "Where's that Funt guy?" the old man asked, pretend primping for a nonexistent camera.

"Can you help me, Pooks?"

"Hell, I'm the Pooks, Jefferson. I knows a few people who might have what you need." Pooks examined Art and Simon sideways for a moment. "But yous is gonna attract attention. Big old brother and a scrawny white boy. You don't see that every day. Not around here anyhow."

That thought had already occurred to Art. He gestured to a paper sack on the floor near Simon's feet. "My last twenty bucks."

Pooks frowned and pulled a small wad of fives from his pocket and peeled off ten of the bills, passing them to Art.

"You still play dominoes, I see."

"I still beats all at dominoes." Pooks corrected him. He opened the passenger door and slid in. Simon scooted very close to Art.

"It's all right," Art reassured him. "Pooks is a friend. Remember?"

Simon, his cards still in hand, flipped through the cards to the proper spot and ceased crowding toward Art.

"What the hell's that?" Pooks asked, sour-faced.

Art fiddled with the loose ignition wires, and the truck's engine turned over without a cough. "His way of keeping track."

Pooks nodded, admiring the system as Simon tucked the cards away. "That's a damn good idea, young fella. Pooks gonna get himself some of those."

"Pooks is my friend," Simon said.

"Hell, yes!" Pooks reacted, slapping a knee and looking toward Art. "All right, Jefferson. Let's get you two squared away."

A sheet of bulletproof glass separated mother and daughter, the handsets of the speakerphone their only connection beyond the visual.

Tears rolled down Jennifer Preston's face, sniffles traveling the few feet to her mother as a wet static.

"Don't do that or I'll start," Anne said.

"I can't believe this," Jennifer said, continually dabbing her nose with a tissue as she stared at her mother, locked up, blue smock the drab attire, a federal marshal standing guard a few feet behind.

"I can't either," Anne said.

"I mean, how could he do this to you?"

The agreeing nod froze, and Anne's expression hardened. "Now wait a minute. He did not do this to me. Someone is doing this to *us*."

Jennifer looked doubtfully away, then drifted back to her mother. "Then why is he running? Why doesn't he turn himself in? Running makes him look—"

"Don't you even think that!" Anne interrupted harshly. "Art is a good man. An honest man. Do you think he'd want me in here? Do you?"

"Then why is he running?"

"Jennifer, running doesn't always mean running away," Anne reminded her daughter.

"I'm not equating this to Dad," Jennifer countered. "God, you are such a damn analyst."

"It *is* my job," Anne said, and they shared a laugh that

lasted a painfully short time. "Babe, you've got to trust Art. There's a reason he's doing what he's doing."

"And what is it?"

A treacherous void of reasons opened before Anne as she considered the question. She looked her daughter in the eyes and said confidently, "I'm sure he'll tell me someday."

He could see the deep holes in the tips of four of the six bullets and could feel the cool metal of the barrel on his forehead. His thumb stroked the trigger up and down.

His eyes squeezed shut.

One.

Two.

Three.

Pull.

Brad Folger, sitting on the edge of the bathtub in the upstairs bathroom, saw himself pull the trigger, knew that he had, believed that he had, but when he forced his eyes open, he could see his thumb still on the slender curve of steel, caressing it.

Heavy breaths, almost gasps, pumped his chest, and somewhere beneath the skin he felt his heart become a runaway steam engine. A roar that he thought might be laughter filled his head, and he dropped the revolver on the mat by the tub and collapsed forward on his knees, hands pressed over his ears, elbows out.

Coward. You couldn't do it.

The roar in his head seemed to agree.

But after a moment the gasps eased, and his heartbeat slowed, and the taunting sounds faded, and when Brad Folger pulled his hands from his ears and sat up, he heard something that could not kill him but that did break his heart.

"Daddy! Daddy!" The cry came from the opposite side of the bathroom door, accompanied by the thump of a tiny fist on wood. "I gotta go."

Brad Folger drew his arm across his upper lip and wiped his eyes with his other hand. "Sweetie, why don't you use the bathroom downstairs."

" 'Cause Tommy used it and it stinks."

Folger's pained scowl dissolved into a grin. He picked the gun up from the floor and tucked it in his waistband, making sure his shirttails covered it. Then he stood and caught sight of his reflection in the mirror.

You are a coward, he told himself. *But not because you couldn't blow your brains out.*

When he opened the door, his three-year-old little girl, stuffed penguin in hand, strolled past him and turned, waiting. "Can I have some privacy?"

Folger smiled at his little girl, nodded, and backed out of the bathroom, pulling the door shut.

"Coward," he said aloud, quietly, the self-pity fading, a new emotion rising. Anger.

He was surprised that he could feel that. Surprised and thankful.

Mr. Pritchard watched the videotape with Sanders, both men seated in an office that sported trophies and plaques honoring the occupant. The scene transfixed them, Pritchard pressing the knuckles of one hand into his chin, Sanders finally stopping the tape with a click of the remote.

"He's smart," Sanders commented. "He knows they'll be watching his friends, so he goes to someone who would be thought of as a nemesis."

"What's his name?" Pritchard inquired.

"Underhill. Walter Underhill. He's a con man Jefferson busted a long time back. He served ten years for dealing in stolen credit cards through the mail. He's still connected but not very active."

Pritchard stared at the frozen scene of Jefferson and Underhill in the front seat of a pickup, the innocent between them. Shot through a long-range lens, the image was grainy, but Pritchard could clearly see that Simon Lynch sat very close to the wanted FBI agent. Very close indeed.

"You're a bright young man, Sanders. What made you suspect he'd be leaving last night?"

"Our surveillance showed the Volvo parked in the driveway," Sanders explained. "It's always in the garage. I knew someone would be going somewhere. It was just a matter of knowing when they left."

A simple tracking device affixed quickly, nonchalantly, under the bumper as a woman out for a walk passed the car had taken care of the rest. But that begged a question. "Will they search the vehicle?"

Sanders shook his head. "They have no reason to."

"And what about the opposition?"

"At this point we can't be sure. But you can be certain they're looking."

Opposing teams, on a crowded field, one team sees the ball amid a forest of legs, afraid to reach for it for fear that their opponents will then see it. Pritchard knew someone would have to make the first move. The difference was that when his team made it, it would be only an opening. If the other side made it, it would be the end.

In this case, he thought, late was not better than never. Late *was* never. Never was never.

Now was the only viable option. Or soon, at the latest.

"Have they laid up yet?" Pritchard asked.

"No."

He thought for a moment, mindful of some of the boys' reservations. "I want to know as soon as they do."

"Yes, sir," Sanders said, clicking the VCR off now, the TV screen collapsing to a single point of light before going black.

chapter 16

Downs and Ups

Just before ten in the evening Brad Folger arrived in the Puzzle Center for his shift, an assistant deputy director answering phones. A de facto demotion he could not protest.

When he entered, he was surprised to see Pedanski swiveling back and forth before the phone console, hands together at his face, thumbs beneath his chin, a finger on each side of his nose. "Leo, what are you doing here? I was supposed to relieve Vik."

Pedanski did not turn toward Folger, did not even glance his way. "I did a double. Told Vik to rest up."

"Oh." Folger laid his jacket over a chair and studied Pedanski. "What's wrong?"

"You didn't log a call," Pedanski said to the console. "The computers logged it, but you wrote nothing. It's my job to reconcile the logs." He swung the chair so that he faced Folger, hands coming to his lap.

"Leo, look, I know I should have, but—" But what? Folger questioned himself. He should have followed procedure. It was all *"for the good of the country."*

As that mantra of G. Nicholas Kudrow reverberated in his head, he realized why he hadn't made any notation. He could not reconcile himself with what was happening, and he could not back out. He did not want to lie, but he could not tell the truth. That voice on the other end of the phone was a real person, a real person who had no idea that he was about to get waylaid by people in the very government he served. For the good of the country, of course.

No, Brad Folger, had he been a man with any backbone, would have told that *real* person what was about to happen. Instead Brad Folger, the coward, had put a gun to his head and tried for the ultimate escape from responsibility.

And now, when it hardly mattered at all, he was an angry man, one who knew not only that what was happening was wrong but that he could do little to stop it.

Let me tell you, his name is Kudrow, and he has this little stooge named Rothchild who can press a button on his computer and make a herd of Cape buffalo stampede half a world away, and together they're destroying this FBI agent so Kudrow can get his hand on a retard who broke our top code. . . . And right after Folger told whatever authority that, the men in white with a big butterfly net would come along. And in a padded cell there would be questions for him. *"You knew this Mike Bell, didn't you, Bradley Folger, and we seem to have stumbled upon certain information implicating you in a fatal hit-and-run some years ago. . . ."*

"Mr. Folger?"

He snapped out of his solitary musing. "What? Yeah, oh, look, I'm sorry I didn't log it but—"

"Sorry?" Pedanski asked, surprised. "No, Mr. Folger, it's not that. It's that . . . well . . . why was an FBI agent calling us?"

Why? Pedanski wasn't relishing his ignorance, Folger thought. What he would give not to . . . not to . . .

Warmth flooded Folger's face, surged at his eyes, spilled

out as streams of hot tears that fell against his hands as they came up. He collapsed into a chair and buried his head on a cluttered desk, Pedanski watching him with a mix of shock and concern. Sobs rocked his body, and before he could stop it, he was on his knees at a trash can throwing up what little food he'd managed to eat. When the heaves ended, he sat on the floor, back against the door, eyes on Pedanski frozen in his chair.

He felt better but not good enough. There was more to purge.

"I need to tell you something," Folger said to Pedanski. Over the next hour he did just that.

Nelson Van Horn let the front door close behind him and was reaching for the light switch when a lamp across the living room came on.

"Shit!"

Standing almost in the dining room, Art Jefferson, head shaved and a day's growth of stubble peppering his jaw, held his Smith & Wesson duty weapon one-handed. It was pointed in Van Horn's direction.

"Don't go for yours," Art suggested. He swallowed hard.

Van Horn held his palms toward Art. "What are you doing?"

"I need something."

"Art..." Van Horn's eyes shifted from Art's strangely menacing face to the pistol, and he noted two things. The menace on the A-SAC's face was not that at all; it was fear. And the muzzle of the shiny Smith was pointed off a few inches to one side, not actually at him. "You're not going to shoot me, and I'm not going to shoot you, so put that away and we can talk."

Art held his position. "Who do I trust, Nels?"

Van Horn weighed whether he should answer.

"I was set up," Art said.

"No shit. Did I do it?"

"No, but your job is to take me in."

"You're my supervisor. Order me not to."

"I'm a wanted man."

"Innocent until proven guilty. Order me."

Art lowered his weapon a bit. "Don't arrest me; don't cause me to be arrested; don't contribute to my arrest."

"Order received," Van Horn said with a nod, and wheeled himself toward Art. "Put the gun away."

It disappeared under a loose blue sweatshirt, tucked into a high-riding holster.

"That's better."

Art went to a chair in the corner and sat, head back on the soft cushion. "I need something, Nels."

"This all has something to do with that Kiwi ciphertext, doesn't it?"

"Yeah." Art dug a scrap of paper from his pocket and handed it to Van Horn. "Put an eight hundred in front of that number and find out where it is."

"This is from what I decoded the other day. The stuff you wouldn't let me keep a copy of."

"Yeah. The trace? Can you do it?"

"Of course I can."

"Will you?"

"You could order me."

"I'm asking."

After a few seconds Van Horn nodded, becoming an accessory to the flight of a federal fugitive. *Well, that was easy enough.* "Nice haircut."

"I'm trying not to look like me."

"You look like a bald you. So, how do I contact you when I get the information? I imagine you're not at the Hilton."

Art sat forward. "I figured that out. Listen up."

Pooks Underhill had more than one place to flop, but he had offered his "nicest" accommodations to Art, a two-room third-floor apartment fifty feet from the Dan Ryan Expressway with a northern exposure that overlooked the railyards. It was in an area of the old South Side where old brick buildings dominated the landscape, where the lost and downtrodden congregated, and where those wanting to get lost could do so.

Art tramped up three flights of creaking stars and tapped on the door of 3B twice.

"Who's that?" the familiar voice challenged from inside.

"It's me."

Pooks undid the three latches and let Art in, resetting the locks again quickly.

"Did your friend show up?" Art asked.

Pooks pointed to a shoe box on the dulled wood tabletop. "Credit cards, two phones, and keys to a Chevy Nova. It's parked on Fifty-fifth."

Relieved, Art put a hand on Pooks's shoulder. "When this is over, I owe you."

A grimace and a shake of the head were Pooks's response. "Shit, Jefferson, you stopped the Pooks from getting into deeper shit when you busted me. I was old and stupid then. Older and wiser now."

Art nodded and looked toward the door to the bedroom. It was open just an inch or so. "How was he?"

"Fine," Pooks said curtly.

"You cut his hair, right?"

"Yep," Pooks confirmed sourly. "And turned that blond mop brown. Yep. Your little friend is A-okay all right."

"What's wrong with you?" Art asked.

"I taught him how to play dominoes," Pooks said. "And the little snot goes aheads and beats me!"

Art chuckled and half sat against the edge of the table. "He beat the Pooks."

"Jefferson, if you tells a soul . . ." Pooks made a bony fist and held it toward Art.

"Not from me," Art assured the old man. "How long did it take him?"

"First game!"

The chuckle rolled into a laugh as Art doubled over.

"Then he up and takes all my dominoes into the bedroom and starts playing alone with 'em! You believe that?"

"Yeah," Art answered, wiping his eyes. "Yeah, I do, Pooks. Is he still playing?"

"He's doing something with 'em," Pooks said, waving a dejected hand as he turned away. "I don't care."

Art left Pooks to sulk in defeat, probably his first in a decade, and eased open the door to the bedroom, his smile draining away and his eyes bugging in wonder at what he saw.

"Jesus . . ."

Simon stood on a chair by the bedroom's only window, looking out to the north, the stepped black form of the Sears Tower rising in the distance, and on the flat top of the dresser next to the window the same structure rose in miniature, constructed of dominoes. A near-perfect replica at least three feet tall.

As Art came into the room, Simon's head rolled his way, eyes more visible now that the blond locks were shorn. "Black is up."

"Yeah," Art said, marveling at the display. "Way up."

"Beats me and then makes that thing," Pooks commented from the doorway to the front room. "Where the hell you find him, Jefferson?"

In a blue house on Vincent Street, where his mother and father were murdered. Art could have explained it that way, but he didn't. He chose to offer no answer at all. Instead he had his own question. "Pooks, can you hang around awhile longer? To keep an eye on him?"

"You got somewhere to go?"

"I've got something to do," Art answered. Or try to do. Damn, there was so *much* to do.

"Hell, just lock the door and tell him to stay," Pooks suggested. "He listens real good."

"This could take awhile," Art said. "I don't want him left alone too long."

Pooks saw something strange in Art's expression, a look he'd never thought the man capable of: helplessness. "What you gotta do?"

Art considered whether he should tell the old con man. But what could it hurt? "I've got to get word to my wife. They've got her locked up. I've got to let her know what's going on. Why I'm doing this."

"Your wife?" Pooks repeated thoughtfully, old, twiglike fingers scratching the stubble beneath his chin. His eyes narrowed, the same way they had when long ago he would dream of cons and how they could be played. After a moment he smiled. He hadn't lost the touch. "Jefferson."

"What?"

"Your wife . . ."

"Anne," Art prompted.

Pooks nodded, creased lips twisting into a grin. "Anne. Does she got an uncle?"

chapter 17

Hoods, Inc.

Unlike the previous day, when a collective disbelief had brought many off day workers into the office, Nels
Van Horn found it sparsely populated, even for a Sunday.
Possibly the opposite was true today. Maybe people sought
distance, like people fleeing an offending odor or an annoying sound.

One of the few agents there waved at Van Horn as he
wheeled past on his way to the com room. He returned the
gesture and continued on, his eyes shifting nervously,
wondering if anyone would note that he was in on an
off day, and if he noticed, would he care, and if he cared,
would he—

Geez, get hold of yourself. You're not robbing a bank.

No, you're just committing another felony. That's all.

After a moment Van Horn convinced his little voice to
shut up and coded his way into the com room.

He wheeled up to the main terminal, powered it up, and
placed the slip of paper Art had given him above the F keys
on the keyboard. When the screen came to life, he began
entering commands. Requests, actually. Normal, everyday requests.

He thought.

———

Even the guards had refused Breem's request to have one of Anne's ankles shackled to the interview room's table, so she sat across that flat surface from him now, the urge to strike out very real, even if only to inflict a minor, painful annoyance on him.

But then Anne suspected that Angelo Breem—who was turning out to be just what her husband had described him to be—was, probably believing it as gospel, just doing his job. He was not the one trying to destroy their lives. He was being used as much as she was. As much as Art was.

And he sure as hell was enjoying it.

"I'd advise you to say nothing," suggested Bertram Hogan, a lawyer to whom Chas had referred her. He sat by her side, relaxed, quite in contrast with her rigid arms-folded-on-the-table posture.

"You don't have to talk," Breem said, writing something on a legal pad. "Let me remind you of the evidence so far. Bank records from three countries. Phone records showing calls from Kermit Fiorello to your husband's personal cellular phone. And Kermit Fiorello himself. Where is he? We go to arrest him, and he's gone just like your husband. Both running at the same time. But no, you don't have to say anything. Just remember, however, silence can be incriminating."

"That's a bowl of cold soup, Breem," Hogan said with just the right amount of bombast.

"Juries hate people who are afraid to talk," Breem observed, continuing to make notes. "That's a fact."

Hogan leaned close to Anne, touching her on the elbow. "Don't say anything."

Anne considered the advice, then said, "I want to say something."

"Good." Breem stopped his scribbling, a ploy in any case to make his quarry think him uninterested, not in need of further evidence. He gave Anne his full attention. "I'm listening."

"You can look under every trash can in this city, in this country, or in any country club, in any courthouse, in any jail, in any police station. You can look high and low. You can ask anyone any question you want to ask, and you can listen to their answers, even if those answers are lies. And after all that you won't have any more evidence against me or my husband than you do now. Because what you have is a lie. And you know the one incontrovertible fact about lies, Mr. Breem, don't you?"

Breem sighed, disappointed that all he was getting was a speech.

"Lies have short lives, but the truth is always there, just waiting to be found."

The sun was deep into its downward arc when Bob Lomax parked his car and decided to walk the remaining few blocks to the Green Oaks Social Club.

Not a gathering place for seniors on a canasta binge, Green Oaks had for decades been the place where the crème de la crème of Chicago's mob elite came on occasion to socialize, to talk business, to complain, to make ever-so-subtle comments that would result in someone getting whacked. It had been raided half a dozen times, and everyone there, from the bosses inside to the lowliest crew members standing a casual guard out front, had seen the inside of a prison.

And still it lived on, in a way with the blessing of the authorities. It was the place where a boss could always be found if a warrant required serving or simple questions needed asking. It was a constant in Chicago's long history with the mob.

Lomax came up the sidewalk in front of the Green Oaks, seven hoods eyeing him cautiously, those he passed forming up behind.

At the entrance he stopped. He had to. A man of considerable girth stood on his way. "Is Milo in?"

The big man snickered and traded looks with the rest of the crew. "You gotta be kidding, Lomax."

Two fingers from Lomax's right hand reached up and pinched the big man's nose, pulling his face close. "Look at my face. Real close. Do I look like I'm kidding?"

Two minutes later, sitting in one corner of a room dominated by a pool table, Milo Prosco lifted a glass of bourbon toward Bob Lomax, who politely raised his in return.

"You took my guys a little by surprise, Lomax," Prosco said in the empty room. He was not the boss of bosses, but he was a made man, an insider, and had such a piece of the construction industry in and around Chicago that it was said anyone building anything should talk to him first, then get permits. Bob Lomax had been trying to put him away for more than a decade. "Walking up all unannounced."

Lomax sipped as Prosco sipped. "Sorry about Tiny's nose."

"It'll heal fine," Prosco said, minimizing the incident. "So, no warrant. To what, then, do I owe this visit?"

"Fiorello," Lomax answered.

A swallow of bourbon swished in Prosco's mouth, puffing his generous cheeks. He was not inclined to say anything.

"No one can find him, and I was wondering if you were having the same problem."

"This sounds almost unofficial," Prosco commented suggestively. "An off-the-record sort of thing."

"I thought the same thing," Lomax confirmed.

Prosco stared at the ceiling for a moment, then tipped the remainder of the bourbon past his lips. "My guys can't find him neither."

"You know what Breem thinks."

"Breem. Ha! The prick wouldn't know shit if it came out of his own ass." Prosco leaned forward, a finger wagging at Lomax. "Let me tell you something. Kermit, he hated the coon. Couldn't stand him. He got the biggest kick out of him testifying and getting him off. A big fucking laugh, man. But no fucking way would he do no thing with him. No way." The chair's cushions exhaled as Prosco sat back. "I know that much. I just don't know where the guy is. You find him, you tell me."

No surprises to be found, just confirmation of what Lomax had figured all along. One scoop of answers into the hole and umpteen more to go.

Sitting in his den, a cup of coffee by his side and the latest Tom Clancy open on his lap, G. Nicholas Kudrow relaxed as the day marched toward its end, a new week looming. When the tan phone on his desk rang, he looked at it and let it ring twice more before putting his book aside to answer it.

"Kudrow."

"Someone is getting nosy," Rothchild said.

"Oh?"

Rothchild explained the incident in less than a minute.

"Why would he be doing that?" Kudrow asked. "Was he being watched?"

"He's not on the list."

"He is now," Kudrow said. "I'll notify Willis."

A laugh embedded in a cough crackled over the line. "Jefferson doesn't know when he's beat."

"He will," Kudrow replied confidently. "Soon enough."

chapter 18

Lion Eyes

As expected, there was a line at the drive-through, a long procession of desperate morning commuters in need of a cup of hot black heaven to get them ready for another Monday. Nelson Van Horn let his thumbs tap the steering wheel of his van, keeping beat with a Fleetwood Mac tune, turning the stereo down only when he reached the order board.

The three cars ahead took their turns at the window, drivers accepting bags of Egg McMuffins and Danishes, paper trays with steaming cups of coffee, the infrequent orange juice. When Van Horn's turn came, he handed over exact change and took his order. He pulled away to a spot near the exit, where he removed his Sausage McMuffin and hash browns from the bag. Then he put something in.

As he drove away, the bag flew from the window and into a line of shrubs bordering the lot.

"Litterbug, litterbug," Georgie said as he watched the act through powerful binoculars from a vehicle parked in a strip mall across the boulevard.

"I'd say that's a dead drop," Ralph commented. He turned on the video camera and the recorders.

All they had to do was wait.

They didn't have to wait long. Twenty minutes to be exact. A rusted red Chevy Nova pulled into the McDonald's lot and close to the line of shrubs. The driver's door opened, and a black man with no hair leaned out and reached into the bushes to retrieve the bag. In the passenger seat was a white kid with dark hair.

Ralph put a radio to his mouth as the Nova left the lot, making a left and passing right in front of them. "Fox Five."

"Fox Five," came the response.

"East on Washington Boulevard, red Chevrolet Nova, 'eighty-one, license is—" Ralph paused to read the tag number.

"Never mind. Passing us now. We're on them."

Ralph patted Georgie on the shoulder. "Let's get moving."

"Some cosmetic changes," Georgie commented, pulling the van into traffic.

"It's them."

"When they get wherever they're going, who do we notify?" Georgie asked. The plans had been changed.

"Whoever answers at this number," Ralph answered, touching his shirt pocket. He was glad they weren't going to be the ones to make the move. This whole operation had the feel of desperation, and more troubling was that he suspected the most desperate were calling the shots.

"I prefer being the messenger," Georgie said, unwittingly agreeing with Ralph's doubting thoughts.

"Me too."

As they drove, Georgie suddenly looked at Ralph and asked, "Have you got a place to lay low, you know, if they ever throw you to the lions?"

"From day one."

Anne hadn't seen her uncle Frederick in ten years and was utterly surprised to hear that he had come to see her. But that surprise changed to bewilderment when she laid eyes on the man through the bulletproof glass of the visiting cubicle.

He winked once at her and put the handset to his ear. Anne sat, eyes studying him, and took her end from the cradle.

"Annie, you look strong. Strong." The old eyes moved a fraction in a silent gesture, adding more to the words.

"Thank you," Anne said in a cautious cadence, her words tiptoeing through a strange landscape.

"You look like you could use a sundae."

A sundae? A sundae. Anne's gaze changed, finding common ground with that of the stranger, who she thought now was not a stranger. *A sundae!*

"Your G-man could probably use one too," Pooks Underhill said, his eyes checking the location of the marshals. When none was looking, he gave Anne the "okay" sign.

Anne swallowed and put her fingertips to the glass. "I hope he's all right."

"I'm sure he is," Pooks said.

"And Simon," Anne added hopefully.

"I'm sure he's just fine."

Anne nodded, a sheen making her eyes glisten. "I'm glad you came, Uncle Frederick. What else can we talk about?"

"Oh," Pooks answered, "lotsa things."

chapter 19

The Stranger

How could a number not exist?

Art punished himself with that question as he and Simon walked up the stairs to 3B.

If you call a number and someone answers, it exists.

Then a converse thought muddied his reasoning.

Just like bank accounts with Anne's name. Those exist, but they don't.

Reality didn't matter apparently, Art was beginning to believe. At least the kind he knew and understood didn't.

At the door he almost knocked, then remembered that Pooks was gone. Would not be back. Not after doing what Art wished he could be doing himself. Eyes might be on him now. Eyes that might follow.

Art opened the three locks with the keys Pooks had left him and, following Pooks's habit and his own skittishness, reset them as soon as they were in.

He only got to number two before Simon said, "There's a stranger."

Art looked over his shoulder and saw a man through the open door to the bedroom, sitting on the bed, eyes cast upon Simon's creation on the dresser.

"Shit," Art said as he drew his weapon and pushed Simon to the couch, bringing the Smith to bear at the stranger, advancing in cautious sliding steps toward the bedroom. "Who are you?"

"My name is Mr. Pritchard." An awesome creation, Pritchard thought as he looked upon the replica of the tower, comparing it with the coal-black rectangle reaching for the clouds to the north.

"What do you want?" Art demanded. He was in the bedroom now and eased around the bed, checking the bathroom and the closet, both of which were clear. Behind Pritchard now, he said again, "I said, What do you want?"

Tearing his eyes from the sculpture of dominoes, Pritchard stood and faced Art. "You can put that away. You'll no more shoot me than you would have shot Agent Van Horn Saturday evening."

The pistol came down a degree, Art's head cocking curiously to one side.

"That wasn't the smartest thing to do," Pritchard said. He came around the foot of the bed and looked into the front room, smiling briefly at the back of Simon's head, then continued. "You were doing things right until then. And sending Mr. Underhill—"

"Just who the hell are you?" Art asked again, wanting more than a name now.

Pritchard looked at the gun. "Do you think I would be sitting in here alone if I were here to arrest you?"

"I'm not worried only about the people who want to lock me up."

Pritchard smiled. "If I were here to take him, would you have made it more than a step inside the front door?"

The stranger was not a good guy, and he was not a bad guy. That lack of definition did not soothe Art's concern, but he could not deny the truth of Pritchard's analysis. He lowered his weapon but kept it in hand at his side.

"I don't have a weapon," Pritchard said.

"I feel better that I do," Art replied.

"Very well." Again Pritchard glanced toward Simon. "How is he?"

"He's fine," Art answered suspiciously. "And why do you care?"

"My entire reason for being here now is that I care. As do a number of other people."

"Other people."

Pritchard nodded. "You seem surprised."

"Pardon me for doubting any implied benevolence, but my life is not exactly on track at the moment, and *his* is worse."

"People care," Pritchard said.

"Right."

Another tack was needed, Pritchard saw. "Tell me, Agent Jefferson, who do you believe is doing this to you?"

Art stared warily at Pritchard.

"The bank accounts, et cetera, et cetera. We know about it all. Who do you believe is doing this to you?"

Art sighed, not sure what to make of this Pritchard fellow but feeling less than threatened by him. "Someone in the National Security Agency."

"I see. Your government is doing this to you?"

"No, I said some*one*." Art corrected him. "Or ones. I don't know."

"Someone with considerable resources?"

"I'd say so," Art said.

Pritchard brought a finger to his lips. "So let me understand this. A person or persons of some authority inside a massive government agency are conspiring to destroy you to get at him. At Simon. Is that it?"

"Pretty close."

"Hmm." Pritchard folded his arms, the pose of the guilty or the confident. "You believe that?"

"Yes."

"Then is it not possible that the exact opposite might be true?" Pritchard said.

"What do you mean?"

"Could not some people in positions of power conspire for the greater good?"

Art considered Pritchard with a doubtful, sideways gaze.

"You believe the opposite," Pritchard reminded him. "Are you so cynical that what I suggest is only fantasy?"

"The government itself is supposed to function for the greater good," Art said.

Pritchard chuckled. "Oh, come on. You're a cynic and not a realist? Please . . ." He narrowed the distance to Art. "Have you ever seen a guilty person go free?"

"Plenty."

"Or an innocent person go to jail?"

His position worked against Art's admitting that, but, especially now he could relate to that point. "Of course."

"Fraud, waste, corruption," Pritchard said. "All parts of this government, which *works for the greater good*. Agent Jefferson, the government, despite the founders' greatest hopes, is a machine that hums along regardless of good or evil. It doesn't care. It can't. The government has no feelings. That is what the masses who complain about the ills of government, and those who tout what good it can achieve, that is what none of them understand. The government is nothing more than a concept drawn from the thoughts of men who died a long time ago.

"And"—Pritchard continued—"it is populated by *people* who do things for their own reasons. Some good, some bad, some indifferent. There is no Department of Evil Doings, no

Agency for Righteous Undertakings. People, Agent Jefferson. People function in those roles."

"All right," Art said. "On whose authority do you operate?"

Again Pritchard chuckled, softly this time, dipping his head until it subsided. "We have no charter, Agent Jefferson. We operate when the need arises."

Art holstered his weapon finally and walked past Pritchard. He stood in the doorway where he could see Simon. "And what is the need?"

"You won't be surprised when I say it is the young man in there."

Now Art's arms folded over his chest. "Why? What makes him so important to you? The same thing that this so-called evil side wants him for?"

"If we wanted him for that reason, remember . . ." Pritchard made a gun out of his hand, pointed it at his temple, and said, "Boom. Boom. When you walked in that door."

"Then why?"

"To save him."

"That's what I am trying to do," Art said insistently.

"You'll fail," Pritchard said sullenly, with surety.

Art shook his head. "Once this is all cleared up—"

"He will be even more vulnerable," Pritchard interjected. "Where will he be? With you and your wife? In a foster home? A care facility? All places where he will likely receive wonderful, loving care. And places he can be found."

Art looked into the front room. Simon had gotten up from the couch and was standing in the empty corner of the room near the door, in his fretting stance, Art could see. Was he wondering where the red rocker was? Would he always?

Worry over the chair in which his father sat in to sing to him and the secrets to breaking the unbreakable code, all in that mind. The mind of a retard? The mind of a genius?

Gray matter worth more than its weight in gold.

"This doesn't end if and when your life is back in order," Pritchard said. "The people I represent do not choose to intervene in every case where an innocent is involved, only in those where our efforts can bring a resolution to a threat."

"So stop these people," Art said. "Whoever's doing this, shut them down."

Pritchard shook his head. "Active measures of that scope would expose us. Exposure would render us useless, Agent Jefferson. We often operate outside the bounds of the law, as our opposites do. We, however, do so benignly. But in the harsh light of judgment that would matter little."

"So what the hell can you do?" Art asked.

Pritchard came to the doorway and added his eyes to those already playing over Simon's back. "Allow us to take him."

Art shook his head.

"To arrange for a new life for him," Pritchard tried to explain, to convince. "We have made similar arrangements before for other innocents."

"I don't know you from a hole in the ground, mister," Art said firmly. "You come in here and tell me you're with some kind of group that sounds like a bunch of wannabe superheroes and tell me to *give* Simon to you. He's not mine to give."

"Then before long he won't be yours at all," Pritchard said.

Simon turned from the corner and approached Art. He stopped when he saw the stranger's feet very close to his friend's. His hand felt at the cards beneath his shirt.

Pritchard crouched down. "That's a nice building you made."

Simon twisted and said, "I was up on the chair."

Pritchard stood again and looked at Art. "Will you walk me to the stairs?"

"Why?"

"He remembers what he hears, I presume. There is something I don't think he should hear."

Art thought it over, recalling Pooks's very true comment that Simon would stay if told, then walked his young friend into the cramped kitchenette. "Simon, I have to walk with this man to the stairs. I'll lock the door. You stay in here and don't open it. Okay? Only I can open it. Got it?"

"Art can open the door," Simon confirmed in his own way.

Art patted him on the shoulder and led Pritchard into the hall, where he twisted the keys in the three locks.

"Which stairs?" Art asked.

"I'm parked in the alley," Pritchard answered.

They walked down the hallway and turned where it ended at the rear of the building.

From the front of the building Keiko Kimura turned onto the hallway and made her way toward 3B.

At the door she stopped and listened, both to the footsteps descending the far stairwell and to scraping footsteps from inside the room. She wondered who the man was with Jefferson, but his relevance was minor, if consequential at all. They were gone, possibly for a minute, possibly for an hour. All she needed was a minute.

From her pocket she removed a small ring of three keys, which the building manager had willingly surrendered from his neatly arranged pegboard after Keiko had cut his throat. No time for anything beyond that, and no desire. Too old, too dark. She inserted each key, undoing each lock, and opened the door to a shabby room. An empty room.

She closed the door and stepped farther in, eyes searching the corners, ears picking up the shuffling feet to her left. There was an open door. Through it she saw what she had come for.

Her tongue slid past her lips and wet them with a slow stroke.

"Hey," Keiko said, passing from the front room to the bedroom. The young American stood there, his feet nervously moving against the old wood floor, one finger touching a dresser where a building made of dominoes rose in tribute to its inspiration out the window. She closed on Simon and swung her hand at the miniature tower, scattering it into hundreds of pieces that clicked off the walls and the floor.

"You're a stranger," Simon said as he retreated to the window in the corner.

"No, I'm your friend," Keiko said, reaching a hand with blue nails toward Simon. "And you're coming with me."

Pritchard stopped before exiting the stairwell on the ground floor and faced Art. "I want to give you a number you can call."

"Why couldn't you do this upstairs?"

"Our young friend's having a phone number he should never have seen is how this all began." Pritchard removed a card from his wallet and held it out so Art could see it. "Remember this number. Call it from any area code in the country. On the third ring press the number five."

Art studied the number, committing it to memory, but he was not sure why.

Pritchard was more certain. "You will call it."

"What makes you so sure?"

"Because they'll never stop looking."

That statement clicked a switch in Art's head. "Will they if you have him?"

Pritchard had no answer to that. At least they would not know where to look. But that was not a denial of Jefferson's point. "Please don't believe that you alone can save him."

"I'm not that good," Art said.

Pritchard wasn't so sure that Jefferson didn't believe it.

The nails dug into the shirtsleeves and into his arm, and Simon's head flopped back as another hand came over his mouth to staunch a scream.

"Shut up!" Keiko commanded, and grabbed for the window shade with the hand that covered Simon's mouth and pulled it down. "Let's go! Now!"

Simon resisted. This was a stranger. He was not supposed to leave. Only Art could open the door. Only Art could tell him to leave.

"Come on!" Keiko said harshly, tugging at the arm.

"You're a stranger," Simon repeated loudly, and pulled his arm free of the stranger's grip. Her nails scratched him, and it hurt, and she reached with the other hand for his face.

"You're coming, you little—"

Never go with a stranger. Simon knew that, and as her fingers touched his cheeks, he tried to push them away. But they came back. He pushed them again. They came back.

"You're a stranger!" Simon said very loud, and swung at the hands reaching for him, swung hard, swung and swung until his arms were flailing, and his fists clenching. "You're a stranger!"

Keiko tried to snag one of the fists pecking at her like some annoying barnyard fowl, but when she did, the other slipped through and crunched against her chin.

199

"You damn little—"

Simon felt the pain in his hand just before a sharper pain stung his face just like the time the man with red hair had—

"Dumb little Joe!" Keiko swore as her hand pummeled Simon's cheek a second time and knocked him to the floor.

In a building a hundred feet west, a woman pulled her face back from a spotting scope. "Did you catch that?"

Her partner, an elderly man, nodded and kept his eyes on a small video screen, the image of the drawn shades yellow in the waning light. "Something is wrong."

"Call him," the woman suggested.

Pritchard was about to offer his hand to Art when his cell phone rang. He folded the compact unit open and listened, saying nothing, his eyes locking on Art's after a moment. "Someone's up there with Simon."

"Who?" *It could be Pooks,* Art told himself. *It could.*

"A woman."

"Dammit!" Art said, turning and bounding up the steps.

Pritchard closed his phone with an angry snap and resisted the urge to follow. He was out the door and in his car before Art reached the third floor.

"Come on!" Keiko prodded, urged, ordered, pleaded, as she pulled Simon into the front room by his shirt, dragging the body that had become a defiant human tornado of arms and legs toward the front door.

She reached it and pulled it open and was knocked over as Art bolted into the room.

He tumbled over her, rolling toward the kitchenette, and she released her grip on Simon as she was smashed against the hard floor.

Art bashed against the low island of cabinets that set the kitchenette off from the front room, his eyes searching back over his path, one hand bringing the sweatshirt up as the other reached for his Smith. Simon was crawling toward the bedroom.

And on the floor two yards away a woman with black hair was coming up from all fours to her knees, a boxy black gun in one hand.

Shit!

Art rolled right as she fired, bullets coming not in singles or in double taps, but in steady burps that peppered the cabinets and followed the wall behind Art across the front room. He gave Simon a shove, sending him sliding across the floor into the bedroom, and fired back twice, blindly.

One round impacted the edge of the door just left of Keiko's head, sending a spray of wood splinters over her. She rolled backward and fired a last burst at the couch, through the couch, as she tumbled into the hallway and scrambled to her feet.

The sound of feet beating a retreat brought Art up slowly from where he lay atop Simon. The last volley of fire had shredded the couch and had punched a half dozen holes in the wall between the front room and the bedroom.

"Simon? Are you all right?"

Simon came to a curled sort of sit, something Art had not seen before, an almost fetal position.

"Are you all right?"

"She was a stranger," Simon said.

Art stood and checked the front room and, thinking as fast as he'd ever had to, grabbed the items Pooks had gotten for him and lifted Simon to his feet. "We've got to go, Simon."

"To the basement. The loud noise, and Mommy and Daddy aren't—" The recital ended in several short breaths.

"Dammit," Art swore, and took Simon's hand in a firm grip and led him out of the apartment, checking the hall in both directions, and then to the back stairwell.

As they exited into the alley, sirens were approaching from all directions.

chapter 20

Price of Admission

Kimura • • •

Nothing made any sense now, Lomax thought.

The week sucked; the day sucked; everything sucked. That was Bob Lomax's estimation of life at the moment as he gazed uselessly out his window to the traffic below. And the real bitch of the matter was he saw no way to make it any better, no way to understand it even.

Sure, he could peck away at the incriminating cloud that surrounded his number two, he could seek answers from the lowlife scum he endeavored to put away, and he could swear at Breem under his breath every chance he got.

But for what? Art was still out there, running, and Lomax hadn't the foggiest idea what was really going on.

And then the newest hole to fill: Kimura.

"Damn," the SAC said, tapping the cool glass with the edge of his fist, leaving fat, muddled smudges on the window.

"Sir?"

Lomax turned, surprised to see Van Horn wheeling in.

"I knocked, but there was no answer."

"Come on in," Lomax said. He rolled his shoulders once

and assumed the position behind his desk. After several years piloting the damn thing he still hadn't gotten used to the feel. "What's on your mind?"

Van Horn steadied himself with a breath. "Sir, Art Jefferson came to my house on Saturday night."

After a moment's absorption of the admission Lomax sniffed a brief laugh. *Son of a bitch, Art.* "And why was that?"

He'd expected maybe a dressing down first, at least, or maybe a question as to where the fugitive was now. Not a *Why?* "He wanted something."

"Money? What?"

"A trace of a phone number," Van Horn answered.

Lomax looked off and shook his head. "He's still investigating. That's a strange thing for a guilty man to be doing."

"You don't think he did it . . ." Van Horn quizzed the SAC.

"Hell, no, Nels. I just wish I knew what—" *A number? What number?* "What number?"

"That's what I was coming in here to tell you. I promised Art I wouldn't, but after that shoot-out, well, sir, I'm worried."

Shoot-out. It wasn't much of that, Lomax knew. Only two slugs matched Art's duty weapon. The remaining *thirty* came from someone else, someone shooting at Art and at Simon Lynch.

And then there were the fingerprints, matched to Art, Simon, Pooks Underhill, an unknown, and, lo and behold, Keiko Kimura.

What in God's name is she doing gunning for my number two?

"I'm worried too, Nels."

"Anyway, he came to me and gave me this number to

trace." Van Horn passed the slip to the SAC. "It's an eight hundred number; only it doesn't exist."

"Excuse me?"

"No listing, sir. I ran it up and down."

"So, it was a mistake," Lomax observed.

"I don't think so," Van Horn said.

"Why is that?"

"Because he got that number out of a page of Kiwi ciphertext. From a magazine."

From a what? Pieces began to fly in Lomax's head. Kimura. Vince Chappell. Betrayal by Mayfly. And now Kiwi. "Nels, from the top, tell me everything you know. Everything."

Rothchild was at lunch, away from his office, when Kudrow stopped by and let himself in. The monitors glowed weakly, and the darkness they could not defeat surrounded him like a shroud. At this moment he found comfort in the din.

He had come for that and to be reminded of his position.

Kudrow eased into Rothchild's chair and felt the warmth it retained. He scanned the numerous controls associated with the systems, finding with little trouble the series of switches that Rothchild had once explained to him. The left switch first, and a picture window appeared on the large monitor before him; then the switch next to it, and an image flooded the window.

I can do this, Kudrow told himself. Things could go wrong, and still he could do this, could, with the flip of a switch, watch the President of the United States sit at his desk in the Oval Office and go about his business as if nobody were the wiser. *If you pick your nose, I have it on tape. If you call the Russian president, I have it. If you speak unkindly of a friend, I have it.*

Art Jefferson might still elude him. Simon Lynch might still be out of his grasp. But not this.

I have this. And I will have them.

"So you decoded these two pages of Kiwi for him," Lomax said. "You don't remember what they said?"

Van Horn shook his head. "Just the number when Art gave it to me Saturday. That stuck in my mind. And—"

"And what?" Lomax pressed. It was no time for reticence.

"Well, I remembered something from the academy. A lecture I attended about a year ago, just before I took over com. The guy giving this one talk went heavy on the anecdotes, and he was telling us how some of the people who develop codes put pieces of them in puzzles and then put those puzzles in magazines, or textbooks even, with messages in them. It's a test to see if anyone might see something they missed. He said that kind of thing has been going on since the sixties."

"And—"

"Well, I remembered one thing from the pages of Kiwi Art showed me. One was a photocopy, and down at the bottom were a page number and, it looked like to me, the name of a magazine. Something called the *Tinkery*."

"And being the diligent agent that you are, you checked that out," Lomax theorized.

"This morning. When I heard about the shoot-out, I decided to do some checking. In case Art needed help."

"Of course he needs help. So?"

"The page of the Kiwi ciphertext was placed as a puzzle over two years ago in this *Tinkery* thing. It's one of those egghead magazines."

If Lomax had been an egghead, he might have been

offended. As it was, he was far from offended. "Who placed it?"

"They have no record of its being placed," Van Horn answered.

Okay, a phone number that didn't exist, pulled from a puzzle that wasn't placed, made up of the code now in use by every arm of the United States government. The day didn't suck anymore, Lomax decided. It simply made no sense.

"Is any of this going to help?" Van Horn asked.

"Who the hell knows?" Lomax fiddled with the slip of paper Van Horn had given him. "Have you tried it?"

"No."

Lomax picked up his phone. "What can it hurt to call a number that doesn't exist?"

He pressed the eleven digits and, after a second, heard the first ring.

The buzz of the phone would never bring anything close to joy again, Pedanski thought as he waited through three rings. Just before the fourth, with the recorders and trace gear up and running, he picked up the receiver.

"Hi, you've reached the Puzzle Center," he said, not even an attempt at enthusiasm punching his words.

"I'm calling about Art Jefferson," the voice said before Pedanski could go on.

Oh, shit.

"Who is this and where are you?" the voice asked as though an answer were expected, part schoolteacher, part drill sergeant.

Pedanski froze.

"Hello . . ."

An indicator on the trace gear flashed, and Pedanski hung up. His breaths came in small eruptions, feeling more like air leaving than coming. A losing battle.

Telling himself that he wasn't hyperventilating, that he was just scared, that he should breathe more slowly, Pedanski very precisely maneuvered his fingers over the keyboard hooked to the trace system and pulled up the information on the number that had just called them.

It said it belonged to the Federal Bureau of Investigation.

"Sh-i-it."

Chicago field office.

Pedanski managed a swallow between the rushes of air ebbing in and out of his lungs.

Office of the special agent in charge.

"Oh, God . . ." *Deep, deep, slow breaths.* But telling wouldn't do. Pedanski grabbed a bag that still held the remnants of day-old doughnuts and dumped it onto the floor, then put it over his mouth, and breathed in and out, doing so for more than a minute before the rise and fall of his chest edged toward normality.

Oh, man, this is out of control. Mr. Folger was right.

But for Folger to be right, it would mean that someone else had to be wrong. Dead wrong.

Art had made one stop at a discount electronic store before choosing a motel near O'Hare International, and once in the small second-floor room with its two twin beds he plugged in the tape player and set it next to a chair by the window.

"Simon," Art said, patting his lap, "come here."

"Daddy's gonna sing."

"Yes, he is," Art affirmed, and helped Simon into a comfortable position, cradled in his arms. The shades were partly open, and he could see downtown in the distance, the buildings dotted by lights that shaped them against the black sky.

"Daddy's gonna sing," Simon said expectantly as he nuzzled his head close under Art's chin.

Art reached over and pressed the play button.

"Wander boy, wander far, wander to the farthest star . . ."

Simon's thumb crept into his mouth. His eyes closed as the song continued.

The words, though, were lost on Art. His attention was elsewhere. On the events of the day before. And on what he was beginning to see in the near future.

At first he had thought Pritchard simply one piece of an attempt to wrest Simon from him at Pooks's apartment, but that possibility he soon decided made little sense. Too much show was involved. The story, good and evil players, walking the man downstairs only to have him warn of someone in the apartment.

If anything, the confluence was chance. That was what Art believed. It was what he had to believe.

"Wander boy, wander far, dreams are what you're made of . . ."

And the woman who had nearly killed him or whom he'd nearly killed. Which he didn't know. He did recognize her, though, from supporting information in the Chappell file. Keiko Kimura. In the States, as Lomax had told him. Closer than that, he had learned first hand.

She wanted Simon.

So did someone else.

Or were they all one?

The tape droned on, to simple humming now, and Simon's breathing took on the rhythm of sleep, slow and deep.

Art could not sleep yet. Staring out the window, eyes fixed on the speckled skyline, he thought of what Pritchard had said. *They'll never stop looking.*

Pritchard, discounted as an enemy, now only a cryptic unknown, albeit one Art was having less trouble believing than before Keiko Kimura had nearly killed him and Simon. His fanciful declarations now seemed not just possible but plausible, and the only part that troubled Art was that he wondered if he wanted to believe so much that he was ignoring his better judgment.

Or could it be as Pritchard said: good existing with evil. It was a given in dogma. Why not in the institutions that governed everyday life?

Faith in man. Art thought it an odd concept in this situation, different from faith in himself. Different, yes, but he believed. He had to.

He could not let Simon exist as a pawn his entire life, always running. Whatever his life was, it should not be that.

And as the night wore on, and the constant of Simon's breathing soothed him, Art looked down upon the quiet, innocent face that lay against his chest, and he understood what was at stake, and he knew what he would do when the new day dawned.

chapter 21

Marked

Of all places, they met in a toy store, Pedanski arriving looking like death not even warmed over and Folger
with wonder plastered on his face as they strolled down the
aisle where video game cartridges were conveniently placed
at eye level for a nine-year-old.

"Don't tell me," Folger said. "You know this aisle well."

Pedanski actually smiled. It did not feel right. "Vik's pulling half of my shift."

"Sounds good," Folger said. "Listen, thanks for listening
the other day. I know I shouldn't have dumped all that—"

"This has to stop," Pedanski said, cutting Folger off, a
crack in his voice. He turned toward a row of game cartridges
and took a box covered by colorful, action-packed art in hand
and tried to pretend that he was really interested in the drivel
presented in small print.

Folger stopped mid-aisle and stepped up close behind
Pedanski. "What happened?"

"Just another call," Pedanski said. He replaced the box
and took another. His eyes were puddled, and his hand
pushed the glasses up awkwardly and wiped the gathering
tears before they could fall. "I didn't plan on this when I

came to Z, when I came to work for Mr. Kudrow."

"None of us did," Folger said.

A small furry creature on a jet-powered tricycle zoomed over rocky terrain on the box Pedanski focused on now. "What you told me was happening to the FBI agent—"

"Jefferson," Folger prompted while Pedanski sniffled.

"That shouldn't happen."

Folger's eyes drifted to the far end of the aisle, past a young boy trying out a new game on a display set right at his level. Price was mentioned nowhere. It was not for him to consider. Others would worry about that. "A lot of things shouldn't happen."

"Well," Pedanski said, thumbs tapping on hollow cardboard, "I'm done with it. I'm out. I'm leaving."

"You can't," Folger said, looking back to Pedanski now. When he'd spilled his guts to the younger man in the Puzzle Center, confessed his and Kudrow's sins freely, there was one he'd left out. "He won't let you."

"And how can he stop me?"

"He can kill you. Just like he did Dean."

A shudder burned through Pedanski's upper body, and he slowly turned toward Folger. "He what?"

"He killed him. He shot him because he said he was selling information to someone outside. Espionage." Folger felt his right eyelid begin to shake and put a pair of fingers to it. "That can carry the death penalty, you know."

It was a weak attempt at humor, not even gallows humor. Induced by nerves, by fear.

Craig? Pedanski should have heard what Folger said and been rocked with disbelief. He was not. He could believe it. He could see Mr. Kudrow doing just that. And what frightened him more, about himself as much as any potential threat, was that he could have imagined Kudrow doing this even before the present situation developed. And he had respected him for that dedication to a cause.

Now he reviled him and a little piece of the naïveté in his own makeup.

Leo Pedanski's thumbs suddenly pressed hard on the game box, collapsing it upon itself, his fingers digging through from the opposite side, punching through the thin shell until he ripped it completely in half and let it fall to the floor. It felt good.

But not good enough.

"Fuck him," Pedanski said in a voice that gained resonance deep in his chest. "I want to see him hurt."

"I understand how you feel," Folger said. He truly did. And the anger, beyond being healthy, as almost everyone who'd ever had difficulty expressing the emotion had been lectured, allowed focus on a target for the desired wrath that one could dream of. If only dream of.

But Folger sensed, saw in Pedanski's profile, in the stony flex of the jaw muscles, in the glassy sheen over the one eye visible, in the unseen grinding of the teeth, that he was doing more than dreaming. He was visualizing what pain he could inflict on G. Nicholas Kudrow as if he really were going to do it.

Pedanski showed Folger his face in its full, furious glory and said, "I want to hurt him. I want to ruin him."

"How, Leo? He's made himself clean. He always has. You and I, we're civil servants who can make a lot of wild claims, but we have nothing concrete to back those up. Hell, I'm on the edge, drinking at work. For all I know, he already may have psych reports on me that say just that."

Pedanski thought, his mind working as it did when tricking algorithms to vex the most determined cryptanalyst, passing over what was useless to consider, looking not only at the likely path of the equation's potential but at the less likely, and the unlikely. And the simply nonexistent.

The back door.

"If you can't beat 'em," a drunk in a bar had told him once, "get someone else to beat 'em for you."

"Rothchild," Pedanski said, no revelrous joy in his voice, no satisfied glint in his eye.

Folger thought he understood and shook his head. "He won't help us. He sold his soul to Kudrow long ago."

"Maybe he'd sell it again," Pedanski suggested, and through the machinations of Folger's expression, his eye steadying even, he could see that this time he truly did understand. But that did not erase the doubt or alter reality.

"Who'd listen?" Folger asked.

"I think I know," Pedanski answered.

It took him only a few minutes to convince Folger. The decision was not hard to make. Anger had steeled their conviction.

In the mirror she studied the mark, turning her head away from the too-bright lamp embedded in the ceiling of the hotel bathroom and then toward it, comparing how her left cheek looked in differing levels of light.

Like hell in either, Keiko Kimura decided, and covered the offending mark, a tear in the skin caused by the shattering wood of the door scraping like sharp, hot rockets across her skin. It was red and raised, an inch and a half long, if not two, the edges puffed pink like the anatomy between her legs, something she had studied in mirrors enough to draw a simile. Except this cleft cut into her face at a perfect diagonal beneath the left eye could not be used for purposes noble or pleasurable. It was a brand. And it would become a scar, she was certain.

"Damn fucking Joe," she said to the mirror, drawing the image of Art Jefferson's coarse dark face on the glass with her mind and a second later driving the very real heel of her palm against the apparition, pieces of it falling away into the sink and dissolving as twinkling bits of silvery noise.

She looked at her hand and saw that a small slice had been cut into the thick meat at the base of the thumb and that a smear of red was rising to a tiny crimson dome over the wound. She brought her hand up and pressed her lips over the cut, drawing what drained out of her back in over her tongue, all while she gazed at the starburst missing from the shattered mirror. Thinking, imagining what she would do to repay Art Jefferson for this mark. What more she would do than just kill him.

A bank of pay phones was cut into a wall outside a department store in the Oak Park Village Mall. Art chose an end unit and dialed the number before turning back so he could see Simon in the Nova parked five seconds away at a dead run. That was how he was seeing separation now. Not in distance but in how long it would take him to get there.

The call he was making would bring that to an end. That was a hope tinged by regret.

One ring sounded, seeming louder than any he could recall before, and in the car Simon's head was down, bobbing gently, the strange dark color of his hair lifting more pangs from low in Art's gut. Maybe it could have been different. Maybe he could have prevented all this from happening. Maybe Simon Lynch could have had a good life, his own life, if only Art had seen more sooner. Had made the right connections.

Maybe. Maybe. Maybe.

Ring number two passed, and as the third ring sounded,

215

without taking his eyes off Simon, Art pressed the number five, creating an annoying, sputtering jingle wrapped around a low howl in his ear, like a hundred mosquitoes vying for a choice vein above the lobe.

Someone answered as the abrasive tone faded.

"Yes?"

"I want to talk to Pritchard."

It could not be called silence that followed: it was more a hum absent depth, but it lasted only a minute.

"I'm glad you called."

"You said I would," Art reminded him. "I'm ready to give him to you."

Now the absence of sound was substantive, suggestive of thought. After a moment Pritchard said, "Do you remember what Simon built on the dresser?"

"Yes," Art answered, his eyes angling down at the receiver, noting something in the way Pritchard spoke, in the preciseness, as if he'd expected this call and had committed what had to be said to memory. A recitation that, still, seemed lacking substance, like slow water gliding over a smooth rock as a wispy, thin sheen. Maybe it was his way. Maybe this was as hard for him as it was for Art.

"You've been, I take it."

"I have," Art confirmed.

"The area people usually gather is closed."

"I've heard." Being remodeled, Art knew from the papers, the Skydeck Observatory had been closed for weeks.

"Can you get there?"

An odd place to present Simon to those who would—and Art still had trouble keeping the cynic down so that he could believe—give him a new life. But this was their call. "When?"

"Nine tomorrow evening."

"I can do that."

"Good then."

"Wait," Art said. It was their call on place and time, but he did have one condition. He gave it to Pritchard not as a request.

"I guess we'll have to manage that."

"I guess you will."

"Tomorrow, Agent Jefferson," Pritchard said, then hung up.

Art put the phone back in its cradle and adjusted the baseball cap on his head, looking to the car and the small figure in the passenger seat. A little more than a day and Simon would be gone. He'd hardly known the kid at all.

Pritchard did not get up from the chair after hanging up. He sat as Sanders watched him, waiting for some words of direction, but after an awkwardly long time the younger man cleared his throat.

"You've been like this ever since you met Jefferson."

"How's 'this'?"

"Contemplative," Sanders explained. "Excessively."

"Well, Mr. Sanders, you are one boldly observant young man." And a correct one at that, Pritchard knew.

"What is it?"

"Something that Jefferson said." Pritchard lifted a dead cigar from the pedestal ashtray next to his chair and slid it between his teeth. "This innocent is different. People will still want him. They'll still look."

"I don't understand."

"We'll have to arrange for special handling. It can't happen as Jefferson thinks it will."

Sanders's face belied his ignorance of Pritchard's point.

"Sanders, I want you to leak the information to the opposition," Pritchard directed.

The whites of Sanders's eyes grew around the dark centers until they looked like plates of alabaster china with dollops of thick gravy in the middle of each. "But that means they'll know. They can stop it. I don't understand, sir. I don't—"

Pritchard lifted a hand. "Having people looking for the innocent won't do. There has to be an absolute resolution."

Sanders understood somewhat now. Exposure. It would mean the end of what they were, what they represented. But what was Mr. Pritchard thinking? How would alerting the opposition prevent that?

How was the question that Pritchard, former army Ranger, drill instructor, jumpmaster at Fort Bragg, had been agonizing over through two sleepless nights and two endless days. How to achieve an absolute resolution.

The answer he came up with was spawned by an adage concerning absolutes or certainties. Death and taxes, he recalled. One was of no use to him. The other was Simon Lynch's only hope.

As long as Art Jefferson behaved as Pritchard believed he would. If he did not, the hope for one would become the fate of both.

"This is what I expect to happen," Pritchard said.

chapter 22

Bait

Bob Lomax tossed his jacket onto the coat-tree just inside his office as he arrived and sneered at his desk.

"Sir?" an agent said through the still-open door behind the SAC.

"Yeah?" Lomax inquired without turning.

"This arrived by courier," the agent said, and when the SAC turned to cast a wary eye upon the bulky package, he added, "I had it fluoroscoped."

Lomax took the package in hand and judged by the shape and heft that it contained about half a ream of material. "From who?"

"The stamp is Fort Meade."

A lightness lifted Lomax's chin, and he turned for his desk, the agent closing the door as he left. Once seated, Lomax drew the sharp edge of his letter opener under the envelope's flap and, trusting that the package's being fluoroscoped meant there *wasn't* anything to worry about, removed the contents, just about what he'd guessed in amount. He gave a cursory look inside the empty envelope for any stragglers, then turned his attention to the stack of pages. A thick rubber band held the pages together.

On top there was a letter, addressed to him, on plain paper.

Agent Lomax,

You will know once you read the enclosed material that a crime has been committed. I was party to it but am by no means at its heart. This concerns an effort to discredit Agent Art Jefferson, through means too incredible to mention or to document. What I can tell you about are those who conceived this and in particular about a man named Rothchild. You would know him as Kirby Gant.

Gant? The name was familiar, but Lomax recalled after a moment that the Kirby Gant he knew of was dead, sleeping with the fishes somewhere if his memory was right. So how could this concern him?

Forty minutes later, after scanning less than half of what an early-morning courier had brought him, Special Agent in Charge Bob Lomax was on the phone with the office of United States Attorney Angelo Breem, demanding a meeting within the hour.

The house in which Nelson Van Horn lived was empty, as it was each morning at this time, so when the phone rang, it was left to a staple of modern life to answer.

"Hi, this is Nels, I can't come to the phone right now, so if you'll leave your name and number, I'll get back to you as soon as I can. . . ."

Beep.

"Hello, I'm relaying a message. Tonight, at nine, the Skydeck Observatory. Bring what you have."

The line clicked off; the dial tone echoed in the house; then silence.

Twenty minutes later Rothchild double clicked an icon on his computer screen and played an intercepted telephone call for Kudrow.

"Who was that?" Kudrow asked.

"Jefferson is getting edgy," Rothchild theorized. "He's even afraid to have his voice heard now. Tired, paranoid is my guess. Getting weak. So he gives someone a few bucks to read that into a phone somewhere."

"Where did the call originate?"

"Near O'Hare," Rothchild answered. "Tonight, nine o'clock. And how convenient—the Skydeck is closed for re-decorating. Boo-hoo."

"Van Horn will be there," Kudrow commented.

"A cripple and a retard," Rothchild observed. "Not much in the way of resistance added to Jefferson."

"There's liable to be shooting just like at the apartment," Kudrow posited. "They'll lock the place down tight. A hundred and three floors is a long way from an exit."

"It's one floor from one," Rothchild said, pointing upward with a straight finger. "A helipad on the roof."

That would mean acquiring transport and putting people atop the tallest building in the world. "What about security?"

Rothchild leaned back, hands laced together behind his head. "At nine on the dot the elevators will suddenly stop working. Security is on the first floor at that hour. That's a long walk up."

"What about the cameras?"

"Glitches come in pairs," Rothchild replied with smug certainty. He loved this, and it showed. Almost better than sex. "Plus, did you see the Chicago forecast for tonight? Fog arollin' in from the lake. No one will see a thing. It's up to the roof, and away they go."

The end. Finally. Kudrow had tasted it for days, bitter when close and then snatched away, sweet now in expectation. Resolution. This entire episode needed to be over.

"Arrange it," Kudrow said, nodding to Rothchild as he left, though he might have spit upon the man if his powers of observation could have reached into the very near future.

"They took the bait," Sanders told Mr. Pritchard, almost surprised that he was doing so. "How did you know?"

"Desire, Sanders." Pritchard clipped the end of a fresh cigar and took his time lighting it. "It makes desperate people predictable." He puffed five times, long and slow, before taking the roll of heavenly, aromatic leaves from his lips. "Are we ready to intercede?"

"We are."

Pritchard replaced the cigar between his teeth and put his feet up on the coffee table. It was all up to Jefferson now.

After an interminable hour watching Angelo Breem peruse the documents at a leisurely pace, Bob Lomax stood from the couch where he'd sat in forced silence and brought a wide, flat hand down on the pages under the U.S. attorney's nose.

"Dammit, Breem, what is it going to be?"

Breem stared at the hand until Lomax removed it; then his eyes came up. They were no longer bright with self-assurance. "This looks real."

"For God's sake, man, what else would it be? Who has any reason to make all that up?"

Breem wanted to say Jefferson did, but even if that were true, there was no way that one FBI agent on the run could arrange this. Jefferson actually seemed inconsequential now. A different thought had caught his fancy, like a bright shiny dime gleaming in contrast with a stale old penny.

And he was not the only one to see the dime. Lomax had even polished it up just to hold it out to him. "You want a name, Breem? This is your ticket to that."

It was more than a ticket to that, Breem could see. Some things were big. Some were mountainous. This was fucking Everest with stairs carved into its side and arrows pointing him to the top. He'd be a fool not to make the climb.

Screw Jefferson, he thought. *Screw Fiorello. Let the minnows be.* Angelo Breem had himself a shark.

A few dabs of makeup had toned down the bright coloring of the wet scar on her cheek, but it would not go away completely. That was fine. Let it be a reminder.

Keiko loaded two weapons into her tote, identical Mini-Uzis, like the one she'd tried to waste Jefferson with in the apartment. And two pistols. And plenty of ammunition for them all.

But from her back pocket she removed her instrument of choice, the straight razor, and opened it to see the light glint off the blade as she twisted it in the air.

"Close enough, Joe," Keiko said to the razor. "Maybe shoot you in the legs to slow you down, then—" *Wheesh. Wheesh. Wheesh.* She sliced the blade through the air and clicked it shut in one snappy motion, then slid it again into the back pocket of her jeans. She reached up and touched the welt on her cheek. It was warm. Like blood.

chapter 23

Hunt and Peck

A two-year-old Dodge pickup was Rothchild's car of choice, though it wasn't registered to him or to anyone who actually existed for that matter. It was registered to a name. A silly name. *How far one could get on a string of letters*, he often thought.

In the afternoon, as the workday ended, and with the weekend just one more day away, Rothchild left his subterranean lair with a satisfaction that buoyed his step and actually made him smile at the main lobby receptionist and found his clean black pickup waiting in the close lot where he always parked it. He climbed in, started the throaty engine, and backed into the traffic aisle without looking. If he hit something, so what? Today was a day not for worries. It was a day to mark in his mental record books. His biggest challenge completed. His biggest scheme brought to a successful end.

There was a bottle of champagne he'd saved for something like this, he remembered as he moved past the guardposts, through the serpentine drive, and onto the roads of Fort Meade. Yes, a bottle of bubbly, as the ever-so-cosmopolitan characters in the movies used to call it. Bubbly

SIMPLE SIMON

and a babe. He had the former. The latter he could rent.

Leaving Meade proper, he thought of what kind of babe he'd like this night. One of the top-heavy ones for some raucous titty fucking or an A-cup waif whom he could maneuver around the bed like some female Gumby doll.

Choices, choices. Maybe both. Yeah. Both. He could handle that, and he could certainly arrange it.

Driving with one hand draped over the top of the steering wheel, Rothchild lost himself in a daydream of the possibilities, thinking of little else and never noticing the four cars that took turns tailing him both back and front.

It was an old Royal that he'd dug out of a storage closet, something so archaic that he was surprised it was even allowed in the Chocolate Box. But it was, the glorious old machine that Brad Folger placed on the blotter on his desk after locking his door.

He drew a breath in, held it, and rolled a sheet of paper into the machine, exhaling as he pecked at the sticky keys with one finger of each hand. Yes, it was old, it was slow, it was an implement of inefficiency, but there was one thing it had over its modern counterparts: a total lack of wires.

Brad Folger wanted this last bit of information to be available to no one, until the time came. When he finished, he put it in an envelope with instructions and wrote Pedanski's name on the outside.

It was not a suicide note. At least not his.

The amazing thing about being where one wasn't supposed to be was that most people didn't give a damn who was where as long as no one was making a fuss. Art knew that from years of having to pull information from witnesses like teeth, things that one would think the person must have seen, but, oh, well, didn't think it too strange the man had a rifle in one hand as he walked down the street.

Getting on the service elevator in the maintenance garage had been exceedingly easy. It was after five, leaving just a few workers milling around, and all the effort it took was putting two hard hats on his and Simon's heads and waiting until a few backs were turned to the corridor leading to the elevators.

Art never had any illusions about trying for the lobby elevators. They would be crowded with people. People who watched the news and might notice a big black guy and a scrawny white kid together, even if they didn't match the photos, his from his bureau file, Simon's ripped from a frame in his dead parents' home.

But a couple of hard hats, however odd, would be par for the course in a building where some renovation was being done. Although Simon's less than macho posture, head dipped, could have drawn a curious eye, it did not. Luck? Timing? Art didn't care. Once on the elevator, an express to the top twenty floors, he pressed 103 and let out a breath as the doors slid shut.

Trooper Wayne Dupar of the Indiana State Police lit up his rack as he pulled in behind the late-model Taurus with three occupants, male, it appeared from his vantage, following the vehicle as it glided to a stop on the shoulder of the interstate.

He gave his position to his dispatch center, knowing that if another unit were in the area, it would be sent to do a roll-by as a matter of practice, and left his cruiser to approach the car from the driver's side, hand on the top of his pistol.

"Gentlemen," Dupar said. "Good evening."

Georgie already had the window down and his wallet out. "Officer. Was I speeding?" *Just give me the ticket. Fast.*

Dupar leaned low and looked across the front seat. Ralph looked back at him, smiling casually. In the backseat a stern man sat on the far right, a bag on the seat next to him. Dupar had ridden as observer in a state police chopper more than once, and he instantly recognized the item as a pilot's bag. *So, planning on doing some flying, are we—*

"No, sir, you weren't speeding, but we had a report of a vehicle matching this one driving recklessly about fifteen miles back that way on the interstate."

"Reckless?" Georgie repeated with a sprinkling of shock. "I promise you, Officer, that wasn't me."

"Well," Dupar drawled, "I'm going to have to satisfy myself about that. I'm going to have to ask you some questions and give you a field sobriety test." He looked at the other two men. "I'm going to have to give you field sobriety tests also, gentlemen."

"What?" Ralph protested, leaning toward the window.

"It happens that sometimes a passenger was driving, then someone switches off," Dupar explained in a painfully slow, meticulous cadence. "Like I said, I'm going to have to satisfy myself that you all are all right to be operating a motor vehicle."

Son of a bitch. Ralph looked at his watch. Twenty minutes. They had to be at the airfield in twenty minutes. "Officer, can we hurry this up, maybe? We've got someplace to be."

Dupar scratched his square chin, once, twice, three times. "Sir, hurrying causes accidents. I'd hate to see you all hurt in an accident. I'd hate to see that." *Not . . .* "I want you to drive away from here alive and in good shape tonight. All right?"

Fine. Fucking fine. Just do it. Do it. Ralph nodded and sat back in his seat.

Officer Dupar showed rows of bone white teeth to the driver and asked, pronouncing every syllable as if talking to a foreigner, "Okay, sir. How about we get you done first?"

"What do you think?" the supervising FBI agent asked, showing the hours-old photo to two of his subordinates on the hastily arranged operation. "I think it looks like him."

The other agents looked to the photo of the man driving the black Dodge pickup, then to an older mug shot of a man named Kirby Gant, aka Mr. Tag.

"If it ain't him," one of the agents commented, "it's a twin."

The supervising agent tapped the photos together on the edge of the fold-down desk in the back of the surveillance van and picked up the phone, dialing the number he'd been given.

"Yes?" a voice answered after just one ring.

"Mr. Breem . . ."

The lobby elevators were good enough for Keiko when she arrived a few minutes after eight, darkness having settled upon the city, and a quietness to the massive building that she found exciting. There was nothing like the shrill edge of a scream ripping an unsuspecting silence to shreds.

She imagined a cry resonating from Jefferson as the elevator began to move. Closed her eyes and made it real in her head.

Her stomach pressing low from the upward rise, the sound playing as if real, she felt a warmth trickle up her thighs and plant itself between her legs. Alone in the elevator, she pressed them together, surprised that thoughts of one so old could excite her.

Maybe pain was pain, and pleasure just pleasure, regardless of age. She would soon know. If so, it would mean a far broader horizon.

chapter 24

Dead No More

There was nothing to which Art could compare this sight. Nothing. As he and Simon walked past sawhorses and the idle tools of carpenters' labors and approached the east side windows of the Skydeck Observatory, all the world below seemed to be a sea of undulating white mist that rolled inward from Lake Michigan, lit with a radiance borne of a thousand man-made lights below. And from this sea the Sears Tower rose, a rectangular island of black against a star-flecked indigo sky, the moon barely a scythe above.

Simon released his grip on Art's hand and pressed himself right up to the glass wall, his breaths laying steamy ovals on the surface. His head came up, eyes also, the jitter somehow steadied, and he looked out upon the world high above the world below.

"This is up," he said, and moved along the floor to ceiling window, hands walking along the glass like a mime searching for an exit from the transparent box that imprisons him. "Up . . ."

"We're way up," Art said in agreement, losing himself in the moment, in Simon's discovery of another place, maybe another universe altogether as he saw it. However he saw it.

Simon's head twisted as though he were pressing an ear to the glass, eyes to the ceiling, trying to get the best view possible. "We're in the sky."

Art followed along as Simon neared the corner of the stripped room. "What do you see?"

"Simon sees up."

And what did that mean? Art wondered. Did Simon even know? In the end did it matter?

"Up," Simon said once again.

Art put a hand on his back and tipped his wrist to check the time. It was almost nine.

This was the night it would end, and Rothchild was gone. Kudrow had made the trip from the Chocolate Box to Rothchild's office to monitor developments. But the man who did not exist had gone home for the day, treating it as any other. That might have been appropriate in most cases, but not this one. He should have realized that, Kudrow thought. Damn right he should have.

So back to the Chocolate Box Kudrow went, through checkpoints he had just come in the opposite direction, back to his office and to a small phone book he kept in the safe with the master cipher books for Kiwi. In the back of that phone book, on a page with more scribbles than readable text, Kudrow ran his finger to the third phone number from the bottom. It had a line through it like most of the others.

He dialed it standing behind his desk.

"Hello?"

An unseen hand might have reached out and lifted Kudrow's chin, but it was his own reaction to the strange male voice at the other end of the line.

"Hello? Who's there?"

Kudrow's throat constricted involuntarily, lest an errant demand be loosed on the person who had answered Rothchild's phone.

No one answered Rothchild's phone but Rothchild. That was the agreement. That was the rule.

"Who the hell is there?"

His breathing might have traveled over the line, and Kudrow thought maybe the thump of his heart as it slammed against the inside of his chest at a pace he could not remember, even during the most grueling treadmill tests he'd been subjected to.

This was a muscle out of control, fed by adrenaline and whatever other chemicals his brain was telling the glands to release into his system. This was panic.

"Is anybody there?"

Kudrow laid the phone back into its cradle, keeping his hand on it as if to hold it in place, standing as still as he could, feeling the *bethump bethump bethump bethump* in his chest go on until he thought it might let loose, like an engine that had thrown a rod, ripping a hole right there and letting the blood spurt out against his blazing white shirt.

He wondered if he was having a heart attack, and then he wondered if he should be wishing that it were so.

The supervising FBI agent spun a chair around and sat facing Kirby Gant in his kitchen.

"Can I have something to drink?" Rothchild asked almost meekly as he remembered doing long ago.

"You got anything?" the agent asked.

"Fruit punch, in the fridge," Rothchild said, and one of the dozen FBI types in his apartment poured him a glass. He sipped from it, draining half, then set it on the kitchen table. "Thanks."

The supervising agent nodded. "Now, how is this going to go? Easy or hard?"

Rothchild had already been read his rights. He knew that he could have an attorney present during questioning. And he further knew that no attorney in the land could do for him what he could do for himself.

"Your name is Kirby Gant," the supervising agent said when no reply came to his question. "Correct?"

Oh, old Kirby. Kirby was dead. Kirby could do Rothchild no good at all. Zero.

"You don't want to talk to Kirby," he told the agent. "You want Rothchild."

Because Rothchild was the one with value, and Rothchild understood the game. Kirby had shown him how to play.

"Rothchild has much more interesting things he can tell you."

Art looked at his watch again. Nine o'clock sharp. And as if on cue, emerging from the sea of mist as a dragonfly might broach murky water, a helicopter appeared and gained altitude as it neared the tower.

They're here, Art thought, his hand sliding from Simon's shoulder to his back, where it rubbed soft circles.

Simon caught sight of the helicopter also and tried to point at it but stubbed his finger into the glass. "It's coming up."

"It's coming," Art said, knowing what he had to say next. "Those are friends, Simon."

Friends? How could that be friends? Friends were not that. That was up. Friends were like Art and Dr. Anne, and Dr. Chazzz.

"Come on," Art said, turning Simon from the window and guiding him back toward the exit from the Skydeck.

The *thrump-thrump-thrump* of the helicopter penetrated the windows as it passed and circled to the north, turning to head back for a landing on the roof. It was a sound that fascinated Simon, requiring Art to keep a firm hand on his back as they wove between the stacks of construction materials nearer the room's center.

Another sound drew Art's attention, though: the soft squeak of a door opening and sliding back on its hinges. He slowed as they neared the turn around the elevator core, which had let them out directly into the Skydeck. He slowed and kept one hand on Simon's back but let his other lift the side of his sweater, and he could feel the cool grip of his Smith & Wesson on his palm as Keiko Kimura came around the corner with a gun in each hand.

chapter 25

One on One on One

Art did two things at once, three if it mattered that he was cursing at the top of his lungs. He gathered Simon's sweatshirt in his fist and heaved him to the floor several feet away behind a pallet of dwarf I beams, and with his other hand he drew his weapon.

He might have fired if Kimura hadn't had the same idea, and as the first muzzle flash spurted from her weapons, he dropped to the floor and rolled toward Simon.

Bullets were not her concern. She had plenty, and therefore Keiko had set both compact submachine guns on full automatic. As she squeezed the triggers, she swung one left and the other right, driving sixty rounds into tools, and materials, and fixtures, and the ceiling, and the bare floor. But the greatest result of her wild firing came when stray bullets, of which almost half of them were, peppered the large window panels on the east side of the Skydeck. At fourteen hundred plus feet in the air, with the tail of a Canadian low-driving fog in from Lake Michigan, the wind load on the exterior of the tower was enormous. And on the window panels in particular. They were designed to accept the load, but not when being punctured by dozens of hollow-point rounds that sent spiderweb cracks in all directions from each point of impact. They were strong but not that strong.

The winds, gusting upward of fifty miles an hour, slammed into the suddenly pulverized panels, which exploded inward, showering the unfinished room with hundreds of thousands of tiny, crystalline blocks. Keiko Kimura fell back as the shower swept over her. Art, in covering Simon, felt the sting of hundreds of the tiny particles pecking at his skin.

And then there was the wind.

Art got to his knees and was almost pushed over by the gusts now invading the east side of the 103d floor. The howl caught his sweater and lifted it over his head, and he was forced to pull it off entirely and discard it. He grabbed Simon and pulled him along the floor by his sweatshirt, toward the elevator core, keeping behind pallets until he reached a spot of open floor where it seemed a million tiny sparklers danced on the floor in the little light there was.

The elevators were across the open space. The elevators were a way out. Kimura had come in the door.

The elevators it would have to be.

Keiko, huddled behind a stack of boxes containing heavy ceramic tiles, reloaded her weapons and shook as much of the glass as she could from her hair.

She peered over the boxes and went to her stomach, covering the major part of the room from just south of the door. She could hear nothing but the cry of the wind and the crackle of glass still being torn from the window frames.

This was not a good position, Keiko knew. The stacks and pallets of construction materials ran north to south in rows, cutting the room off every ten feet or so. She needed a field of fire down the rows. Down each if she could clear them. One at a time. Make her targets' safe zone smaller and smaller.

With a plan now, she came to a crouch and duck-walked south, toward the beginning of the rows.

Art helped Simon to his knees and tried to tell him something, but the noise was just too intense. Simon's hands were pressed to his ears, his eyes flitting open only sporadically. He would have to lead him to the elevators. No, carry him. Or at least drag.

Son of a bitch! Where had she come from? Art allowed himself that brief venting, then took Simon's shirt in hand once again, and, keeping his weapon in the direction he had last seen Kimura, made a low dash for the T-shaped elevator core.

He moved as fast as possible, his eyes moving, looking up the rows between the pallets, then taking a quick check of the space between the two elevators, the doors of which opened into the vertical base of the T. Beyond the elevators, two small alcoves that would soon be walled in formed the cross of the T, and looking back to the room from just outside the elevators, Art could see nothing but debris being swirled in minicyclones.

He could not see Kimura, and considered that a possible break in his luck, until he pressed the elevator button and saw that there was no light behind it. Nor above in the readout of its location.

The elevators were not working.

"Shit!" he said aloud, losing the word to the wind.

The only choice now was the door to the hallway and then to the stairs. Art pulled Simon up again and eased back toward the spot where the T let into the room, his weapon sweeping the path ahead, his eyes moving, moving, looking for anything that migh—

Brrrrrr-rrrrrrr-rrrrrr-rrrrr.

The bursts of fire caught Art completely by surprise, coming up the row that looked directly down the base of the T, driving hot spikes into his arms, and sending him backpedaling, still holding Simon's shirt through pain that seemed to course through him from fingers to shoulders on both sides, and sending him into one of the alcoves at the top of the T, where he collapsed against a pile of cardboard refuse, Simon at his side.

Keiko came up to a half crouch and set one of the Mini-Uzis on a stack of boxes. She'd emptied it, saving the other, and now wanted to have a hand free. She moved down the row and, even in the low light, could see the spray of red on the floor and the bare gypsum wallboards.

She had made contact. Removing the straight razor from her pocket with her free hand, opening it with a snap of the wrist, she hoped, actually prayed, that she hadn't killed him. Not yet.

Art looked down at his arms and saw immediately two neat punctures in the skin over each bicep. His weapon was still in his hand, loosely, and when he tried to squeeze his fingers around the grip, the reply was a buzz of hot sparkles that dazzled his senses and forced a scream from his lungs.

Unfortunately, in the windbreak of the alcove, he could hear himself perfectly.

"Shit! Shit! Shit!"

Now what? Now fucking what? Art would have liked to wait for an answer to present itself, but he knew there wasn't time. Either Kimura would make her way to him, or he'd bleed to death. He had to do something, something to save Simon. But what? He was alone and wounded.

Well, wounded, yes, but not alone . . .

No. No. Art repeated it again, over and over in his head, telling himself that there was no way, absolutely no way he could . . .

Then you die. And he . . .

Art looked to Simon, who had let his hands come away

from his ears and was blinking and twisting, his body rocking where he sat on his knees, blood dotting one side of his
face. Art's blood.

Oh, God, why?

Do it! Now! Before it's too late!

"Simon," Art said, grimacing as he pushed with his feet
until his back was against the wall. He let his weapon slide
out of his hand and to the floor. "Simon. Can you hear me?"

"Simon hears Art. My friend, Art. There's a loud noise."

Art nodded. "Simon, I want you to do something for me.
All right?"

"For my friend Art."

"Simon . . ." *Forgive me. Please.* ". . . take out your cards."

"So," Angelo Breem said, then cleared his throat, all the
while Anne's gaze crossing the distance over the U.S. attorney's desk to peck at his frightened eyes whenever they
chanced contact with hers. "We are extremely sorry for what
has happened. But you have to understand, this was an or-
chestrated ploy. We were as much victims of it as you and
your husband."

If her jaw had been removable, it would have detached
itself and taken the elevator to the lobby. Was he really saying this? Was this an apology? Had he learned tact from
some Nazi?

"So . . . you are free."

Lomax, standing behind Anne, could only shake his head.
"Breem, you are one smooth fellow."

"Pardon?" Breem said.

Anne slowly stood up from her chair, still wearing the
smock from her time in detention. "What are you doing
about Art?"

"Well . . ."

The door to Breem's office opened, and Janice Powach poked her head in. "Agent Lomax. Call for you out here. Urgent."

"Be right back," Lomax said, and left the office to take the call. "Lomax here."

"Sir, it's Nels Van Horn."

"What is it?"

"Sir, I've got some strange message on my machine. I think you should listen."

In his office Breem stammered through what efforts were being made to find Art, to notify him that all charges had been dropped. Anne would not release him from her stare. Not until Bob Lomax burst into the office and grabbed her by the arm.

"Bob? What is it? Where are we going?"

He pulled her toward the door. "Sears Tower. No time to explain. Come on."

Keiko was now at the elevator core, where the base of the T began. She was about to begin her advance past the elevators when, moving from right to left, Art Jefferson bolted from one of the alcoves, arms dangling, and dived for the other.

She fired a quick burst at him, aiming low, but saw the bullets stitch along the base of the far wall. But even above the roar of the wind she heard a cry born of a terrible pain rise from where Jefferson had landed.

They were hers. Him now, the kid later.

Keiko moved with cautious steps toward the alcoves at the top of the T.

Every square inch of skin on his arms felt as though someone had bathed them in hot oil and had then taken a wire brush to them. Art pushed himself to the back of the alcove, though it wasn't very deep. His arms lay almost limply at his sides, hands in plain view, his skin covered by curving streams of blood. He lay there and looked out of the alcove and saw Keiko Kimura ease into the space where she could see him and, in the opposite alcove, Simon.

Keiko gave Art a good look, her weapon covering him, and then a less careful once-over of the kid, who sat on his knees, some sort of book thing that hung around his neck held in both hands. He looked to be reading from it. Good. Whatever kept him occupied.

She looked back to Art. She had quick work to do.

"Hey, big man," Keiko said, a tributary of the wind pushing strands of black hair across her face. She brought the straight razor close to her cheek and touched the wound ever so gently. "Keiko's gotta give you something." She eased into the alcove, facing Art fully now, standing over him near his feet, the submachine gun held low and casually, the straight razor her weapon of choice. " 'Cause you gave her something."

Her nails were blue, Art saw, and she made a face at him that might have been mistaken for a smile, but only because she was showing teeth. He saw it as a silent growl.

"I'm gonna cut you bad, big man," she said, and took another step toward him, between his legs now. "Real bad."

"Mayfly!" Art said as loud as he could, right at Kimura's face, and she instantly puzzled over his use of that word.

Why the hell would he say that?

But Simon knew why. He had his cards out. He had been listening. Art had said "mayfly." And it said on his card: IF ART SAYS MAYFLY, THN TAK TH GUN OUT FROM UNDR YOUR SHIRT

AND HOLD IT LIK ART SHOWD YOU AND POINT IT AT TH STRANGRS
BACK

Art was his friend. The card told him what to do. He took
the gun out and held it with one hand the way Art had
shown him. He looked over the long top part the way Art
had shown him. At the end of the long top part he saw the
stranger's back.

He was doing what the card told him. But there was more
on that card.

"Say good-bye to your face, big man," Keiko said, beginning to bend toward Art, the sharp flat blade of the razor
coming his way.

"Kiwi!" Art screamed.

For a second Keiko paused.

Simon glanced at the card again.

IF ART SAYS KIWI THN PUT YOUR OTHR HAND ON TH GUN LIK
ART SHOWD YOU AND PUT YOUR FINGR ON TH TRIGGR LIK ART SHOWD
YOU AND PULL TH TRIGGR

Simon let the cards drop so they dangled by the lanyard
around his neck, and he put the other hand on the gun the
way Art had shown him, and he put his finger on the trigger,
and he pulled the trigger—

BOOM!

Bending as she was, the bullet that might have hit Keiko
Kimura mid-back instead ripped through her spine and tra-
versed her torso toward the front, cutting a swath of vital
muscle from her heart and pushing her onto Art Jefferson
like a puppet whose strings had been snipped.

The straight razor fell onto his chest. He felt a warm ooze
trickle onto his stomach from the front of Keiko Kimura. She
wheezed once but never moved. He rolled her off of him with
a lift of one knee.

In the alcove opposite him, Art saw Simon sprawled back

on the pile of flattened cardboard boxes, the gun on the floor, his small head shaking from side to side. Art wriggled his way to his feet and went to Simon. "Are you all right?"

"That was a loud noise," Simon said.

Art went to his knees and put his head against Simon's. "Have you got your cards?"

Simon took them in hand.

"Take the card you just wrote, with 'mayfly' and 'kiwi' on it, and tear it out."

Simon did, pulling the three-by-five piece of sturdy stock away from the tiny ring binders with a zipping sound.

"Fold it up," Art told him, and when Simon had, he said, "And put it in my pocket. Good. Like that." *No one is going to think you did this. I pray to God you forget that you did this.*

Simon looked to the gun on the floor, eyes dancing all around it. "Loud."

Art struggled to his feet and had Simon get up with him. "We've got to go up."

"Up, up, up!" Simon said.

A smile beat through Art's pain. *Let that mean he forgot. Please.*

"You follow me," Art said. "Understand?"

"Simon follows Art." Art was his friend. He would follow a friend.

chapter 26

Downfall

Art and Simon emerged onto the roof with little trouble, and Art could see that Kimura had likely spent some of the time before ambushing them opening doors that would let out to the helipad.

And as Art stepped into the wind that slid across the roof like an endless, invisible tsunami, he suddenly wondered if the helicopter he could see sitting a dozen yards away, its rotors turning, three men jumping from it and running his way, might not be there for her. If it was, he had just fought a losing battle.

He was both right and wrong.

A youngish man, blond hair whipping in the tumult, came close to Art, and the first thing that was obvious was that he carried no weapon.

"Jefferson?" the man yelled.

Art nodded, his arms held awkwardly against his body.

"Pritchard sent me!"

"Who are you?" Art asked.

"That's not important!"

"It is to him!" Art said.

The man looked to Simon, who huddled behind Art, something in his hands. "My name is Sean!"

Art turned to face Simon and crouched. "Simon, this is Sean! He's a friend!"

A friend. Art was telling Simon that Sean was a friend. A friend could tell you who was a friend. Simon took the pen clipped to his cards and flipped to the proper spot. Beneath POOKS UNDRHILL he wrote SHON.

"What's that mean?" Sean asked.

"It means he trusts you!" Art answered.

Sean stood up from his crouch, as did Art. "Where's Kimura?"

"Dead!"

"Where?" Sean pressed.

"In the Skydeck! By the elevators! Why?"

Sean waved the two men with him past. They disappeared into the building.

"What's that about?" Art asked.

"Listen, Jefferson . . . you've got to trust us!"

"I'm giving Simon to you, dammit! What more do you want?"

"It wouldn't have worked any other way!"

Art grimaced at Sean. "What are you talking about?"

The two men returned, carrying Kimura's lifeless body and her weapons. They took the body to the helicopter and strapped it into a passenger seat in the back, sitting it up, as if it were alive.

"Jefferson, believe that he'll be all right! No matter what you see!"

"What?" Art asked, confused, something in Sean's eyes making him understand just a little. *If Kimura is found, they'll know she didn't get him. This way there might be a chance people would believe that she got him . . . and they wouldn't need to look.* That comforted Art, but only briefly. *But when she doesn't turn up, won't people start—*

"We've got to go!" Sean said.

Art nudged Simon so he would come around to his front, and when he did, he felt the slender body press against his. He knew. He knew what was happening. At least some of it.

"Simon, I want you to go with Sean! He's your friend! Right?"

"Right," Simon said, his voice barely audible in the turbulence.

Sean put his hand out, and Simon put his in it. They began to walk toward the helicopter. Art stepped forward, pulled by the departure, and said as loud as he could, "I love you, Simon!"

Simon paused, pulling on Sean's hand, and his head swung back toward Art, the green eyes sweeping up until they met the big brown eyes for the briefest instant. But in that instant Art knew that Simon understood.

A minute later the helicopter lifted off into the horrid wind, the pilot fighting it until he had his bird heading out toward Lake Michigan.

The phone in the Puzzle Center did not make Pedanski jump this time. It was an expected call on a normal line.

"Pedanski."

"You found the envelope I left for you?" Brad Folger inquired.

"I did."

"Start faxing it now," Folger instructed him. "To Senator Grant first, and work down the Intelligence Committee from him. Then the rest."

"Okay. Are you—"

"I'm across the street right now," Folger said.

"You'll be all right."

"I can't be any worse," Folger said, then hung up.

Five minutes later fax machines in dozens of Senate and House offices began spitting identical pages. The first words were: "By the time you read this, G. Nicholas Kudrow, deputy director, COMSEC-Z of the National Security Agency, will be the focus of a federal investigation into violations of wiretap statutes, extortion, tampering with evidence of a felony, and assorted other crimes."

Over water now, Sean began to get himself and Simon into harnesses, as did the other crew members. Keiko Kimura was left alone.

"Do you like to fly, Simon?" Sean asked.

Fly. Like the birds. Way up. "Up in the sky!"

Sean nodded. "Yeah. You got it."

The desk sergeant of the evening shift looked up when the well-dressed man approached with a woman by his side. "Can I help you folks?"

Brad Folger nodded and took a breath. "Yes. Sometime back there was an accident. . . ."

The lights were barely lights anymore, Art thought, and he wondered if it was distance or blood loss that was making the strobe of the helicopter go faint. But in the next instant he had no trouble seeing what happened.

Far over the water, about where he thought the helicopter was fading, a brilliant flash lit the mist below, and then a trail of yellow orange spun wildly against the dark sky before trailing off into the fog, pulling a ribbon of fire with it.

Art ran against the wind to the edge of the helipad and

was about to scream to God above not to let it be true when what Sean had said just minutes before struck him and completed the picture. *Trust us . . . Believe he'll be all right. No matter what you see . . .*

And he understood. Nothing could be expected of the dead. Nothing but silence. The dead were truly the only ones who could rest.

It was too far off and too windy to hear, but Art could imagine the remains of the helicopter slamming into the water, pieces coming apart. The lake had swallowed larger things. Some it still kept.

"What was that?" Anne asked Lomax, staring through the patchy fog out over the lake. "It looked like fire."

"I don't know," Lomax said, but then he didn't really care either. He had only one thing on his mind. Get to the tower, get to his number two.

First they had to get the elevators working again. Then Lomax had to get through a gauntlet of Chicago PD intent on keeping everyone below 103. Once they were persuaded to get a move on and clear the building up to the roof, he escorted Anne to the helipad, where Art had been found huddled in the stairwell leading up to the helipad.

"Oh, God," Anne said as she knelt next to him.

"Paramedics are on the way," a cop said.

"Art! Art!" Lomax said loud and right in Art's face.

"Babe. Do you hear me?" Anne prodded.

Art half opened his eyes. "I tried. I tried. But they got him. And the helicopter went . . . went . . ."

Anne put her hands on either side of his face as his eyes slid shut. "Art!"

At home, in his study, with a fire glowing warm across the room, G. Nicholas Kudrow sat at his desk after his wife had gone to bed and picked up the phone. It was late, but there were calls he had to make.

"Hello?" a somewhat gruff and groggy voice said.

Kudrow smiled before speaking. He was not conscious of doing so. "Senator Grant. Kudrow here. I need to speak to you about—"

The abrupt click and return of the dial tone unnerved Kudrow, but he told himself that there were those in any position of power who were prone to fits of weakness.

He simply moved on, going to the next number in his book.

"Yes?" an equally disturbed voice answered.

"Senator Franklin. Kudrow here. I—"

The hang-up came quicker this time. And in the next call about the same. And in the one after that even quicker.

After the sixth silent rebuff, Kudrow walked over to the fire and slid his book of names and numbers through the mesh spark screen and into the flames. He watched it become embers, changed from what it had been to something very different.

His life was over. He knew that. Not over as in the end of breathing or waking each morning but simply over as he had known it. That he accepted quickly, the best way to accept anything that was bound to be difficult.

And this would be difficult. He would have to give up much. His wife. His family. His home. His career. Almost everything.

Except his freedom. That he could retain. Of course he would have to lose himself, become a new person, find a place where he could live unaccosted, free from fear of arrest.

There were places that would offer him that because he could offer them something. Much was locked away in the only vault no one could ever search.

But to do all this he would need something. Something to get him places, to trade for favors, to sustain him. And he would need it now. Cash. Total liquidity.

He did not have it in his home, and he could not chance a large withdrawal at the bank. He had no great sum of money available for immediate use. But he knew where he could get some.

Epilogue

Stars

It was amazing what one week, a few stitches, and two and a half pints of blood could do to restore the vigor to one's step. And though Art Jefferson would not be throwing curveballs for some time to come, he was alive, and with his wife, and fulfilling a promise he had made to himself before all hell broke loose.

This, he knew, was for Anne.

"Take a left up ahead," Art said from the unfamiliar spot of the passenger seat. Behind the wheel Anne followed his directions perfectly, her eyes focused on the country road ahead, the gleam he'd come to love not yet back. She was still grieving.

"Where are you taking me?" Anne asked.

Art, both arms in casts and practically laced across his chest in slings, kept his expression serious. He hoped to God she would understand.

"A nice place I used to visit," Art answered as convincingly as he could. This was not hard. The funeral had been hard, seeing an empty casket lowered into the earth next to the grave of his parents. Art had really started asking himself if this was right just about then.

But it was right. For Simon.

"What brought you out here?"

He looked out the window, at the trees and the green fields and the old barns teetering on the edge of collapse but obstinately defying the elements and physical laws to remain upright. It had been years since he had been here, to this place in the country, but he loved it.

It was the right place for this to happen.

"Turn again," Art said. "Left. It's a kind of dirt road."

The Volvo lurched as Anne steered it off pavement and onto the mix of gravel and dry earth. "Really?"

"It's worth the drive," Art said.

The lane wove through a field, with split-rail fences on either side, and swung right past a gathering of old buildings that looked as though the next winter would do them in. A minivan was parked behind the tallest of the structures, a barn with more angles to its roof than Anne could count, and standing outside the vehicle was . . .

Anne slammed on the brakes, the skidding tires drawing a dust cloud from the earth and throwing it forward of the Volvo.

"Simon!" she yelled, fingers wrapped so tight on the steering wheel that Art could imagine her snapping fist-size pieces off at any second.

"Well? Are you going to stay here or go see him?"

Anne looked at Art, her eyes at first severe, then quizzical, then disappointed. Then they simply melted into two big brown puddles, and she jumped out of the car and ran to Simon.

Art had to use the tip of his shoe to open the door, and then he got out. As he reached the front of the Volvo, watching Anne embrace Simon nearer the other vehicle, Mr. Pritchard walked over to greet him.

"Agent Jefferson," Pritchard said, the blue of his suit far too formal for the setting. "This was your condition, correct?"

Art nodded and leaned on the warm hood of the Volvo. The night sky above was clear, unburdened by clouds. One could see for miles and miles. "They found Kimura's body two days ago. The fish got to most of her. I saw the pictures."

"They're raising the rest of the wreckage tomorrow, I understand," Pritchard commented.

"How did you pull it off?"

A snicker slipped from Pritchard's mouth. "I used to be Airborne, Agent Jefferson."

"Parachutes?" Art asked with quiet incredulity. "Simon?"

"A tandem rig," Pritchard explained. "It's used commercially all the time to give the experience of a jump to those who can't make one on their own."

"Sean?" Art wondered aloud.

"An extremely experienced man at leaving perfectly good aircraft in mid-flight."

So that explained that, but not everything. Not how Kimura had found him. Art wasn't sure he wanted, or needed, to know more than he did. "I'm not going to ask you what I could ask you."

"I never intended . . ." Pritchard said, staring briefly at the casts on the man's arms before looking back toward Simon.

"Retirement was looming in a few years anyway," Art said. There would be some loss of motor abilities in each arm. Not enough to matter much but enough to bring his career with the bureau to an end. "Have you found a place for him?"

"With a wonderful family in another country," Pritchard said, adding, "It's best you don't know more than that."

"Believe me, I understand."

Pritchard smiled. "You know, if ever you are looking for some part-time work."

"I have your number," Art said. He knew he'd never call.

"Well, it's best we be going," Pritchard said. "His new family is anxious to meet him."

Art nodded and watched Pritchard walk away, watched Anne take Simon into her arms for the last time. He could have gone to him and stolen his own time, but they had had their moment together on the top of the world, as he liked to think of it.

When the moment came that Simon was back in the minivan, Anne walked back to Art, her eyes cast upon the ground. When she reached him, though, they came up to his.

"I think I understand this," she said. "I think. So you will explain it to me someday."

"I will."

"Otherwise I'll beat you silly."

Art had the urge to hug her, almost felt his arms reach for her. She knew that he would want to and leaned against the hood of the Volvo, her head easing onto his shoulder. They stood together and watched as the minivan's lights came on and as it drove away and disappeared down the lane.

Anne sniffled and wiped her eyes with the back of her hand before looking to the sky. "A pretty night."

Art let his own gaze drift to the heavens, to the wide field of stars arrayed above from horizon to horizon. "You know, my grandma used to say that on the eighth day God put the twinkle in the stars."

Anne looked up from where her head lay on Art's shoulder and said, "Your grandma was a brilliant lady."

———

The man slunk out of the shed behind the Iowa farmhouse just before midnight, a bulging suitcase safely in hand, his future secure.

But not the one he had envisioned.

"Hold it," Darrell Dean said as the stranger emerged from his clinking and clanking around in the shed. He held a double-barreled shotgun, which was pointed at the stranger's chest, and when he saw what the man had in one hand, he was mighty glad he'd grabbed the old duck gun before coming to investigate.

The man nearly tripped over himself with surprise, the sight of those wide side-by-side barrels bringing the hair on his neck to attention. He had a gun, of course, but it was in a pocket, and he dared not venture for it just yet. Talk first. Reasoning.

"I suppose you're wondering—"

"Put it down," Darrell said, motioning to the ground with the muzzle.

The man complied.

"Keep your hands up and step over there," Darrell ordered in a low, less than pleasant voice, its edges serrated with a nasal twang.

He raised his hands, just as the petty criminals did in grade B westerns, and side-stepped away from the shed, away from the suitcase.

"Right there," Darrell Dean said, already knowing how this little dilemma would be solved. He'd caught himself a thief, all right, red-handed, mind you. But he could no more call Sheriff Jackson to turn this old bird in than he could tell him what it was he was stealing. This was *the* money. The money his brother, Craig, had . . . acquired.

Poor old bugger, Darrell Dean thought, then gave the thief both barrels in the gut, tossing him back into the dirt.

He replaced the suitcase of money where it had been

hidden successfully for years. Then he dragged the thief's body into one of his fields and, after digging a good-size hole with the backhoe, rolled G. Nicholas Kudrow in and covered him up.

In short order he'd plant corn over the spot.